AMY MYERS was born in Kent, where she still lives, although she has now ventured to the far side of the Medway. For many years a director of a London publishing company, she is now a full-time writer. Married to an American, she lived for some years in Paris, where, surrounded by food, she first dreamed up her Victorian chef detective Auguste Didier. Currently she is writing her contemporary crime series starring Jack Colby, car detective, and in between his adventures continuing her Marsh & Daughter series and her Victorian chimnney sweep Tom Wasp novels.

By Amy Myers

Dark Harvest

AMY MYERS

Allison & Busby Limited
12 Fitzroy Mews
London W1T 6DW
allisonandbusby.com

Hardback and paperback editions published in Great Britain as *Dark Harvest* in 1997 under the pseudonym ALICE CARR.
This paperback edition published by Allison & Busby in 2015.

A CIP catalogue record for this book is available from
the British Library.

10 9 8 7 6 5 4 3 2 1

ISBN 978-0-7490-1926-6

Typeset in 10.55/15.55 pt Sabon by
Allison & Busby Ltd.

The paper used for this Allison & Busby publication
has been produced from trees that have been legally sourced
from well-managed and credibly certified forests.

Printed and bound by
CPI Group (UK) Ltd, Croydon, CR0 4YY

To Carol with love and thanks

Prologue

'The girl I left behind me . . .' Matilda Lilley listened to the nonchalant whistling of the young soldier on her right at the ship's rail, as the steamer drew away from Admiralty Pier. Everyone was leaving behind someone loved. Including her. Tilly allowed herself the rare luxury of heartache and self-doubt.

At Ashden Rectory they would be in the middle of family prayers – if they still kept up the ritual in the midst of war and, knowing her brother Laurence, they would. Gathered beside the breakfast chafing dishes would be her sister-in-law Elizabeth, her nieces dear Felicia and rebellious Phoebe, her young nephew George, the formidable Mrs Dibble, her hands clasped in prayer that the Almighty might continue to accommodate her in her endeavours to keep the Rectory wheels turning, her husband Percy – But why go on? Together they made a whole, the Rectory, despite the fact that two faces were missing: Isabel, now married, and darling Caroline, actually here in Dover, working in a Voluntary Aid Detachment. She had snatched a brief hour with her yesterday. Brief because Caroline had to hurry back for an emergency meeting about the Zeppelin threat, sparked off by the previous night's long-expected attack on Norfolk, which promised to affect every man, woman and child in England – even in slumbering Sussex.

What was Ashden making of the Zeppelin threat, Tilly wondered with some amusement, picturing old Jacob Timms pontificating on the seat beneath the oak tree, believing himself comfortably separated from war by sixty years since his service in the Crimea. What would he say if through the darkened skies over the village slithered a silver cigar-shaped monster? She wished she could be there to see it, but she had donned her tin-lined hat and that was that.

'If I should die . . .' Tilly impatiently dismissed Rupert Brooke's poem which she had read in a magazine last year and which now popped unbidden into her mind. Did she regret her decision? No. Had she any intention of fertilising some corner of a foreign field? She had not. Did those white cliffs, receding into the distance, fill her with sentiment for her homeland? They did not. Was she deserting her comrades-in-arms left behind in England? No. If women were equal to men politically, they should take their share of the dangers. And if that danger, in this cold, rainy January of 1915, meant driving ambulances with the First Aid Nursing Yeomanry from the front line to base hospitals, so be it. She was 'Miss Lilley' now; 'Lady

Matilda Lilley' had vanished along with her past life. But her heart had not vanished with it.

No, her heart remained in Ashden. In Sussex; rail against its imperfections as she might – forever England.

Chapter One

Home at last! Caroline jumped down on to the familiar platform. The wooden canopy of Ashden railway station still had not been repainted. Good! Side by side with Lord Kitchener's accusing finger pointing out from his recruiting poster, the old advertisement still bravely exhorted the world to come to Hastings for a sunny holiday. One day she'd actually go! The cubbyhole window through which her sister Phoebe served tea for the war effort was shuttered against the early March winds, but Caroline could see the station cat Ruby (she was black and white) asleep as usual on the windowsill of the booking office, and inside she could hear Mr Chappell whistling 'If you were the only girl in the world'. She sighed with happiness.

The porter, young Arthur Mutter, took her ticket with a murmured word of greeting for the Rector's daughter.

'How's the list, Arthur?'

He was suddenly animated. 'Saw the old Brighton *Bonchurch* last week, miss.' To the never ending disgust of his father Harold, one of the two village carriers, Arthur had developed a passion for the railway. Without parental consent he had become a porter, and spent all his free time doggedly travelling the railways despite the wartime delays.

'Caroline!'

Her mother, breathless and looking uncharacteristically flustered, hurried into the booking office. Caroline's pleasure was complete. She found herself running, almost hurling herself into her mother's arms, relaxing as she caught a waft of the familiar lavender scent. The mere sight of her mother, the old blue hat crammed over her dark hair, hatpins at all angles, signalled all was right with the world.

'Where's the trap? Nothing's wrong is it?' Caroline asked anxiously as she disengaged herself, and straightened the feather in her mother's hat which she had knocked in her enthusiasm.

Elizabeth Lilley gave her daughter a welcoming pat before taking one of Caroline's two small suitcases. 'Nothing. I walked. Poppy is growing more and more cantankerous in her old horsey age. She *is* nineteen. I told her she'd get taken by the Army as so many horses have, if she didn't prove how indispensable she was, but I'm afraid she still refused to move. Mutter delivered your trunk yesterday, so I knew you wouldn't be carrying much luggage.'

'It's so unusual to see you out walking.'

'It's the war,' her mother said blithely. 'You'd be amazed how much I'm out nowadays.'

It did amaze her. In Caroline's imagination her mother

dwelt within the red walls of the Rectory garden; the rambling red brick house was filled with her as by the warm aroma of baking bread. Her mother *was* the Rectory.

'I see the war hasn't persuaded you into the new shorter skirts,' she teased.

'All in good time, Caroline. It may be the first of March, but it's still winter and no fit time for my ankles to appear on the world stage.'

Caroline had a sneaking hope that her mother never would adopt modern fashions. Selfishly, she wanted her never to change, for if she did the Rectory itself might change. Her mother's striking looks and tall, well-built figure suited the flowing length of the pre-war fashions, though she would be the last person to care for such considerations.

The hedgerows were just beginning to show signs of life, Caroline saw with pleasure as she walked down Station Road, and the ploughed fields, earth still clogged with the heavy winter rainfall, gave at least a promise of growth.

'How's Isabel?' Caroline asked, as they passed the track which led to Hop House. Her elder sister's letters were full of complaints of how the war had ruined her life; her husband thought more of playing soldiers than of her, and staff were unobtainable – save for the terrible Mrs Bugle. Caroline, irritated, nevertheless felt sorry for her; despite the fact that Isabel had been only too eager to leap into matrimony with Robert, the son of Ashden's wealthy brewer and hopgrower William Swinford-Browne; it was a hard fate then to find herself left alone as a young bride after the noisy family life of the Rectory. Though not,

Caroline reminded herself, nearly as hard a fate as many young wives were experiencing.

'Coping wonderfully,' Elizabeth replied airily.

Caroline laughed. 'I'll soon find out, anyway. I'll invite myself to Hop House for supper.'

'I shouldn't if I were you. Isabel's cook is so bad, Isabel might cook it herself – and she's worse.' Elizabeth nodded to Tom Cooper sitting in the doorway of his almshouse and he waved his cap at them. 'Anyway, you'll see Isabel tonight at Rectory dinner.'

'Morning, Miss Caroline.'

Tom's greeting was as casual as if he saw her every day. True, she had been here at Christmas, and indeed had only left Ashden for the first time last September after the outbreak of war, but to Caroline it seemed a lifetime. While she had been away, Ashden had become an imaginary village that rose up occasionally in her conscious mind, before sinking again, submerged by the frightfulness of a war whose results she had to deal with every day in Dover. Now that she was back in Ashden it was hard to believe it was real. Until, that is, they passed the monstrous picture palace built a few months ago by Swinford-Browne. A black and white timber edifice boasting towers and even crenellations, right in the centre of Ashden, it immediately drew the eye from the village's mellow red-brick beauty and the weathered grey stone of St Nicholas, her father's church. The picture palace stood arrogantly on the corner of Station Road and the rise of Bankside, and she did her best to ignore it. She looked beyond it to the pond at the foot of the grassy slope leading down from Bankside. To the right she could see Timms the newsagent, the post office, the general stores and Bertram the butcher's.

She forced herself to look straight ahead to the track by the side of St Nicholas that led to the gates of the Manor, now a hospital for the wounded. Then, her heart leaping with sudden pleasure, she caught her first sight of the Rectory, its white gates open as always. In the front garden a brave daffodil or two was already in flower, dotting the grass. Caroline ran into the Rectory drive. Once inside the gates she executed a neat little hornpipe of joy on the gravel and made for the tradesmen's door, her favourite entrance, since it took her straight into the kitchen. Mrs Dibble had her back to her. Intent on punishing pastry at the oak table, she was loudly singing 'Soldiers of the Cross Arise' in honour of the season. Caroline's hand stole round her to steal some sultanas. Mrs Dibble jumped and pushed the hand away. 'It's Lent, Miss Caroline, even if you are a nurse now.'

'I'm not.' She munched away. 'I drive ambulances and make tea. How are Mr Dibble, and Lizzie and Joe? And Fred, of course,' she added quickly. Not that Fred was ever likely to be different. He managed a few jobs in the Rectory, like lighting and filling the oil lamps and chopping wood for the boiler, but mostly he pursued his amiable way in his garden workshop.

'Muriel's had the little one last week, a girl, Josephine.' Mrs Dibble glowed with pride. 'Joe will be pleased as punch when he gets back.' There was a brave defiance in the 'when'. Joe was a Territorial with the 5th Sussex. 'Left for France, he did, just a week before she was born.' The words were cheerful enough, but her eyes told a different story.

'Have you heard from him?'

'Not yet. Still, hunger's the best sauce, that's what they do say. Talking of which, there's the carrots to peel.' Caroline fled.

'Have you heard from him?' What a stupid question. Caroline knew the answer was probably no. Her last letter from Reggie had arrived yesterday, yet was written ten days earlier. Then, he said, he was kicking his heels with nothing to do. By now he could be in the midst of battle, wounded even – no, she must not think that way. There was little enough that women were allowed to do in this war; what they could do was keep strong hearts for those they loved who were far away. Her fiancé Reggie Hunney was a second lieutenant with the 2nd Royal Sussex, fighting on the Western Front. At Christmas he had been near a town called Ypres in Belgium, but now she suspected the battalion had moved. The need for self-censorship by officers and imposed censorship on the troops made it hard for those at home.

She had last seen him at Christmas. It had been easy to be strong then, surrounded by loved ones, but it was more difficult in the bleak winter evenings that followed. Listening to the waves crashing on Dover beach and the rain, the endless rains of January, lashing at the windows of her hostel bedroom, how could she help but worry over what was happening to Reggie? Mud, Reggie had written, was fighting on the German side, by which she gathered that there could be no British offensive till spring. The German trenches, he had told her, were much better dug and equipped than the British, which were often taken over from those hastily prepared by the French, designed for immediate cover, not the permanent occupation which, since the disaster of Ypres in November, he gloomily predicted. Then he had seen her face, remembered to whom he was talking, and made an effort to be cheerful. Why should he though, she reasoned. He needed a listener, and who better than she? At least, with her VAD experience, she had some conception of what war meant, with the hospital ships arriving constantly all through that autumn and winter. How Reggie must have suffered in the rain of this long winter, but spring was surely about to come.

In Ashdown Forest, which lay a mile or so from the Rectory, the ferns would be stirring, waiting to unfurl pale fronds hidden beneath the dead bracken of last year. Spring usually brought hope. This year it brought the probability of a new British assault, and with it the hope that this would be a prelude to winning the war. But it would mean more casualties, more heartbreak.

She knocked on the study door, not expecting her father to be there, for this was usually his parish visiting time. It opened even as she knocked. Laurence Lilley had heard her voice, and had been waiting patiently till she came to find him. Of all his five children, Caroline was secretly the most dear to him.

'How long for, Caroline?' He kissed her, drew her in, sat her down, and then quietly asked this all-important question.

'I don't know, Father.'

'Were you not satisfied as a VAD? It is valuable work.'

Caroline produced her prepared answer. 'My six-month contract has ended, and I didn't like your having to pay for me to live away from home.' This was true. It had always worried her that she was unpaid as a VAD; she felt she should contribute to the stretched resources of the Rectory.

'I thought it had just been agreed that VADs should receive a small salary.'

Her heart sank. She had been banking on him not having heard the news. With a salary of twenty pounds a year, she could live away from home perfectly well, even though the cost of living was shooting up.

'You're not disappointed I'm home?'

'Do you see it as a failure on your part?'

'No!' she burst out. 'It's just that I'm not a very good VAD. Lots of people could do the job as well as I do, and probably better. I don't know quite what I should do. But I *shall* do something.'

'So if you are sure your feet are still on the path God has chosen for you, and that you have not—'

'Ambled into the forest?' she finished for him, remembering the theme of many sermons. A track led from their orchard down to one of the gates into Ashdown Forest. As a child she had pictured being lost amid the heaths and woods of the forest, wandering through the green glades – delightful until one grew hungry. 'Oh yes, I am sure. Perhaps I *should* go to the front like Aunt Tilly and Felicia.' Her aunt had transformed herself from militant suffragette to determined war worker and was driving ambulances, and her younger sister was preparing to join her very shortly. Her father remained silent. 'You don't want me to, do you, any more than Reggie does?' She had given Reggie her promise that she would stay in England, however much she disagreed with his reasoning.

'I admit I'd be relieved if God decided no more of my daughters should feel called to the front.'

'And what about George?' Her brother was the youngest of the family, but he was sixteen.

'I don't know, Caroline.' She saw the sudden anxiety on his face, and was sorry she had spoken. 'He is a man, after all. That makes a difference. I can only pray for the war to end quickly.'

'What *difference*?' she asked gently. 'I know women are still confined to looking after the men – cooking, cleaning, nursing, comforting and so on. I know they're essential, but there's so much else we could do as well. We could step into many of the jobs that men do now and release enough manpower to overwhelm the enemy. Why doesn't the government see that?'

'Governments move slowly because public opinion moves slowly,' he answered her. 'Besides, you are wrong. Wives are taking over running their husbands' shops. I even heard of a lady becoming a window-cleaner in Tunbridge Wells. Soon you too may be a wife, and you'll have Reggie's job to consider.'

Before the war Reggie had run the Manor estate for his father, who had been occupied in London much of the time in the War Office. Now Sir John was away permanently, except for sporadic short visits, and the estate had to struggle on as best it could with a manager.

'You sound like Lady Hunney.' Caroline tried to joke. 'I'd meddle in the estate over her dead body, I fear.'

'And she is all too much alive. Living in the Dower House has done little to diminish her presence.'

'I'll have to go and see her,' Caroline said dismally. But *tomorrow*!

When she had gone, Laurence sat for a while, unable to return to the correspondence that only half an hour ago had seemed so vital, as he wrestled with something that he acknowledged at last to be fear. While only one of his five children, and the least likely one at that, had chosen to go abroad, it had been bearable. When the war was over, Felicia would return and normal life would come back to the Rectory. And to Ashden.

He saw his role in this war as twofold: firstly, the need to keep abreast of his parishioners' troubles. With the squire away in London and unable to play his part, it grew more and more difficult. There was Mrs Hubble who hadn't been right in the head since young Timothy's death at Ypres; Mrs Tilbury the younger, facing eviction by Swinford-Browne now Paul was called up; and always, always the Mutter-Thorn feud. On the outbreak of war the hatchet had been temporarily buried, but last week a Thorn had accused a Mutter of spying by signalling to the enemy. Joe Ifield, the village policeman, bound to take 'official' notice, had come to him for a solution. It had taken time to discover that Mrs Mutter had left her blinds undrawn by mistake a week earlier, and to diffuse the incident by suggesting Joe issue an 'official' reprimand. If

Ashden battled thus, what hope for peace in Europe?

And now Caroline, whom he had privately hoped was home to stay, was clearly restless. Of course, when Reggie came home and they married, she would settle down. Wouldn't she?

He was equally sure of the second part of his role, but the path to it was less clear. He prayed for light. His parish must be held together somehow, so that when its menfolk returned, their jobs, their families, their way of life could remain unchanged. For this reason he was still in two minds about women doing men's work. For a woman to take over her husband's job to keep the business going seemed to him a different matter from what he suspected Caroline had in mind: organised use of women's labour. But if it had to come, it would, and his task would be all the harder.

'Call me Canute,' he thought wryly, hoping it would not fall to him to convince Ashden that tides could not be turned by men.

Caroline flung open her bedroom window, regardless of early March winds. The larch still had its winter brown cones, but as she looked out over the gardens she could see signs of life. Fred Dibble was idly kicking the compost heap. Poor Fred – though why, she wondered, should she think of him as poor? He seemed happy enough. Thank goodness all that nonsense about his being a peeping Tom had died down. Harriet, their housemaid who had first accused him, seemed much happier now Agnes Pilbeam had left and she was the housemaid-cum-parlourmaid. Less than a year ago Caroline had been standing at this very window, wondering what life held for her. Since then so much had happened – too much. The choice had been simpler then: stay in Ashden or go away. But then there had been no Reggie, no war. The war called her away, Reggie wanted her to stay in England, preferably in Ashden. Why couldn't she be a VAD at Ashden Manor like Felicia, he had suggested hopefully at Christmas. She had laughed, not taking him seriously. Lady Hunney disapproved so strongly of their engagement that he must know such proximity would be impossible.

Time to tackle the trunk. It had been carefully packed with the help of Ellen, her Dover roommate. She was going to miss Ellen's cheerful company, but she was determined not to lose touch with her. Ellen hailed from the East End of London and had never seen a cow before her train journey to Dover. Caroline had solemnly promised her a much closer introduction.

It was time to change for supper. Daringly, she extracted one of her new shorter-length dresses from the trunk. Well, not exactly new, she admitted. It was several years old, but it was fashionably full-skirted. With the skirt chopped off just above the ankle by Ellen's nimble fingers and two rows of military braid tacked on the bottom by her less accomplished ones, she decided, as she swirled in front of the mirror, that she could grace the fashion pages of *The Lady*. She wondered idly if Lady Hunney wore short skirts yet and giggled at the image it conjured up.

Outside she could hear voices, doors slamming, as the family arrived home from their various daily occupations. She drew a deep breath and threw open her bedroom door – the sign, that she was prepared for visitors. The fire in the hearth, specially lit for her return, obligingly crackled into life.

It was Phoebe, naturally, who catapulted through the door first. The puppy fat had completely vanished now, leaving her figure comfortably rounded like Mother's, unlike Caroline's own more slender build. Five years her junior, Phoebe was now nearly eighteen.

'You're back,' Phoebe cried happily, embracing her briefly. 'I suppose you couldn't sew on this button, could you?' She held out a serge skirt which Caroline recalled had started life as a gown of Mother's.

'I could not!' Start doing things for Phoebe and she would never stop. 'How's the tea business?'

Phoebe pulled a face. 'Boring. I know it's for the war effort and it was my idea, but you've no idea how I groan inside at making yet more cups of tea and smiling my head off when I'm frozen half to death. And the rain in January! Caroline, you can't imagine what it was like. In June at least I'll be old enough to be a VAD like you and Felicia, and do something *interesting*.'

'You'd find that can be boring too, and you'd be tied to a contract.'

Of all of them Phoebe most longed to escape from Ashden, and had been going to finishing school in Paris when the war had intervened. Unfortunately Phoebe, when bored, was likely to get into mischief. Caroline had her suspicions that her sister's boredom lay behind the departure of their nice curate Christopher Denis last year. They'd been landed with dour Charles Pickering as a replacement. Even Phoebe hadn't considered setting her cap at him. Her idea of serving teas to train travellers had succeeded in keeping her occupied, but now Caroline recognised – with foreboding – signs of trouble.

Phoebe giggled. 'I'm glad you're back.' Caroline squeezed her hand, and arm in arm they walked down the stairs to dinner. 'With Felicia going, and Patricia Swinford-Browne away, and Eleanor going to be a vet, I hate being left to dole out cups—'

'A *what*?' Caroline stopped in surprise.

'Oh, that. Dr Cuss needs an assistant.' Phoebe was delighted with the effect she had had. 'Eleanor's working for him.'

'And what does Lady Hunney say to her daughter becoming a vet?'

'Quite a lot. But Eleanor's still doing it.'

She'd been away too long, Caroline decided. She was missing all the fun. 'You've got Isabel for company.'

Phoebe raised an eyebrow and it was Caroline's turn to laugh as she warmed herself at the stove in the entrance hall. Only a few weeks now and they would lose its comforting heat, when the ritual day came and Percy and Fred staggered outside with it for storage till autumn.

The youngest sister, between George and Felicia, Phoebe always came off worst in battles with Isabel. Impossible though her elder sister could be, Caroline had always felt close to her, and realised she was eagerly waiting for Isabel to walk in. The front door of the Rectory had always been kept unlocked, so it was with surprise that she heard the sound of the bell. She turned an inquiring eye to Phoebe.

'It's Rector's Hour,' her sister explained. 'It gets so busy now, Father decided he must regulate it by knowing who was waiting to see him. Besides, someone is pinching the coal. Father thinks they take a lump or two each time they come.'

'*Coal*?' Caroline repeated, horrified.

'Mother says it's because times are so hard and the family allowances don't stretch far enough. There's a coal shortage.'

'I know. I haven't been in Outer Mongolia,' Caroline said patiently. 'It affects Dover as well as Ashden.' Sometimes Dover had *felt* like Outer Mongolia, a different world of sadness and horror, and she had to teach herself not to brood in her few free hours about the endless stream of stretchers being ferried from hospital ship to ambulance, to yet another train and another hospital. That each stretcher might be carrying Reggie had been her immediate fear, though she tried not to let it show as she raised a smile for those conscious enough to appreciate it. When it was her turn to do canteen duty, how she had longed to be back in the Rectory kitchen, listening to Mrs Dibble and Mother discussing the rising price of sugar over a cup of tea. She had vowed that when she returned, the kitchen would be the place she'd visit first, as if to reassure herself it was still there. And so it had been.

The Rectory *was* a little different, though. Before the war the days had an order to them, the steady clock of Rectory life. Matins, Family Prayers and sacrosanct mealtimes, Evensong, Rector's Hour – and so each day chimed away. The year too had its order, ruled by spring-cleaning ('On the first of March the fleas do jump' she was accustomed to hearing from Mrs Dibble as she prepared for the spring battle), bottling, preserving and harvesting, as well as by the Church festivals. She had loved it all. Now this life was threatened as the war became a reality for Ashden like the rest of England. The Kaiser's raids in January had set off a Zeppelin panic. Mother had confided to her that Percy Dibble was sent out nightly to scour the skies before he was allowed to go to bed, in case the five hundred foot monster had set its sights on them.

There was another ring at the door. Caroline reluctantly moved away from the stove.

'There's Isabel,' Phoebe announced confidently. 'You can always tell her ring. She's the Lord Kitchener of Ashden. Come forth, all ye who would serve Isabel—'

'Phoebe!' warned Caroline.

Isabel's face brightened when she saw Caroline. She was still the prettiest of them all, Caroline thought, with her fair curls and blue eyes and tall slim figure, though Felicia was undoubtedly the most beautiful. If only Isabel would smile more.

She rushed to embrace her sister. Even in her excitement, she noted that the patriotic urge against buying new clothes had not affected Isabel; that full swirling taffeta skirt and elegant simple blouse had come straight from the dressmaker – and not the village seamstress, Mrs Hazel, either, Caroline thought indulgently. Behind her she could hear Felicia's voice and the pounding of feet that declared George was on his way. And so, bursting with happiness, she went in to dinner.

As her father said grace, she wondered what Reggie might be eating at this moment, and where he was. In a trench? In his billets behind the line? In an exotic *estaminet*? No, she would not think about Reggie now; she would join in the grace and appreciate where *she* was. As Harriet brought in the soup, she even gave thanks for Mrs Dibble, who for all her quirks and oddities had obviously been determined to provide her favourite dishes. George had teased her on the way in that they were reduced to nettle soup and stewed cow heel, but here was the familiar leek and potato, and even an early roast of lamb, normally only served for the first time at Easter.

She listened to her family chattering about the events of the day and the latest village dramas, content just to be back here. At last George could wait no longer to ask what was uppermost in his mind. 'Did you see any Zeppelins?'

'I'm afraid not. I've seen a few aeroplanes. British, that is. Oh, and a seaplane or two.'

'You were lucky being in Dover,' he moaned. 'Everything's happening there. Not like Ashden.'

'It's happening everywhere, George,' her father pointed out. 'Even here.'

'The day a Zep appears over Ashden, I'll eat my school hat.'

'The shadow lies over us all,' Elizabeth commented quietly. 'They could strike anywhere. But this is not the time or place to discuss it.'

'You always said we should talk over the important issues of the day at dinner. And the chaps at Skinner's

27

were talking about what we're going to do when we're old enough.' Or before, he thought.

Caroline caught a glance between her parents, an odd silence which her mother quickly smoothed over with a reference to the apple pie before them. 'This is the last of the apples in the applety, as Mrs Dibble still calls it.' The applety was one half of the hayloft above Poppy's stable, where Percy and Fred carefully stored the apples from the orchard each September. 'Goodness knows how much we'll have to pay to buy more. Ever since the Kaiser announced he was going to start blockading food supplies, the general stores seem to be putting their prices up every week.'

'What was all that about?' Caroline later hissed at Felicia as they went upstairs for a private talk, before rejoining the family in the drawing room. George had left to escort Isabel home with a dimmed torch.

'There was a stink in January because George announced he wanted to leave Skinner's right away and go into the Royal Flying Corps.' Felicia eyed Caroline's bed, strewn with her Dover belongings, and opted for the armchair.

'But he's far too young.'

'He'll be seventeen next December, and that's their minimum age. He fancies himself shooting down a Zeppelin, and is desperately hoping that the war will last long enough for him to volunteer. You can imagine what that's doing to Mother.'

'Yes.'

'It came about because he decided – without telling Father – to apply for one of those scholarships Skinner's offers for Tonbridge School, so that he could train in commercial studies instead of going to Oxford as Father wants him to. Then he got cross because, being George, he left it too late and found he couldn't apply after his sixteenth birthday, and Father refused to pay, so he's had this idea instead.'

'Commercial studies? He can't even handle his pocket money.'

'He wants to become a commercial artist. Did he tell you he sold a cartoon about a Zeppelin to *Bystander*?'

'No. He's not the best of letter writers.'

'He was so proud of it, he wanted to put it in the parish magazine too, only Father forbade it.'

'Why?' In Caroline's view, her brother was doing an amazingly good job of editing the magazine in her absence.

'He doesn't want Ashden infected by Zeppelin panic more than it is already.'

'But surely to laugh at it is the best remedy.'

'I agree, but he also considers the parish magazine is not the place to discuss war, and that I agree with too.'

'But is it right to ignore it?'

'I don't know, Caroline.'

Caroline glanced at her sister and realised she had been less than considerate. In comparison with Felicia's problems, a parish magazine must seem small beer.

'How is he?' she asked gently.

At first Caroline thought she had gone too far in asking about Daniel Hunney, for Felicia's usually serene face clouded. Her sister was the only one of them who always preferred to keep her own counsel. When they were growing up, it had been taken for shyness, but the few weeks that

Caroline had worked with her sister as a VAD had shown her that shyness hid a strength of purpose that outshone them all. Today, however, with her departure so near, she seemed glad of the chance to talk of Daniel.

'It looked so hopeful. He went to a Belgian hospital in Calais for treatment, and had to have another operation there because the stump wasn't healing properly. Now he's back here, and they can't fit an artificial leg until it does. Oh *Caroline*, the pain.'

She did not say whether the pain was his or hers. Even now it seemed unbelievable that Daniel Hunney, Reggie's strikingly handsome and energetic younger brother, who last year had had such high hopes of travelling the world after coming down from Oxford, now lay semi-paralysed in a hospital ward in his former home, and with only half a left leg. It was for his sake that Felicia had trained to be a VAD so that she could at least be near him, showing a single-mindedness in her devotion to him that was not returned. Or if it was, something – Caroline did not know what – had gone awry: the family had been shocked to hear of Felicia's intention to work abroad as soon as her first contract was over. Under Red Cross rules, at nineteen she wasn't nearly old enough to work overseas. Caroline had reminded her at Christmas, and all Felicia had replied was that 'there are ways'.

Though she had not said so, Caroline had a shrewd idea that she had arranged to join Aunt Tilly. Tilly had gone to join the FANYs, who since Christmas had taken over responsibility at Calais for transport of the wounded. Would her aunt be content to serve under orders? Caroline still found it hard to believe that the woman she had taken to be a retiring, submissive daughter to the formidable Dowager Lady Buckford was not only a suffragette but a militant, who had been in prison more than once.

'An artificial leg, although he's paralysed?' Caroline queried.

'The doctors still aren't sure how permanent the paralysis is. Paralysis from gunshots can wear off, and the effects of Daniel's shrapnel wounds too perhaps. Lady Hunney is insisting he knows that he's to be fitted with a leg to give him an incentive to fight the paralysis. She's installed some new machine called Zander apparatus which helps encourage movement. Not to mention a whirlpool bath worked by compressed air, which helps some of the pain coming from the missing limb. Sounds odd, doesn't it? But it works, and you know what she's like.'

Caroline knew only too well, and felt envious of Felicia's freedom to travel, whatever the sad reason. Because she loved Reggie, Caroline had agreed to stay for there was much for women to do here in England – if only the government would let them.

My darling one,
Your lovely letters of the 12th, 13th and 14th arrived together and I would have liked to read them in correct military order. I was too impatient for that and seized one sentence from the first, another from the second and another from the last . . .
I wish I had something to tell you to show what a hero I have been, so that you would be proud of

*me. All is quiet though, leaving one too much time
to contemplate whether in action one might fail to
do one's Hunneybest or, even as I write this, fall to
a sniper's bullet. I much prefer the action: one does
what one has to do, and thinks after.*

*The dawn is breaking here, the same dawn that
is kissing you awake in Ashden. Lucky dawn, don't
you think? Oh my darling, remember our orchard,
remember our Christmas, only remember, as I do,
and then we shall be together.*

Caroline folded up the letter once again and blew out the
candle, but sleep was a long time coming. If there had been
no war she would have been married to Reggie by now,
and though she respected his view that they should wait till
the fighting was over, she couldn't understand it. He loved
her, she knew that, even more now than when they realised
they were in love last summer. Daniel's tragedy must have
had a lot to do with Reggie's decision for it had affected
him deeply. During his brief leave at Christmas she sensed
a part of his mind was still on the Western Front with his
men, and he did not seem to have the energy to discuss
their marriage.

Her head told her that was the reason, but her heart
could not share its certainty. He was fighting for their
future, he had told her, fighting for what his forefathers
had built and the future security of Ashden. Then why
not marry and create an heir, she had thought rebelliously.
Perhaps he did not wish to leave her a widow? Why not?
If he were killed, leaving her like this was just as bad.

She was sure that their marriage would give him extra determination to fight on. Did this work for her too? She supposed so, but most of the time she could only remember Reggie's arms around her and his words 'I love you', which held her as a comforting blanket in the uncertain chill of March.

Chapter Two

Margaret Dibble stirred and woke up with sudden pleasure as she remembered Miss Caroline was home again. Normally the house revolved round Mrs Lilley, but today was special. She'd make a bacon pudding for luncheon, she'd got a nice swede tucked away, and the sage was growing again in the garden. Had she enough bacon left? Just about. She'd use the last of the bottled plums in a nice fool.

Time to get going. Things were harder now Agnes was gone and expecting; Harriet was efficient enough, but somewhat less than willing and the tweeny Myrtle was willing enough but less than efficient. Talk about Jack Sprat and his wife. Harriet and Myrtle made a good couple, she supposed – for a three-legged race. That reminded her of poor Mr Daniel and she rose briskly, as if by being at her post she was helping beat the Kaiser. Every time she scrubbed the kitchen table she imagined it was the Kaiser's face and scrubbed all the harder. He wouldn't have no moustache by the time she'd finished with him.

'Immortal, invisible.' she hummed, then burst into song, casting a scathing look at Percy. 'But nought changeth thee!' *He* was in no hurry to beat the Kaiser. Not like her Joe. She'd say a morning prayer for him today, like she did every day. Rectory prayers were getting shorter now, what with fewer staff and the family here, there and everywhere.

She was always in a quandary whether to pray for Rudolf – her Lizzie's husband who had been hauled back to his native Germany to fight for his country, leaving Lizzie to face the result of being married to a German. Twice she'd had her windows broken, poor lamb. They were that nasty, the Rector had found her a cottage on the Hunney estate so she could make a new start. Hunwife, they had called her. Just as well Lizzie had no young 'uns or they'd be in trouble too. Would she ever have any? War had a lot to answer for.

She decided, since she had nothing against Rudolf personally, she would pray for all those who were caught up in this war against their will – Rudolf wouldn't choose to fight for the Kaiser, she was sure of that. He'd rescued a baby rabbit from a fox once and given it to Fred to mend, he wouldn't go round nailing babies to church doors or do nasty things to nuns like the Huns in Belgium. Not Rudolf. She wondered if it were treason to think kindly of a German and decided she didn't care if it was.

She hurried downstairs to make a nice cup of tea before Harriet came in, but to her surprise found the housemaid there already.

'Morning, Mrs Dibble.' Harriet's handsome face looked almost cheerful.

'Morning, Harriet.' She was guarded in her warmth. On the surface all was well between them after the unfortunate happenings of last summer, but you never knew, and she always ensured Fred was out of Harriet's way when she could. 'What you doing early?'

'I dunno.' Harriet shrugged. 'It seemed a nice morning. I thought I'd take Miss Caroline a cup of tea.'

It was on the tip of Mrs Dibble's tongue to say she'd do that, thank you all the same, seeing it was Miss Caroline's first morning home, but good humour made her generous. 'Good idea, Harriet.' The Rector had stopped early morning tea for the family now there were only the three of them, that's if you didn't count Percy – which she seldom did – and Fred, poor love.

She turned her head as the door opened, and there was Mrs Lilley, still in her nightdress and old dressing gown with her dark hair flowing down her back.

'I thought, if you don't object, Mrs Dibble, I'd take Caroline a cup of tea. It *is* her first morning.'

After breakfast, Caroline decided to put off the evil moment for as long as she could by walking the long way round to the Dower House. Instead of taking the garden gate out into Silly Lane, she made her way through the churchyard, with a quick visit to St Nicholas to draw strength for the coming ordeal.

Parker, the butler, opened the door of the Dower House to her with the same degree of condescension, she noted, as he had at Ashden Manor. An imp of mischief had made her bring a calling card: she would be as formal as Lady Hunney herself. It also prevented Parker's sniff when he asked 'What name shall I say?', ridiculous since she had been calling on, and indeed working for, the Hunneys all her life. She had put on her longest skirt, so that only a hint of ankle could be seen and even that was chastely hidden by her boots.

She told herself that anyone who had braved Grandmother Buckford had nothing to fear from Lady Hunney, but was all too well aware that where she was concerned, Lady Hunney remained an implacable opponent who would not hesitate to involve Reggie in her campaign to break the engagement. She braced herself, adopted her best Grandmother Buckford walk, and sailed into the morning room to find to her surprise that Lady Hunney was not there, although she was quite sure it was her 'At Home' time.

'Her ladyship is at her committee meeting,' Parker informed her smugly, as though some kind of victory had been won. 'She will be with you soon.'

Committee? The hospital, Caroline presumed. Or had Lady Hunney started an organisation of her own for the war effort? Caroline hoped the latter; if that steely will were set to conquer the Kaiser instead of her, the war would be over and Reggie returned to her extremely quickly.

'Good morning, Caroline. I am pleased to see you.'

Caroline swung round in surprise, suddenly conscious that, despite her efforts, in this setting she still managed to feel dowdy beside Lady Hunney's Bond Street wool costume. She could not bring herself to return the false compliment but greeted Lady Hunney politely.

'Do sit down. Will you take coffee before you begin?'

'Begin?' In her confusion, Caroline sat on too low a chair. She'd forgotten Lady Hunney's Red Queen tactics of surprise.

'I assume,' Lady Hunney rang for coffee, 'that you've come to resume your duties.'

Caroline was nonplussed. 'The hospital is fully staffed, Lady Hunney. They have already replaced Felicia.'

'Not nursing duties, Caroline. I'm glad you've realised you are unsuited for that. I meant, in the library.'

Before the war she had worked in the Ashden Manor library, but that was a long time ago. Surely Lady Hunney could not be serious? 'But the hospital staff wouldn't want me getting in their way there now.'

'I told you last autumn. Many of the books have now been transferred to the Dower House and I naturally assumed you had come to help restore some order.'

'I'm afraid not.' Panic made Caroline abrupt. A maid brought in the coffee.

'I understood you wish to work for the war effort. Reggie told me in his last letter. Why not here at Ashden? The perfect opportunity.'

'I cannot agree, Lady Hunney. Books can wait until the war is over. And it will be over all the sooner if everyone, not just men, contributes to the battle.'

Snap went the dragon's triumphant jaws. 'Then I have the perfect solution. You may join my committee.'

Caroline knew she had fallen into the trap. 'Committee?'

She fumbled with the sugar spoon, conscious of The Eye upon her, however sweetly The Face might be smiling.

'Mrs Swinford-Browne and I are collaborating on entertainment for the troops at Crowborough and King's Standing. Your sister Isabel has been kind enough to help us with her advice. However, we need someone to do typewriting and clerical work. It will give Reggie pleasure to think of us working closely together.'

Trap? It was a pit and a pendulum, worse than anything Edgar Allan Poe could have envisaged. Refuse outright and she was dammed; accept and she was lost. She would say she would consider it. No, she wouldn't be that hypocritical. 'You're very kind, Lady Hunney, but I don't think it would suit me.'

'Is being *suited* relevant?' The voice was icy. 'You must learn not to put yourself above tedious tasks just because you are Reggie's fiancée, Caroline. It is your duty to help where you can.'

Caroline seized at the first straw. 'I need paid employment.'

'And what paid employment, other than that which you have abandoned, will you find?' A very slight emphasis on the 'you'.

'I'm sure something will present itself.' Caroline felt like Mr Micawber.

'Reggie—' Lady Hunney began, but Caroline's patience snapped.

'I hear Eleanor is working for Dr Cuss,' she said warmly. 'That's splendid news. You must be very proud of her.'

Lady Hunney did not reply, and Caroline squirmed

at her perhaps ignoble victory. She remembered how her ladyship had travelled through the war zone to find Daniel when he was believed dead and felt conscience-stricken.

Eventually Lady Hunney spoke, and in quite a reasonable tone. 'When this war is over, Caroline, the hospital will leave Ashden, and the Hunneys will live in the Manor again. As Reggie's wife you will have a position to maintain. Take care that you keep the respect of the village meanwhile. Work if you wish, but at something which clearly divides you from them. If you make yourself as they are, they will treat you accordingly. We cannot allow that.'

'I respect your views, but can't agree with them.' Caroline knew her voice was shaky.

'Then I bid you good morning, Caroline.'

Was there a grain of truth in what she said? And who were *we*? The royal we? Herself and Sir John? Herself and Reggie? Surely not. Deciding to take a long walk to recover, Caroline told herself that for every grain of truth, there were ninety-nine of falsehood or at least blindness. Committees might do wonderful work, but *all* women should be involved in the war effort, not just educated and aristocratic women. What was so terrible about honest toil that the village might no longer respect her? She found herself walking in the direction of the school house and decided to see whether Philip Ryde were free, though she felt guilty at taking his precious time. He didn't seem to mind, though, and ushered her into the parlour of the school house.

Caroline was relieved that Beatrice Ryde was out. Beatrice cosseted her younger brother like a baby chick and viewed Caroline with deep suspicion, for Philip had been in love with her. Even Reggie's ring on her finger had not served to soften Philip's sister. Philip had a limp which excluded him from volunteering for the Army, but if he resented this his face did not reflect it. To Caroline it looked the same: long, thin, intelligent and gentle.

'So you do see, Philip,' she finished her outpouring, 'why I feel I have to do something to make a place for women to work in this war.'

He thought for a moment. 'You say women are unable to contribute save peripherally, but that's not true, Caroline. Have you looked around you?'

'At what?'

'At who's trying to run the farms. Owlers, for instance. Mr Lake's wife has been out *ploughing*. And not the second or third ploughings either, but the fallowing. And did you see who was behind the counter at Naylor's? Mrs Naylor is the draper now. My sister is helping me here in the school, and taking more and more of the responsibility now I'm away such a lot.' There was some pride in his voice. He had told her he was a special constable in Tunbridge Wells, detailed for the areas where the troops were billeted.

'Yes, but what of all those women who don't have jobs they more or less have to take over?'

'There's always work if they seek it out.'

Caroline thought this over as she walked home down Station Road to the Rectory. No, she wasn't satisfied. Women weren't used to seeking work, it wouldn't naturally occur to many that they were as capable as men of doing most jobs. They needed to be told, to be recruited. Women needed their own Lord Kitchener to call them to factories, shops, offices and farms.

A wagon passed her which she vaguely remembered as belonging to the Swinford-Browne estate, and its driver glanced at her as if waiting for her to acknowledge him. Did she know him? She realised she did. It was that strange man Frank Eliot, manager of the Swinford-Browne hopgardens and oasthouse. She wondered idly how the hops would fare this year. Would the pickers come down from London as usual? Already this month the hop stringing would be in progress. Or would it? She turned to shout after the wagon, then ran up to it as Frank Eliot, surprised, tugged on the reins.

'Mother!' Caroline rushed upstairs and burst into what was called 'Mother's boudoir'. Far from being a place of dainty lace and feminine fripperies, it was her workroom and as cheerfully untidy as a room could be. Heaps of clothing for refugees occupied most chairs, her own sewing was piled on the floor, and the desk had almost disappeared under brown paper, string, sealing wax and tissue paper.

'Don't distract me, darling, I'm busy. I can't recall whether Edith said mark the parcels Serbia or St Omer for the woollens.'

'Address some to both. I *want* to distract you. I've had the most wonderful idea and you're going to help me.'

Laurence had just returned home from visiting old Sammy Farthing, the bootmaker, who was laid low with a quinsy, when he heard a shriek from above. Alarmed, he dashed up the stairs, and was relieved to find Caroline looking exuberant and, though white with shock, his wife still in good health.

She leapt up from the chair into which she had collapsed on Caroline's announcement. 'Laurence, Caroline has gone completely off her head. She wants to go into *farming* – and what's worse, she says I'm to help her.' Elizabeth looked despairing.

He burst out laughing, glad it wasn't serious. 'I don't see you in trousers and boots.'

'Not in that way, Father,' Caroline interrupted. 'I've been talking to Frank Eliot. I asked him how he'll manage with so many of their labourers and casual hop-pickers having volunteered. He said that he'd applied to see if any of the troops in the camps around the Forest could be spared, but it didn't look promising. The government, you won't be surprised to hear, is dragging its feet. So I want Mother to help me organise the women of the village, everyone doing a week or two, when and where the work is needed. It would mean going round to see the farmers to explain and sort out rates of pay, then finding volunteers and running the rota system.'

A hard fist seemed to thump Laurence in the midriff. So soon to have to face this dilemma, and in his own household.

'You see?' Elizabeth looked in appeal at her husband. 'Caroline doesn't understand. It's hard enough organising the church flower rota, let alone something like this.'

'Your mother's quite right. Can you imagine Mutters and Thorns working side by side? She's very busy now, and—'

Laurence knew he was temporising. That wasn't the issue.

'But she could make it the excuse to resign from Mrs Swinford-Browne's Comfort Our Troops committee.'

Elizabeth regarded her balefully. 'Sometimes I think, Laurence, that Caroline has inherited your guile.'

'No, Mother.' Caroline was indignant. 'My plan is common sense, and after all. Father, it's only a slight extension of what Mrs Lake is doing on her husband's farm.' What a good thing she had visited Philip!

'More than slight, Caroline.'

'Ashden depends for its livelihood on its farms and this is the only way they can survive. Where is the extra labour to come from? It's Ashden's survival, not just the farms'.' She was convinced she was right.

'It is worth consideration, Caroline.' He could hardly deny it, he realised. 'But I insist you approach the *farmers* first and only when and if they are enthusiastic should you approach the women.'

'Mother?'

'What do you think, Laurence?' Elizabeth turned to her husband.

No! he wanted to shout. *No.* But he couldn't. 'If you're convinced that Caroline is right and you have the time and are willing to help, why not?'

'It's hardly a role for the Rector's wife,' she said doubtfully.

At that he had to laugh. 'And when, Elizabeth, has that deterred you from something you felt called by Our Lord to do?'

At last, at last, Caroline thought, as she ran down the stairs for lunch half an hour later, I have something to *do*. I'm on my way. She twirled the loose top of the banister at the foot before walking into the dining room where she could smell Mrs Dibble's bacon pudding.

Chapter Three

Agnes Thorn opened her eyes. The walls of her huge bedroom at Castle Tillow looked no less bleak than they had yesterday. She didn't feel like Agnes Thorn, she still felt like Agnes Pilbeam, despite the mound under the bedclothes which was an ever-present reminder of Jamie. Only a few weeks now; it was the middle of March, and she was due early May. Already she was 'wriggling like a chimney sweep', so Mrs Hay the midwife said, the first of May being chimney sweeps' day.

Agnes had done her best to make the room homely. The photograph of her Jamie had pride of place, taken in Dover while he'd been at Shorncliffe training to be a soldier and looking so proud of his new uniform (he'd told her later it was borrowed, there weren't enough to go round).

She hadn't seen him since Boxing Day. He was one of Kitchener's men, and was with the 7th Sussex in Aldershot.

He wrote that he was longing for the order to go overseas. She couldn't understand it. Why did he want to go and leave her? Now of all times – to have their baby alone and *here*. She felt like Cleopatra or some other ancient queen stuck in this huge bed in a vast bedroom with only a chest, washstand and one chair to fill it. Only she had no servants like a queen would have. She *was* a servant.

She could see from the bed the dead embers of last night's fire, but they were giving out no heat at all. She felt no inclination to hurry to wash in the cold water she'd brought up last night, then clamber into her clothes to go down to that barn of an old kitchen and struggle with the fire. Johnson would be nowhere to be seen, for all he was supposed to light it, and Mary who came in from the village would be late again. Miss Emily and Miss Charlotte may be eighty-seven and eighty-five respectively, but they still expected their breakfast sharp at nine.

What was she going to do? Here she was, living in a ruin with two eccentric old recluses at the top of Tillow Hill, way above the village. Before she came no one knew much about the two Norville sisters in their tumbledown castle. Now it had barbed wire all round and a 'moat' (which was nothing more than a pond) in case the Kaiser invaded Sussex. They were looking forward to having a baby in the house, so she'd persuaded Jamie it was best for her to stay on until he got back from the wars. They did not talk about why, but they both knew the reason. Mabel and Alfred Thorn were still insisting she went to them to have the baby. His parents didn't want *her*, she knew that; they wanted someone there to help run the ironmongery like Jamie had done. She wouldn't do it! She wouldn't do it because of Len. Jamie's brother had made his life a misery last year and his eyes crawled over every girl in Ashden. She couldn't go to her own parents either. Even though she was married now, they didn't have room in their hearts or their cottage for her.

No, she'd have to stay in Castle Tillow, heating water on the range day after day. After all, women had managed this way for centuries, she told herself, tears gathering in her eyes. Why not her? Mrs Hay, the midwife, would be there when the baby came, so all would be well. Even Johnson had promised to toll the invasion bell he had rigged up last summer at the Norvilles' behest, only this time it would be to warn Joe Ifield that the baby was on its way so he could cycle out to Mrs Hay who might not hear it where she lived. So why wasn't she content with that?

Agnes struggled out of bed, shivering in the cold, and washed. She felt a little better after that, but not like she used to feel in the nice warm Rectory, old Dribble Dibble or not.

The thought of the Rectory, and the news she'd heard yesterday that Miss Caroline was back home, made her weep a little more, and she had to wash her face all over again in that icy water.

Felicia crept down the stairs to avoid waking her family or alerting Mrs Dibble in the kitchen, on her way to walk to the railway station. Her trunk had been collected by the carrier yesterday so all she had was one suitcase. It was much too early for the first train which wasn't due until twenty to eight, but she could not bear another farewell. She was still afraid her resolution might break. Even now she wished she could convince herself she should remain, because she could help Daniel best by staying here. It was too cruel to be leaving at this moment, when the doctors had at last confirmed that the paralysis might not be permanent. When she went to say goodbye yesterday Daniel had just been given the good news – Lady Hunney, against the doctors' wishes, was convinced it would give him the will to fight. If so, Felicia had not detected it.

He had been sitting in his invalid chair in the conservatory overlooking the gardens, listlessly looking out towards the world he had longed to travel. He had not even turned his head, but he must have sensed her arrival.

'I'll miss you,' he said.

There was a daffodil in the stone pot on the terrace steps. She saw every detail of it still, etched in her memory.

'I could stay.' She was not as strong as she had thought.

'No.' Daniel's voice was detached. 'Even if the paralysis improves, nothing else will.' He slightly emphasised the 'nothing' and then that too lay between them. She knew it was not the leg he was thinking of but that he would never be a normal man again.

'There is a perhaps, though?' The words ground out of her; she couldn't help them. There was no one else for her, only Daniel.

'No, Felicia.'

Had it not been for the sudden throb in his steady voice, she would have been fooled into believing he was relieved she was going. He had never told her otherwise; in fact he had encouraged it. She changed the subject. 'Did I tell you about the rota of local women to help on the farms? Caroline has talked Mother into helping her organise it,' she said brightly. 'The local branch of Women's Farm and Garden Union heard about it and got in touch.'

'I thought they existed only to promote Gertrude Jekylls.'

'Hydes too, apparently,' she managed to joke. 'They're interested in steering their activities towards war work. Caroline went along to talk it over with them, and now the idea is to approach the Board of Agriculture for their cooperation. I can see Caroline conquering Whitehall, can't you?'

'It's Ashden she'll have to win round, especially if my mother has anything to do with it.'

'Why?' Felicia was immediately wary. She was tolerated by Lady Hunney, but was well aware of her implacable opposition to Caroline and Reggie's marriage. 'Surely it's an excellent idea?'

'A woman's place is in organising concerts to terrorise the troops, especially wounded ones who can't get away.' He might laugh at his awe-inspiring mother but Felicia knew how close the bond was between them.

'But women have always helped on the land everywhere, not just in Ashden. Caroline is merely organising it more efficiently in view of the war situation. She's encouraging women who might not have considered it, whether they do it for the war effort or for the money.'

'Not *all* women. Not women like you and Caroline. Especially Caroline. I fear the pitchforks will be out for her. I take it she doesn't intend to have a personal hand in the work.'

'I don't know, but if so, a pitchfork won't stop her.'

'Reggie might, if Mother digs her heels in.'

'Surely he wouldn't.'

'Not if these were normal times, but he's out *there*.' Daniel was quiet for a moment. 'Where are you going, Felicia?'

'Wimereux,' she told him promptly. 'The new hospital run by Dr Louisa Garrett Anderson and Dr Flora Murray. They were running a hospital in the Hotel Claridge in Paris, but they've had to leave it. They've found a large house, Château Mauricien near Boulogne and they need staff.'

She had answered too promptly. 'And what exactly will you do there?'

Go straight to the front, but she could not tell him that. 'Whatever they need. Maybe I'll go on to another hospital. Rouen. Even Paris perhaps.'

'This is the first time you've ever prevaricated with me. You normally talk direct to my heart. That's why I—'

Please, please don't say it. Not now. She could not bear it. Those words that would have meant so much last summer would be bitter-sweet now, and the last shreds of her resolve would vanish.

'Know you're lying,' Daniel finished jerkily, and she relaxed.

'I must be going. I promised Ahab I'd take him for a last walk.' Speak cheerfully – if you can.

'Lucky Ahab.'

She kissed him on the cheek. 'Goodbye, Daniel.'

'Keep safe, Felicia, keep safe,' he called after her as she went out through the garden door.

She did not look back, but she knew he would be watching until she turned the corner by the chestnut tree.

She could not face another such ordeal this morning, but she should have known that Caroline might guess she'd do something like this. When she opened the front door her sister was there, shivering on the porch, hunched up in her navy blue coat, and there were Poppy and the trap.

'It's Poppy's fault I'm here. I heard her neighing and when I came down to investigate it was obvious she was set on trotting to the railway station.'

'How very kind of Poppy.' Felicia flung her arms round Caroline's neck. 'And you,' she whispered.

The clip-clop of Poppy's feet broke the silence that fell between them. There was for once nothing to be said. They both knew why she was going and where.

'Give my love to Aunt Tilly,' Caroline said at last, plunging to the heart of the matter.

'I can't have any secrets from you, can I?'

'Do you have joint plans?' Now that she'd pried so far, she might as well go further.

'Of course,' Felicia replied blithely. 'We thought we might spend a few days in Cannes. It is the height of the season, after all.'

Caroline laughed as she reined in Poppy outside the dark red brick of Ashden railway station, and asked no more.

She remained with her sister on the platform until the train for East Grinstead and London steamed in; it would be her last sight of Felicia for goodness knew how long, and she drank it in: the dark hair piled up loosely under the green felt hat, the neat navy costume and coat. Soon she'd be back in VAD uniform presumably, like Aunt Tilly, though attached to the FANYs; her beautiful dark eyes would be looking out from under a coif. She still felt protective of her younger sister, quite unable to believe her apparent transformation.

'Keep safe, Felicia, keep safe,' she whispered as the train bearing her sister puffed away into the blue and grey distance.

'I'll put a paragraph in the parish mag if you like,' George offered. Caroline was hunched up over the desk in the morning room, surrounded by pieces of paper and home-made alphabetised books for names and addresses; she was glad of something to concentrate on other than the offensive at Neuve Chapelle and whether Reggie had been in it. The attack had been a great success, thank goodness, with gains made and held. There had been casualties, of course, they had read. How many wasn't yet clear. Nor who they were . . . No, she would not think of that.

'Would you?' She looked up grateful at George's offer. 'Paid volunteers wanted for farm work, men and women of all ages.' Well nearly, she didn't want Jacob Timms staggering up offering his services, two sticks and all. Not that he'd want to. He'd miss his mornings putting the village to rights from the seat under the oak tree, a task continued in the Norville Arms on Bankside at lunchtime over ale, bread, cheese and a ha'porth of pickles, and in the evenings over more ale. He claimed he had a right to comment on the news. He'd been newsagent for forty years. 'That won't work alone, of course,' she continued. 'I'll have to bang on some doors, but at least they'll be prepared. And we're also looking for women who will look after babies and children at their homes if the mothers want to work.'

'I could even get a bit in the *Leopard*,' George announced in a burst of enthusiasm. 'Not looking after kids though. Help on Saturday afternoons picking, that sort of thing. That's if chaps aren't barred in your missionary fervour for women hogging the jobs that men could do.'

She flung her book of addresses at him, but he dodged. 'That's a generous offer.' She meant it. For George to give space to her doings in the Skinner's school magazine meant recognition indeed for women's right to work.

'Makes a change from reading what the old boys are up to in France,' he grunted. 'I might as well help that way, there's precious little else I can do. Pa won't even let me join the Volunteer Training Corps at the Wells. Not exactly helping the war effort to spend my time reading in the *Courier* about Skinner's old boys being POWs in Germany.'

'You sound almost envious.'

'Pa's still set on Oxford. I ask you. Now. When he knows I'm just hanging around waiting till I'm old enough to do my bit. Do you know, I nearly got a white feather last week, till she saw the Skinner's uniform and even then she hesitated. The war will be over by the time I'm seventeen.'

'I hope so.'

'Yes.' George had the decency to flush. 'I know you want

Reggie back and all that, but you must see it's different for me. I'm a chap.'

Different for him? No, she didn't see. After she'd given him a piece of her mind, she tried once more to organise her lists. She had had no idea of the varied jobs that farmers, or rather those who entertained the idea of paid women workers, required. Even in the winter there was dairying and stock care, cleaning and oiling machinery, chaff cutting and food mixing – not to mention mending, that bane of a woman's life anywhere it seemed, and on farms it was sacks. Now in March there was a need for potato planting, weeding, cabbage planting, and grass seeding.

In a rough division of work, it had been agreed that Mother would organise the rotas into times, days and jobs with the workers, and Caroline would negotiate with the farmers and seek out volunteers. It had not been easy. Some farmers even refused to see her, word having got round about her mission. One simply told her, women to the stove, men to the field, adding triumphantly he was applying for soldiers, and boys to be let off school, to help the harvest. She simply couldn't understand it.

Then she had had an idea. Meeting a refusal from Cyril Mutter at Robin's Farm, she mentioned idly that George Thorn had also refused and it was nice to see them in agreement about something. Next day his son Norman Mutter had appeared at the Rectory to announce they had changed their minds, they'd be only too pleased. They would undoubtedly deter as many Thorns as encourage Mutters into adopting her scheme, but she banked on mercenary motives bringing the Thorns into line in due course.

Women had been quick to volunteer: women like Lizzie Dibble, left on parish relief of five shillings a week and what her parents could spare after Rudolf was recalled to Germany; or Ginny Patterson, trying to manage on the stingy family allowances with four small children. The last of the Mutters had finally fallen into line with his clan, 'I need a gel to turn manure muck ready for me mangold wurzels,' he announced belligerently.

'You shall have one,' she had replied cheerfully, 'even if it has to be me.' That had silenced him.

This morning, however, she faced a formidable assignment and one she had been putting off. William Swinford-Browne's hop farm. His lordship had generously offered her fifteen minutes of his valuable time.

Caroline knocked at the door of The Towers determined on peaceful negotiation. Its butler answered after a short pause. Most of The Towers' staff had volunteered – the Kaiser, it was rumoured in the village, held fewer terrors for them than the Swinford-Brownes. The butler remained, but in the gargoyle stakes he was on long odds against Parker at Ashden Dower House. The Towers, Caroline thought, as she marched in, could have stepped right out of a Grimms' fairy tale, only it wasn't the princesses who dwelt within this one but the beasts.

The dark trees surrounding the house made it seem even gloomier than its architecture. It tried so hard to be grand with towers, gables and crenelated roof edges, that it was bound to fade as soon as one was ushered into the presence of the Swinford-Brownes: William, pear-shaped with his small darting eyes and hands that were only too eager to follow suit (witness his former housemaid Ruth Horner) and Edith, over-anxious, over-fussy in dress and manners, and over-organising. Caroline had been careful to make it clear to William, that this was a business meeting and to choose a day when she knew from Isabel that Edith was in London visiting the headquarters of the Belgian Relief Committee.

'Good morning, Caroline.' William heaved his bulk up from behind his desk.

What a nuisance that being related by marriage through Isabel gave him the right to call her by her Christian name.

'I'm here about our Ashden Agricultural Labour Organisation, Mr Swinford-Browne. I expect you have heard about it.'

'I have, yes. Go on.'

'Your hopgardens. Can we organise you paid women's help for stringing, digging, hoeing, and nidgeting? And in due course, picking?'

'I could take a few. I pay by eight bushels to the shilling.'

'By the hour for stringing and hoeing,' she interrupted firmly. 'Four shillings for one eight-hour day. And most hop farmers are paying five bushels now.'

'Ridiculous. We're talking about untrained women.'

'We're talking about the cost of living, which is forty per cent up from before the war.'

'Maybe, young woman. That's not my concern. What is, is that with men at the front there's less beer drunk. The brewing business isn't thriving. I might grow and brew my own hops, but I have to sell beer at the end of it. That clear to you?'

'Perfectly, thank you. Unfortunately I can't guarantee workers for you unless you guarantee our standard wages.'

She held her breath. It was a gamble, for she needed his support. To her amazement, after drumming his fingers impatiently on the table for a moment or two, he gave in. 'Have it your own way. You can discuss all the details with Eliot. I told him to expect you. Not too hard to guess what you were coming for. You take after your aunt.'

Delighted at her easy victory, and taking his comparison to Tilly as the compliment he had not intended, Caroline escaped. She was still very puzzled – perhaps, she reasoned, he really did have an acute labour shortage, for all his brave words. Many of the farmers freely acknowledged they had a problem. Schoolboys were being paid half a crown a day for scaring crows, and cutting nettles, but there were few jobs of this sort they could do, and their interest in weeding vanished rapidly when faced with muddy fields and a Canterbury hoe.

She set off down the track to Frank Eliot's home, Hop Cottage. It took her past Hop House where Isabel was living. Caroline debated whether to call in to see her but decided to get her business concluded first. As it happened Isabel spotted her going by and ran after her.

'Where are you going?'

'Hop Cottage. About workers for the hopgardens.' Caroline stopped as Isabel reached her.

'I'll come with you. I need some fresh air – I'll just get my coat.'

Fresh air? Isabel? Caroline laughed to herself, but if Isabel needed company, why not? She led a lonely enough life and somehow she couldn't see her sister putting her name down on the government register for women prepared to work, which was being set up this month.

Beside Isabel, Caroline felt dowdy in her old costume which dragged round her ankles. Isabel's new walking skirt showed not only her ankles but some of her calves as well. Her neat little boots picked their way daintily over the rough track while Caroline strode ahead in her well-worn ones. She had had quite enough fresh air in the last two weeks without dawdling.

Isabel, she suddenly realised, was looking remarkable pretty this morning, quite her old self again, her fair hair and blue eyes sparkling in the chilly sunshine. She listened while her sister earnestly impressed on her the advantages of the new 'military curve' in corsetry, until she grew bored.

'How is Robert?'

Isabel's mouth twisted down immediately. 'Enjoying playing soldiers. Excited at the idea he might be going overseas soon. Never a thought of me.'

'Surely he'll have some leave first?'

'I suppose so. I think he mentioned it in his last letter, in between lamentations that he wouldn't be able to get to Wimbledon this year.'

'You don't seem very enthusiastic about it.'

'Oh, I *am*,' her sister assured her. 'You've no idea how dull life is. Organising concerts for Ashden Manor is the most exciting thing I do. Maud is talking about arranging them for the soldiers billeted in Tunbridge Wells. I might even sing there too. She's a splendid organiser.'

Yes, thought Caroline bitterly. Of everything and

everyone. Between Lady Hunney and Mrs Swinford-Browne the whole village was sandwiched, squeezed on both sides. To Isabel, Lady Hunney had been first 'Aunt Maud' and now 'Maud'.

She was becoming uncomfortably aware of a gulf between her and her elder sister brought about by more than Isabel's marriage. She did not understand her any more. The old Isabel, careless, transparent and laughably selfish, seemed to have given way to a more petulant, determined woman who could no longer laugh at herself.

Frank Eliot's eyes flickered in surprise, even as he bowed his head, when he saw Isabel. He ushered them into his parlour.

'I appreciate your taking an interest in the hop gardens, Mrs Swinford-Browne.'

Caroline never knew what to make of Frank Eliot. He had the reputation of being a hard manager, yet stories of individual kindnesses kept circulating round the village, and Phoebe, curiously, would not hear a word said against him. He had a slightly rakish, ungentlemanly appearance, and dressed gaudily, with a brightly coloured cravat that resembled a costermonger's scarf. This didn't help his reputation, Caroline decided, nor did his piercing tawny-brown eyes which had no hesitation in staring at you till they had taken in all they wanted.

'Not at all,' Isabel replied graciously. 'I have already told Caroline I'll be only too happy to help her organise workers for the hopgardens.'

Caroline tried not to look surprised. It was the first she had heard of it.

'How kind.' Frank Eliot was staring at Isabel in a way that suggested to Caroline he was echoing her own amazement.

'I've agreed daily and piecework rates with Mr Swinford-Browne.' Caroline decided it was time to establish her position. 'And now I'll need a list of your requirements, numbers of workers, how many days and which months.'

'I'll draw one up, Miss Lilley.'

'My mother will supply you with a copy of the rota as soon as possible after you let us have your list.'

'Give me a few days to sort out my own men. Some are still talking about leaving the land to volunteer or go into munitions. I'll bring the list down to the Rectory, say next Monday, and you can reckon to have three at work next week.'

'If you let me have the list, Mr Eliot,' Isabel said quickly, 'I'll take it down for you. I could call for it on Sunday, when I'm dining at the Rectory?'

Such thoughtfulness was rare in Isabel. Curiouser and curiouser! Caroline began to feel the gulf between herself and her sister might be more like Alice in Wonderland's rabbithole.

'Have you seen the *Courier*, my dear?'

Laurence put his head round the boudoir door, only to find his wife absent. Surprised by his own annoyance at this departure from routine, he remembered she had said something at breakfast about organising the women assigned to potato planting at Owlers Farm. He went down to the morning room to try to find the newspaper. It was an established rule that he should read the *Courier* first. It wasn't there, and so, he deduced, someone was reading it. The Dibbles had their own copy, but he wasn't going to ask to borrow it when he had one of his own. George was at school. Caroline and Elizabeth were out. He marched upstairs in search of Phoebe.

'And where, young woman, is my *Courier*?' he asked as soon as she answered his knock.

She jumped up guiltily. Not only had she taken his newspaper, but she had been sprawling on the bed. 'Here,' she said carelessly. 'I'm sorry, Father.' Laurence took the bundled heap of newspaper without comment.

After he left, Phoebe, who had gleaned all she needed from the *Courier*, wondered whether she had the courage to go ahead with her plan. She decided she did – only she wouldn't mention it to anyone just yet.

Returning to his study, Laurence wondered idly what Phoebe had found so fascinating in the newspaper. Mrs Dibble cornered him in the hall.

'If you please, sir, Mrs Lilley not being here, I'll have to trouble you for some money. The coalman's called unexpected.'

Laurence looked at her sharply. 'He normally submits his account.'

'I said *unexpected*, sir.' Her voice was heavy with meaning, by which he gathered the Rectory was being favoured above other residences during the current coal shortage. 'That'll be three pounds ten shillings. It's up again. Thirty-six shillings for the ton of best, and thirty-four for the kitchen. I don't know what things are coming to.'

Nor did he. Reluctantly Laurence counted out the required one pound notes, wondering if he would ever get used to this paper money forced upon them by war. He was tempted to tell the coalman to take the coal away again, but decided discretion was the better part of valour: if the village persisted in stealing his lumps of coal, he had at least some moral right for turning a blind eye. Nevertheless his conscience remained troubled. Before the war the path of right had been comparatively clearly marked; nowadays it was becoming increasingly overgrown.

But he had no right to be vexed over such trifles as coal and newspapers beside the problems being faced by many of his parishioners. Three had gone in the village already. Quite apart from the personal tragedy, there was the financial aspect. How could a widow support a large family on the meagre five shillings a week pension she would receive? Parish Relief was already stretched to breaking point, and he had to top it up from his own equally stretched income. Swinford-Browne, the greatest tithe-payer on the Union committee, had vetoed any increase. Elizabeth had pointed out gently that Caroline's scheme could produce valuable income for the needy. He could only agree, but he still fretted at Elizabeth's frequent absences from home. He had understood that Caroline would do the running around and Elizabeth work in the Rectory. It seemed he was wrong. His wife was being constantly called out to the village for some emergency or other. At that moment she came through the study door in such high good humour that he felt ashamed of his annoyance.

'I called in on Nanny Oates on the way back.'

'And how is she?' He put his arm round her and kissed her on the mouth, rather to her surprise. 'When did I last tell you I love you, Elizabeth?'

She smiled. 'In bed?' she asked daringly, for Laurence liked to separate the twenty-four hours into compartments and, passionate though he was, he seldom liked to be reminded of it during the day.

'No,' he answered gently.

'Then it was at Christmas. I remember because—'

'Far too long ago. Why have you not complained?'

'Because I know you love me, Laurence.'

'That's true. I sometimes think—' He broke off. 'Tell me about Nanny Oates.'

'You won't believe it. She's determined to help the war effort.'

He broke into laughter. The idea of his once formidable nanny, now in her early eighties and rheumaticky, on the march against the Kaiser, bayonet at the ready, was irresistible.

'Boadicea put it in her mind,' Elizabeth was laughing too, 'and it really isn't a bad idea.' All Nanny's hens were named after English queens, but Boadicea being the earliest queen began the rota, and was always the favourite, closely followed by Berengaria. There had been six Boadiceas so far. 'When the hens are laying she always gets far too many eggs and has to give them away. So she proposes to go round the village collecting other people's spare eggs and sell them as well as her own from a stall outside her house.'

Laurence looked at her, assuming she had seen the flaw in this plan. 'If it's good laying time then no one will need them.'

'I didn't like to dampen her enthusiasm by pointing it out.'

'And she's too old to take them into the town markets and shops. She needs a pair of young legs to run them into Tunbridge Wells. We could contact the National Poultry Organisation.'

'You know she doesn't hold with organisations.' Their eyes met.

'Fred!' they exclaimed in unison.

How different this Easter was to last year. Caroline loved Easter, particularly Easter morning. It had always been a Rectory tradition that the Hunneys would come to lunch. All five of them. Last year, however, the Swinford-Brownes had cast their blight on the table and the Hunneys had been absent. This year Reggie would still be absent; could she bear to see the others without him? Sir John might or might not be there depending on his work at the War Office which, now the spring offensive had taken place, was heavy.

Although the newspapers had been told, and had duly reported, that Neuve Chapelle had been a success, when the casualty lists began slowly to appear, the extent of the carnage revealed itself. Thousands upon thousands of men lost. Men like Anthony Wilding, Robert's Wimbledon hero. Men like Johnnie Hay, the midwife's son, with freckled face and bright red cheeks, who should be whistling in the general stores, not lying dead in France. Nor had the offensive been the success claimed. A breakthrough sweep on to Lille had been the objective, not flattening one small village, however gallant the efforts had been in taking it.

There had been an outcry against the misinformation given to the newspapers by the government. Surely from now on the truth would be told? Reggie could so nearly have been on the appalling Roll of Honour of fallen officers, but she had received a letter ten days ago assuring her all was well. The 2nd Sussex had been in close reserve but had not taken part. But when would the next offensive be, for he would surely be involved in that? She made an effort to concentrate on Easter.

Isabel would be at luncheon, no Robert though. No Felicia. Only Lady Hunney, Daniel and Eleanor and, thankfully, *not* the Swinford-Brownes. Even Mrs Dibble's lamb followed by her primrose pie could not have compensated for that. Thinking of Mrs Dibble reminded her of last night. She had been in the kitchen when Eleanor arrived at the door, still in her working boots which she carefully removed before entering. This had revealed to Mrs Dibble the horror of trousers underneath Eleanor's long overall.

'And who do you think you are, Miss Eleanor?' she had asked. 'The Empress of China?'

Eleanor laughed. 'Just being practical, Mrs Dibble.' They had always got on well. As a child Eleanor had frequently taken refuge in the Rectory kitchen and would beg to be allowed to help, to stir, to do anything. At home this was strictly forbidden.

''Tis a man's job being a vet.'

'But there are not enough men left to do them all, Mrs Dibble. Besides, I'm good at it.'

Caroline had rescued her friend and borne her off to her bedroom. 'How are you getting on?'

Eleanor made a face. 'Slowly. I'm trained to give first aid to people, not animals, but I'm learning. Martin's a good teacher. I delivered a breech birth calf the other day.'

'Well done!' Caroline detected a slight flush on Eleanor's cheeks when she spoke of Martin Cuss, the vet. Caroline had always thought of him as rather awkward and uninspiring.

'How's your mother adapting to your being a vet?'

'Adapt? The Forth Bridge bends more easily. She ignores it. Short of asking me to leave home, there's nothing else she can do.'

'You can always come here.'

'Thank you. I would, but there's Daniel, you see. Mother would drive him mad if I left. No, she doesn't refer to what I do and nor do I. The arrangement works very well.'

'Perhaps it will work like that for me.'

'I doubt it.' Eleanor was frank. 'She still seems adamant that you'll ruin Reggie's life.'

'I may ruin her *plans* for Reggie's life, yes.' She felt hurt.

'I suspect that's what she senses.'

'What could I do to improve matters?' Caroline forced a laugh. 'Short of typing for the concert committee.'

'Be very careful with your farm labour scheme.'

'Why?' Caroline was indignant.

'She says it's unsuitable.'

'Has she written to Reggie with her views?'

'Only very generally, I think. She may be biding her time.'

Caroline shrugged, though she did not feel at all nonchalant. 'I can't do my work with one eye on what your mother thinks. I shall just have to risk it. You've got away with it, after all.'

'That may make her all the more determined you won't.'

Late in April, as she strolled home from Lovel's Mill with the extra bread Mrs Dibble wanted, Caroline was surprised to be overtaken by Phoebe vigorously pedalling past on the Withyham road towards the Rectory.

'Hey,' she called after her, 'where have you been?' She was surprised when Phoebe, having dismounted, flushed bright red.

'Work.'

'Mrs Chappell was doing the teas at the station today. I saw her.'

'I—'

'Come to think of it, Mrs Chappell is doing the teas a lot nowadays. What's happening?'

Phoebe remained mutinously silent as she wheeled the bicycle towards the stables where they kept their collection of ramshackle machines. Caroline pursued her.

'You've given up the station teas, haven't you? So where have you been?' She was alarmed, thinking of the mischief Phoebe was all too likely to get into.

'You'll tell Father and Mother. I don't want them to know yet.'

'It depends.'

'I won't tell you unless you promise not to say anything for a few weeks. I'm on probation, so if there's going to be a row, I don't want to find it's unnecessary.'

'Probation? What do you mean?'

'To see if I'm suitable.'

'For *what*? And I promise.'

'I've taken a job at Crowborough Warren.'

'That's a long way to cycle.' Then she suddenly realised and was aghast. 'The Warren. But that's where the—'

'Yes, I knew you'd be jumpy about it. It's the Army camp. The new YMCA recreation hut just opened by Princess Victoria. They needed staff so I applied.'

Phoebe let loose amongst thousands of soldiers? It was unthinkable!

'It's fun. I like it. It's only serving tea in the refreshment rooms, but I get paid fifteen shillings a week. And there's something happening all the time, not just when trains come in.'

Was it fun? Phoebe wondered even as she was saying it. It had been terrifying at first. The recreation hut was packed with khaki-clad soldiers milling about, shouting and joking about the Brides in the Bath murder trial which had preoccupied the newspapers, giving her nightmares. And swearing too – at least she supposed that was what it was; she didn't know most of the words. Perhaps she should have let Caroline think it was an officers' recreation hut. 'Remember you promised you wouldn't tell.'

'I wish I hadn't,' Caroline said grimly. 'I'm going with you tomorrow to see—'

'No, you're not! You do your work, I'll do mine. I'll be

eighteen in a few weeks – I told them I was already. I'm grown up.'

Caroline looked at her. In years, in appearance and figure, yes, but Phoebe was still a child in so many ways. But she supposed she was right; she was nearly grown up. 'I'll give you two weeks,' she agreed with reluctance.

'I'm told you've added your name to this government register for women who want war work, Caroline. We won't be lucky enough to keep you here long then.' William Swinford-Browne laughed heartily. 'Just like girls today, isn't it, Mrs Lilley? Start something, change your mind and leave it all to Mother.'

The beef tasted like ashes in her mouth. She should have known she couldn't escape for long the dreaded luncheon. Although her parents disliked William Swinford-Browne, relations had to be maintained, however formally, because of Isabel. Easter Sunday, even with Lady Hunney present and Reggie absent, had been an enjoyable occasion, but now they were reaping the whirlwind a month later. What a wonderful way to welcome May. Especially as, at Isabel's pleading, her fellow committee member Maud Hunney was once again present.

Caroline was about to reply when her mother intervened. 'I was intending to sign it myself, Mr Swinford-Browne but, alas, I'm over their age limit now.'

'But I can give you plenty of work for the war effort,' said Edith, astonished. There were, she informed them, her Belgian Relief Committee in which Mrs Lilley appeared to have lost interest, the Troops' Entertainment Committee, the sewing and knitting circle for Comforts for our Gallant

Soldiers. 'Despite *all* I am doing, I still feel it my duty to take on more.' She lowered her voice. 'The latest emergency, you know.' News of the appalling use of gas by the Germans in their attack at Ypres was just coming through.

'How worthy a cause,' Elizabeth replied. 'But I agree with Caroline that we have to give priority to our poorer parishioners. In order for them to *give* to such worthy causes as yours, Edith, they must *receive*. In the form of shillings and crowns.'

'Oh, quite,' Edith agreed.

'I would have thought the village was as adequately provided for in that respect as it has ever been.' Lady Hunney adopted a tone of sweet reproach. 'I do feel that at such a time we should remain at the posts we were born to as a matter of duty, not give way to our individual desires. Any farm bailiff could easily undertake this agricultural scheme of yours, Caroline, without troubling your mother. Indeed, I would suggest our bailiff Patterson might be suitable.'

Oh, clever. Caroline chewed her way furiously through her mouthful of beef before replying. Help came from an unlikely quarter.

'I can offer women more than having to scratch around in the muck and dirt,' announced William Swinford-Browne.

'In the hopgardens?' Isabel asked.

'The land's finished. It's shells this country needs.'

What was coming, wondered Caroline.

'The brewery's a white elephant now the King's signed the pledge for the whole Palace,' he went on, 'and meddlesome local councils are cutting drinking hours.

Lloyd George is right though. It's munitions the country needs, and if he thinks drink is doing more harm to the war effort than German submarines, then that's that. I'd sell the brewery if I could, but no one would buy it now. I'm gutting and expanding it and converting to munitions. There'll be work enough there for your girls.' The brewery was on the outskirts of East Grinstead, and several of his present workers travelled there daily from Ashden.

'What sort of munitions?' Laurence enquired.

'Shells. There's only the Woolwich Arsenal producing them now, and we need more. Many more. I've heard whispers.' He tapped the side of his nose with a podgy forefinger, as if to convey that he walked in high places. 'That's why we're not winning this war. No shells, no ammunition. Strikes, drink – whatever the reasons, there's a shortage. Girls can fill shells as well as men, and more cheaply.'

'But that's dangerous work, William.' Edith sounded a little shocked.

William glared at his wife. 'You women say you're equal to men; that's what those suffragettes like your sister believe, Rector.' He could not even mention Aunt Tilly by name, Caroline realised with amusement. How he loathed her!

'And as for the hop farm, I'll give it a year and if it doesn't improve I'll grub the lot up and plough it for wheat.'

Caroline felt tears stinging her eyes as the whole family fell silent. She wanted to shout, 'But Ashden has *always* had its hopgardens.' Now she knew why Swinford-Browne had let her have such an easy passage when she called to see him. He did not care. But it was another ominous sign that the war could be nowhere near its end, if there were whispers in Whitehall of a need to build dark satanic factories in Sussex's green and pleasant land.

She noticed George gazing speculatively over at Swinford-Browne and knew just what was in his mind. A cartoon. Swinford-Browne in a beer jug? His Majesty looking forlornly at a brandy and soda?

'My bit for the war effort, eh, Edith?' Swinford-Browne chortled benevolently.

'Yes, indeed, Mr Swinford-Browne,' Elizabeth agreed. 'You and your wife are an example to us all. Now, I wonder, Edith' (although she would never accord her husband his Christian name she felt some sympathy for his wife) 'as you are so willing to do extra work, there is one task for which I know your kind heart has fitted you.'

'And what is that, Elizabeth?' Edith beamed.

'So many women have answered our call that we need others to look after their babies while they are working on the land.'

Oh, well done, Mother. Caroline had to struggle not to laugh at the look of horror on Edith's face.

Agnes kept her head high amidst all the curious looks. She knew what they were thinking. What was the Rector's former parlourmaid doing waiting her turn for Rector's Hour? The next thing would be whether they dared ask her about the Norvilles. Or maybe they were thinking about how the baby was due and she and Jamie had only been wed since Christmas? Well, let them.

The Rector did not show the surprise he felt when he saw her sitting there. He called her in to his study.

'What is it, Agnes?' Then, when she did not speak, 'Are the Miss Norvilles upsetting you?'

'No, sir. I'll stay there with the baby and have it there too. It's the Thorns.'

'What have they done?'

'They keep telling me I should go there and now the baby's late and I *don't* want to go,' she managed to gasp. There, it was out.

'Then don't go. I'm sure Jamie will understand.'

'But he's not here, and there's been a message sent up with Mary that Len and Mr Thorn are coming to collect me tomorrow and this time won't take no for an answer. Being Jamie's father, Mr Thorn says he has a right.'

The Rector was puzzled. 'It would be more comfortable for you at Mrs Thorn's. I'm sure she'll treat you kindly.'

'But I won't get away again.' Didn't anybody understand. 'They'll want me to work there.'

'Would that be so bad?'

She hesitated, then blurted out, 'It's Len, sir. I'm scared of him. And he do hate Jamie so. Up in Castle Tillow I feel safe. When I told Johnson he said he wouldn't let them in, but I know them Thorns. There'll be a fight, all over me, and I'll have to go.'

The Rector thought for a moment. 'Excuse me, if you will, Agnes. I won't be long.' He went outside.

Agnes felt mightily relieved now it was off her chest and allowed herself a little weep. Five minutes later she was recovered when the door opened and both the Rector and Mrs Lilley came in.

'We've solved your problem, Agnes,' the Rector informed her. 'I'll talk to the Thorns. I think you'll find they'll change their minds.'

'And I can have the baby at Castle Tillow?'

It was Mrs Lilley who answered. 'If you wish, Agnes. We'd prefer somewhere else though.'

'Where?' She wouldn't go to her parents, she *wouldn't*.

'The Rectory.'

Chapter Four

'Out, Kaiser Willie, out! And you. *And* you!' Caroline
hoed vigorously round the barley crop at Owler's Farm.
If she convinced herself each jab was a jab at His German
Imperial Majesty, she would truly be contributing towards
the war effort. She hadn't expected to be wielding a hoe
herself, but when Mrs Lake broke her arm after slipping on
muck in the yard, there had been an emergency call from
her husband, incapacitated himself after losing an arm at
Ypres in November. She had welcomed it, because Farmer
Lake had at first been a die-hard, telling her they could
manage without a pack of women squawking around,
thank you very much, Miss Lilley. But now here she was,
advancing hoe in hand to defeat the enemy. And enjoying
it, tiring though it was.

So far her scheme was working reasonably well, with
a few hiccoughs as one or two women tired of the hard

labour. She had heard whispers about the better pay at Swinford-Browne's munitions factory, and there were always more volunteers for sowing and picking than for weeding. Which was why she was fighting the Germans in this field single-handed.

Caroline stood upright to rest her aching back, glanced at her wristwatch (a present from Reggie at Christmas), and realised with pleasure it was time for lunch. Sometimes she brought sandwiches, but with Agnes's baby already overdue – it had been due last weekend, the 2nd May, and now it was Saturday – she wanted to be at the Rectory as much as she could. How busy they all were! Even Mother. Caroline felt somewhat conscience-stricken at how much time her mother was having to spend out of the Rectory, chasing women who had been 'thinking it over', and altering rotas after last-minute changes of plan owing to the fickle weather which obstinately ignored the fact that it was spring and remained cold and grey.

Father also spent much more of his time out in the village. As well as the sick, the elderly and the bereaved, the war had brought practical problems of how to survive when old means of livelihood were threatened and new ways seemed slow to appear. There were far too many problems to deal with in Rector's Hour. Some of the villagers were, in any case, too proud to attend such a relatively public parade of their troubles, but could be persuaded to respond to a personal visit.

Caroline jabbed at a recalcitrant clump of scarlet pimpernel, aware that she was still frustrated to be here while Reggie was facing such terrible horrors on the Western Front. She knew there were two faces to this war, the one put over in the newspapers, full of successes and gallant heroes, and the one she had seen during her VAD work at Dover, which manifested itself in mangled, gangrenous limbs and now, after the terrible use by the Germans of gas at Ypres, eaten-away lungs.

She poked another clump. This was no time for despondency. If every woman added her pile of weeds, yes, it *would* help, for every job done by a woman would free a man for the front. That was the message being put over by the suffragette movement now. Yet so far little seemed to be coming of the government's register of women willing to work. Although she had put her name down immediately, she had heard nothing, nor seen anything more about it in the newspapers.

She leant her hoe against the hedge and hopped over the stile into Silly Lane to return to the Rectory for lunch. As she emerged past the barrier created by the thick May growth of hedgerow, she almost collided with Lady Hunney, the last person usually to be found strolling in the lane. What could she be doing here? Lady Hunney, immaculately dressed in a severe navy costume and hat, eyed Caroline, from the Wellington boots, up the trousers and old smock she wore over them to the battered panama hat of Father's which she had crammed on her head. A large mud patch adorning one knee completed her toilette.

'Is this your usual attire for your new organisation, Caroline? It seems somewhat strange.'

It was a mild comment, but somehow this woman had the power to reduce her to one of Mrs Dibble's less successful jellies. Caroline summoned her strength. 'No, but I'm helping the cereal harvest at the moment. The Kaiser has imposed a submarine blockade, as you know.'

Lady Hunney ignored the Kaiser. 'I greatly regret that you have taken no notice of the guidance I gave you. Good day, Caroline.'

Before she had a chance to reply, Lady Hunney had walked on. Caroline was relieved that she had escaped comparatively lightly. She shrugged off the slight uneasiness the encounter had left her with. After all, the only hold Lady Hunney had over her was Reggie. She must try to avoid conflict with his mother for his sake, and perhaps Lady Hunney felt the same – hence her less than virulent words just now.

The ever-nagging fear when she did not hear from Reggie had been allayed by a letter yesterday; at last she knew that the terrible battles that had taken place at Ypres in late April had not claimed him, for the letter was dated 1st May. He had written of the yellow poisonous gas fumes that left men choking for breath and blinded. It had been the Canadians who suffered most, he wrote, but the Germans would have a taste of what it was like because now *they* had Kitchener's permission to use gas. It would be the Germans whose lungs slowly, inexorably drowned in water. Once again, the insidious thought nagged at her: Reggie may have survived Ypres, but what about the next battle? This afternoon she must hoe twice as hard, she decided, as the Rectory gate clicked home behind her.

She found her father alone and pacing around the dining room. That meant Mother was out, she realised guiltily, remembering this morning's panic about finding extra labour for planting cabbages at Robin's farm.

'Ah, there you are, Caroline. I thought I was doomed to lunch alone.'

She relaxed. He didn't seem to be blaming her, and all had been progressing normally in the kitchen. Still no sign of the baby, Mrs Dibble informed her.

'I'll go to change. Mother will be here any moment, I'm sure.'

'Perhaps. She went to comfort Mrs Swinford-Browne.'

'*What?*' Caroline almost laughed, so unexpected was the image conjured up. Then with sudden alarm: 'Not bad news of Robert or Patricia?'

'No. Her brother was on the *Lusitania*. You read the newspapers?'

'I didn't have time. What's happened?'

'A German submarine has sunk a civilian liner in the Atlantic with terrible loss of life. Over eleven hundred dead. It's no accident, this is a new and terrible policy. They've even boasted of it in the New York press. Any vessel flying the British or Allied flag is at risk, no matter who sails in it. There were over a hundred American citizens lost in the *Lusitania*. Coming so hard on the heels of the American merchant ship sunk a week ago it must surely persuade President Wilson he cannot remain neutral any longer.'

Eleven hundred lost. Caroline remembered that awful day in 1912 when the *Titanic* went down, and the loss of the *Empress of Ireland* last year. But they were accidents, and this new catastrophe was not. Only last month they had sunk a Dutch tanker, violating her neutrality. That could have been no accident either. 'Now the Kaiser acknowledges no rules of war, America *must* enter; that would help bring peace.'

'But at what cost? More and more lives to be lost while the fighting goes on.'

'Don't you believe in the struggle, Father?'

In April there had been an international women's peace congress at The Hague in neutral Holland to seek peace. Her father had welcomed it, and she had been puzzled that not only the government but the Women's Social and Political Union, Mrs Pankhurst's organisation, had been against sending delegates in case, presumably, it diminished Britain's fighting spirit. The other suffrage societies wanted to send delegates, but were unable to travel because, so she'd heard, the government deliberately suspended the ferry service to Holland.

'I believe we must stand firm against the forces of evil. How to reconcile this with man's inhumanity to man in the form of shells, gas and Zeppelin bombs is a matter that one could argue for ever. But now this war means death to civilians as well as soldiers. I just don't know.'

So far the much-feared Zeppelin raids had been fewer than anticipated. April had seen four, however, although they wreaked little harm. But who could tell what would happen now? Caroline felt alarmed. Seldom had she seen her father so distressed. Perhaps the Misses Norville had been right to fortify their house, useless though barbed wire would be to keep out German bombs. Mentally though, *everyone* should fortify themselves.

'God is our strength, Caroline.' Her father's quiet comment came as a relief.

Mrs Dibble plonked down a plate of stew and new potatoes in front of Agnes. 'You work your way through that, my girl. You're eating for two, remember. There's a nice pond pudding to follow.'

'Why so much fuss about a bally Thorn?'

'What did you say?' Mrs Dibble whirled round on Harriet, who had come into the kitchen after a hard morning cleaning the windows.

'Nothing.'

'Yes, you did.'

Harriet's temper flared. 'I don't mind waiting on Agnes. But I ain't a-waiting on that bastard Thorn she's got inside her.'

'We're wed,' Agnes shouted.

'Late,' sneered Harriet. 'And the Rector had a say in that, I've no doubt.'

'I don't know what's got into you, Harriet Mutter.' Mrs Dibble intervened before Agnes could reply. 'The Rectory is no place for Thorns and Mutters to air their grievances. And you remember, Harriet, you're employed here as parlourmaid-cum-housemaid, and it don't matter what your name is.'

'I don't take my orders from you, but from Mrs Lilley.'

'Want me to ask her, poor lady, with all she has to do, whether she approves of you using bad language about an unborn baby? She's a good Christian lady, praise be to God.'

Harriet subsided. She'd gone further than she meant, but she wasn't going to admit it. She had her pride, after all.

'Tea, miss, and make it a strong 'un, me old china.'

Countless khaki-clad bodies pushing and shoving, shouting in the hot refreshment room, the talk and raucous songs in such thick Cockney accents that Phoebe didn't understand most of it. Drink wasn't the attraction here because there was no alcohol, it being a YMCA-sponsored operation. The soldiers came in droves because it was much nearer than Crowborough's and Tunbridge Wells's public houses – and girls were serving the refreshments.

The refreshment rooms in the recreation hall were under the management of a stern-eyed lady called Mrs Manning, who kept her 'young ladies', as she called them, under a strict eye. Not that Phoebe had any intention of misbehaving; she was still too overwhelmed by the strangeness of it all. At the railway station, her own venture, she had felt in control when the troops laughed and joked as she took them tea. This was a different world. The sound of 'It's a long way to Tipperary' and 'We are Fred Karno's Army', not to mention the awful 'Sister Susie's Sewing Shirts for Soldiers' being bawled out night and day filled her dreams, as tiredness refused to let her brain stop working.

Her work colleagues were strange to her too. Helen was the one she liked best. Her father kept a draper's shop in Tunbridge Wells. Marie's was a milkman in Crowborough and Betty's a farmer. Their language and jokes both fascinated her and repelled her, but she was gradually growing accustomed to them, and Mrs Manning's grim eye stopped them in their tracks anyway, much of the time. Only Marie had so far accepted an offer to step out with a young soldier; she had reappeared the next day with never a word to say about it. Phoebe was the only one who dared to ask her. She giggled but said nothing.

There were thousands of young soldiers at this camp and the recreation hall could hold two thousand, so it was not surprising that the faces were a bewildering and ever-changing mass. One group, though, always seemed to be there, and one face in particular. She noticed him because he never shouted and was often silent when his mates were yelling their heads off. She told herself he was homesick for London, and gave him a special smile whenever she could.

'Miss Phoebe's got her eye on you, Harry,' one of his mates observed.

Harry Darling blushed.

Laurence walked briskly up Station Road to the railway station. Briskness was called for – the weather was cold. All around him May was burgeoning forth and the hedgerows were brilliant green, but above the skies lowered day after day, not even sending welcome spring rain. Half the village grumbled that the guns on the Western Front had changed the weather, and the other half that they were paying for last year's heat. He had just come from a brief chat with Isabel which had somewhat perturbed him. He knew the signs of restlessness in his eldest daughter. He remembered the uncontrolled excitement she had shown when she was so friendly with that scallywag from Groombridge – until he had chased him away. He'd been justified. He was an idler, a rich one perhaps, but he'd married the following year and led his wife a sorry dance. He wondered idly what was making her restless now, then dismissed Isabel from his mind. She was safely married, after all.

Walking through to the platform, he was puzzled to find Mrs Chappell serving teas, and no sign of Phoebe. 'Is my daughter here, Mrs Chappell?'

'Not now, Rector. Taken a job, she has. She looks in here from time to time.'

For a moment he did not take it in. Of all his children, he worried most about Phoebe, who had the least common sense and, more important, the least sense of self-preservation. 'Where will I find her?' he demanded, fear making him abrupt.

Mrs Chappell hesitated, glad the train from London had pulled in so she had an excuse not to answer him as busily she handed out teas and lemonade. He must find the stationmaster. But there was no sign of Chappell inside the booking office and, hovering irresolutely, he noticed a young woman questioning young Mutter as she handed him her ticket. A striking-looking woman, about thirty, with neat hair and a dark green suit and hat. Despite his concern for Phoebe, he wondered fleetingly who she was.

'Where can I find Tillow House?' he heard her ask.

'Down the lane, miss, turn left.'

She looked through the window down the length of Station Road and then at her luggage. 'Is there a cab?'

'Only the carrier, miss, and he's just left.'

Curious as to who she was, Laurence came forward. 'If you'll allow me, I'll escort you to Tillow House. We can manage these suitcases between us. I am Laurence Lilley, Rector of Ashden.'

She turned to him gratefully. 'Thank you.' Her face was glowing, alive, a strong face, he thought, even more intrigued.

'You're to stay with Dr Marden's family?' he asked, as they set off down the lane. 'For the moment.'

'Forgive my curiosity, but I realise now. You must be his niece, Rachel, Mrs Smythe's daughter.' Dr Marden's sister had been lost in the *Empress of Ireland* disaster.

'I'm no relation. My name is Beth Parry. I'm his new assistant.'

'A nurse? But Miss Marden is—'

'I am a doctor, Mr Lilley.'

'Phoebe, a word if you please.'

Phoebe, steering her bicycle quickly round the bushes in the hope of evading scrutiny, stopped guiltily at the unusual sight of her father thrusting open his study window and positively shouting at her. He must *know*. It

87

wasn't fair – she had been on the point of telling him. She left the bicycle where it was and went to the study to face retribution.

'Phoebe, I gather you've taken another job. Can you explain why you felt you could not discuss it with me?'

Trust Father to make her feel really mean. She opened her mouth to defend herself, but then realised there was no defence. But she had done the right thing, she reminded herself.

'I *had* to, Father. I felt I ought to do more for the war effort. There was less and less to do at the station, and this way I really am helping the troops.'

'In what way?'

'In the refreshment room of the recreation hut in Crowborough Warren.'

'*What*?' This was far worse than he'd feared. 'In an Army camp? Phoebe, can you really believe this is the right place for you?'

'Yes.' Phoebe quavered. Then she found her tongue. 'The hut was opened by Princess Victoria. It's run by the YMCA, a *Christian* fellowship. I'm just looking after young boys far from home.'

Laurence's lips longed to twitch, but he restrained them, for this was a serious matter. 'My dear child, Army camps are notorious for licentious behaviour. After all, your friend Patricia is a policewoman patrolling such camps to look out for young girls in moral danger.' He stopped as a thought occurred to him. 'Was this her idea?'

'Mine,' Phoebe said hastily. 'She did mention it to me, but it was my decision.'

'Patricia is a lot older than you, Phoebe.'

'I'm seventeen.'

'And no doubt you told them you were eighteen.'

'Underage men are volunteering daily, Father. Why not women?'

'Because, Phoebe,' he was exasperated, 'young women are more vulnerable than young men in such environments.'

'They are—'

'That's enough!' He had tried to be reasonable, but how could he be in the circumstances? 'You will leave immediately.'

'Oh *no*, Father,' she wailed. 'I love it there. And Mrs Manning is very strict and I'm cheering them up and, oh, they *like* me there. Nobody here in Ashden likes me.' She burst into tears.

Appalled, Laurence realised how little he knew of his own child and her problems. What could she mean, no one in Ashden liked her? There was some deep trouble here and he must tread more delicately than he'd planned.

'Very well. I will have a talk with this Mrs Manning.'

Phoebe squirmed. How she would hate being 'talked' about. Still, if it meant she could stay she'd endure it.

'Percy!' Mrs Dibble's yell could be heard even through the study door. 'Quickly, quickly, you largy lummocks. It's coming. Go for Mrs Hay.'

'The baby,' breathed Phoebe, thrilled. She rushed out of the room past her father and up the stairs before he could stop her.

The world he had known, he reflected, somewhat

dazed, was not only changing, it was rushing headlong. His mother had never allowed Tilly to see either of her brothers less than fully dressed. Now Felicia was nursing men in France; Phoebe was mixing with young soldiers at a ridiculously early age, and Caroline was intent on changing the natural evolution of politics and government. His mother had not let his sister leave the house unaccompanied before she was twenty-one; she had been carefully shielded from the facts of life – though look what had happened, he reminded himself Tilly had rebelled and become a militant suffragette.

Percy wobbled by on his bicycle, though blessed if he could see what all the excitement was about. It was only another Thorn about to enter the world.

'Harriet, get up here and help me with Agnes.' Mrs Dibble ran past the Rector and up the stairs, shrieking.

Sauntering out from the kitchen, Harriet quickened her step as she saw the Rector's eye on her.

'Get the water boiling,' Mrs Dibble countermanded her instruction, and Harriet, sighing heavily, returned to the kitchen.

Up in her old room on the second floor, which she'd insisted on in preference to a bigger one, Agnes lay, clinging through the pain to the thought of Jamie. Her Jamie – waiting to go overseas.

'We've got a baby.'

'Young Agnes, is it?' Nanny Oates stopped counting eggs as Fred ran up the grassy slope of Bankside shouting his momentous news. 'Boy or girl?'

Fred thought about this for a moment. 'It's a girl. I like girls.'

Remembering a time when that appeared all too likely, Nanny Oates replied sharply, 'I thought you were here to help the war effort, Fred.'

'Yes. And the baby.'

'You get yourself to the Wells, young man, then you can have all the time you want to think about babies.'

Each time he went, Nanny wondered whether he would ever get there, but so far he had always returned with the money carefully tied into his large red handkerchief.

'You know where you're going today, don't you? Edward Durrant's as was, in the Pantiles, and John Brown's in the High Street. And if he says he's enough of his own, don't take no for an answer.'

He nodded, repeating after her. He couldn't read, but could learn parrot-fashion.

'And mind you don't break 'em on the way,' she called after him. She was doing well. She'd made over three pounds in the three days on the stall outside her cottage, which she persisted in maintaining, just to show young Mr Laurence there were folks in this village prepared to do their bit by buying eggs, even if he were a doubting Thomas. She sat in her basket chair, tapping with her stick and tut-tutting every time someone passed who didn't stop to buy, even when she knew they kept chickens of their own. Boadicea had been laying well this last week, as if she knew there was a war on. Mary hadn't helped much, but what could you expect of a hen called after Bloody Mary? She'd omit her name next time round and skip straight to Good Queen Bess.

Caroline was in Tunbridge Wells too that Tuesday morning, snatching a few hours off between the Lakes' barley and the hop stringing. She was visiting her friend, the Honorable Penelope Banning, who was home from Serbia and convalescing after an attack of typhus fever. Penelope had gone out with Lady Paget's hospital unit in September and had worked in the Skopje hospital.

As Caroline was shown into the morning room where her friend was sprawled on a chaise longue, she was concerned to see that Penelope still looked very pale.

'How are you?'

'No longer smelling of mice.' Penelope made an effort to joke about the horrible smell associated with the disease. 'What about you? What news of Reggie?'

Penelope had been the apple of Reggie's eye only a year ago, Caroline remembered. She'd been jealous of Penelope then, but how differently she felt now.

'Safe when last I heard. He's avoided Ypres.'

'Leave?'

Caroline made a face. 'No mention of it. The offensives, I suppose.' She hated being made to think of the next attack, yet again.

'It seems a funny kind of war stuck in trenches planning your next move, while facing the enemy doing just the same. Suppose they both decide to attack on the same day? It's different in Serbia.'

Penelope told Caroline that the Serbs were still doggedly defending their country. The first Austrian invasion had failed, and when she had arrived their ill-equipped army was waiting for the next. In December it had come, but been repulsed before it reached Belgrade. For Lady Paget's unit it seemed like constant war, only theirs was against smallpox, lack of doctors, vermin – and typhus, to which she and countless others, had succumbed.

'Will you go back there when you're well again?' Caroline asked.

'Yes. I'm going to limber up with a little work here first, starting this afternoon.'

'Where?'

'The National Union of Women's Suffrage Societies' local branch. Sarah Grand is the president – you'll have read her novels?'

'Of course.' Caroline was familiar with the controversial *Ideala*, which had been published anonymously before she was born. 'I thought you were a WSPU supporter, militant to the last. The Pankhursts for ever.'

'I was, but as they have suspended their fight to win the vote and are all working for the war effort, in their different ways, I might just as well support the NUWSS.'

'Recruiting?'

Penelope laughed. 'Much as I'd like to march up and down on a stage singing patriotic songs, I'd scare men, not seduce them.' Penelope was over six foot tall, but her pallor and thinness might scare them more, Caroline thought. 'If you read your *Courier* you'd have seen that they re-opened the clothing depot yesterday at their HQ in Crescent Road. I'm going along to help this afternoon. All good causes. War Relief and the Belgian Relief Fund.'

'But Penelope—'

'Yes?' An eyebrow arched.

'Clothes?'

Penelope understood immediately. 'I know. Just more of the same. Not a real job. In your situation I'd feel the same. Out in Serbia, though, I saw what those old clothes can do for the wounded and civilians shelled out of their homes. It gave me a different perspective.'

'If the Germans broke through at Ypres to the Channel Ports, do you think that could happen here?'

'Of course.'

They were both quiet for a moment, then Penelope said brightly, 'I'll ring for sherry and petit fours, and then we'll *know* it will never happen here. Now tell me about Ashden and the Queen Bee of the Hunneypots. How is she?'

'Formidable. I don't think Ashden is big enough to hold both me and her, Penny.' Caroline's despondency suddenly overwhelmed her. 'The prospect of years under her eye as her daughter-in-law appals me.'

'If you feel like that, why don't you offer your services to the Pankhurst mob up in London? Did you see in the newspapers they're advertising for girls to support the big demo in the summer?'

Caroline had been so preoccupied with the agricultural rota, she hadn't taken it in. 'The one in July to demand the right to work? Don't they want people to march on the day, rather than working for it now? Anyway, I've got a job – organising women's labour here.'

'Ah well, I'm sure I could get you in to help there if you ever need to. We have a London house. In Holland Park. You could live there – Pa won't mind.'

'What won't I mind?' Simon, Lord Banning, in his fifties, with a mild manner which Caroline knew could be deceptive, came into the room. 'Ah, Miss Lilley. How nice.'

'You won't mind if Caroline strikes camp in Holland Park?'

'Not at all. There's only one feudal retainer and his wife there at the moment, but Miss Lilley is resourceful. Like her aunt.' He raised an interrogative eyebrow.

Caroline laughed. 'Aunt Tilly is well. I had a letter yesterday. She and Felicia are both at a base hospital, driving the wounded to hospital ships.'

'I am relieved. Of course you may use the London house whenever you choose. And if you could persuade Penelope to stay there too, I should be eternally in your debt. London might hold more attraction than Tunbridge Wells, and dissuade her from returning to Serbia.'

Later that evening Penelope, exhausted after a mere three hours of sorting clothes, tackled her father. 'Why didn't you tell Caroline about Tilly, Pa?'

'Because Tilly doesn't want Laurence's family to hear about Felicia.'

'And what are they doing? You haven't told me yet. And how do you know? Did she write to you?'

He hesitated, then shrugged. 'I heard through my

contacts in the War Office that they've formed a two-woman team like Mairi Chisholm and Elsie Knocker. They're treating soldiers in the front line.'

'You mean they're under fire?' Penelope was horrified.

'Even the casualty clearing stations seven or eight miles from the front are within the range of heavy shells.'

Penelope thought for a moment. 'You're still being evasive. They're going out into no man's land, aren't they?'

'Yes.'

He looked at her and continued, 'You too have done so.'

'I'm older than Felicia.'

'Does age enter into it?'

'But Felicia looks so fragile.' Penelope could hardly believe that the quiet, reserved girl with her Pre-Raphaelite looks possessed nerve and determination to venture into the front line, let alone beyond it. And Tilly too. She must be nearly fifty. Ancient, like Pa. Not the age to go dashing about on a battlefield. 'Tilly means a lot to you, doesn't she?'

He considered. 'I suppose—'

'Come on, Pa. Forget you're a diplomat.'

'Yes.'

'Miss Caroline!' Startled, Caroline straightened up, feeling the pain in her back. She had thought she was fit after her VAD work, but weeding corn taxed different muscles. She was enjoying herself, though. Last night she had made a recruiting speech for women volunteers in the village hall, with lemonade and buns to get the women talking afterwards, and the response had been good. Twenty new names, and even if a few changed their minds (they always did) it was still encouraging. And weeding corn at Ashden Manor Home Farm had a charm that working in the vegetable garden at the Rectory had never managed to convey to her.

To her amazement Parker, looking ridiculously out of place in his formal butler's black in the middle of the field, was addressing her. 'Lady Hunney presents her compliments, and would be glad to see you at the Dower House.'

'I'll come at five after work.'

'Now, Miss Lilley, if you please. The farmer has been instructed to free you immediately.'

Fuming with indignation, she hurried to the Dower House, removing her boots at the porch. No comment was passed on her baggy trousers covered with a loose tunic-like gaberdine, though the contrast between Lady Hunney's elegant tea gown and Caroline's hartogs (as the village called such comfortable attire) was extreme.

'Have you quite taken leave of your senses, Caroline?'

'I don't know what you mean. I wasn't pleased to be ordered to leave my work by Parker and I obeyed only because I did not wish to involve Farmer Harris, as he is a tenant of yours.'

'I am glad you recalled that fact, Caroline. He is, however, not a tenant of mine, but of Ashden Manor. One day you will be the lady of Ashden, the squire's wife, his landlord, to whom he is indebted for house, farm and much of his trade. Now apparently he is employing you.

What do you imagine will result from that?'

'Nothing, Lady Hunney.' Caroline kept her voice steady.

'Then you have not the intelligence I assumed you possessed. However, Reginald is—'

'Please do not bring Reggie into this.'

'Reginald is my principal concern. I demand that you give up this work.'

'I cannot.'

'Then I shall instruct Mr Harris not to employ you. Moreover, I shall let it be known in the village that I thoroughly disapprove of your being employed by anybody to do menial labour.'

Caroline tried again. 'I believe that if England is to win this war, Lady Hunney, it will only be with the help of women, *all* women, of all classes.'

'Are you implying I have done nothing for the war effort?'

'As I see it, we must each do what we think best. You on your concert committee, I in my agricultural work.'

'Unfortunately you not only see, but are seen. You do not become your upbringing, Miss Lilley.'

Nor you yours, Caroline thought savagely as she left. Her first instinct was to go to London as Penelope had suggested. But that would mean a victory for Lady Hunney. Perhaps she should remain in Ashden and fulfil her duty here. Even if no farmers would let her work for them, she could still organise the rotas, and that was becoming more interesting now that the Board of Agriculture had asked to meet her.

No! She would stay, despite her ladyship's efforts to dislodge her.

* * *

98

Jamie Thorn came marching to the front door of the Rectory as though he owned the place. He felt as though he did. He was fighting for his King and country – or would be soon – and now he had a wee one to fight for too. No Germans would nail his little Agnes up on a church door, like they did in Belgium. In his mind the baby was a tiny version of his beautiful, grey-eyed wife.

He pulled the old-fashioned bell, and came face to face with Harriet. Her face changed. A Thorn, here, on her own doorstep and her answering the bell like she was his servant.

'Round the back,' she snapped. 'Save for Rector's Hour. You know the rules.'

'I'll be coming in here, Miss,' he replied, stepping in and pushing the door back, not rudely, but firmly. He'd been given some odd looks in the village, and he wasn't going to take any more from this broody Mutter. He was a soldier of His Majesty and worth anyone's front door.

His Agnes was sitting in a chair by the window in her room. She looked on the pale side but she grew pink enough when she saw him. 'Jamie!' She flew across the room and into his arms. 'You're early.'

'Wanted to see my baby, didn't I?' His voice, muffled by her hair, was hoarse with emotion as he held her once more.

'Here she is, Jamie.' Agnes sounded almost shy as she indicated the baby in the wooden cot.

He cleared his throat, but it didn't help. 'She's got your eyes, Agnes,' he managed to say.

'Silly. All babies have blue eyes, not grey.'

'Baby Aggie.'

'I'd like to call her something else, Jamie. It's too confusing with two Agneses.'

He looked up in surprise. 'Mabel?'

'No.' Agnes was rather sharp. After Jamie's mother? Never! 'Elizabeth, after Mrs Lilley.'

'If that's how you want it, Aggie, it's all right with me,' Jamie said valiantly. In fact anything would have been all right with him at that moment, even Ermyntrude Boadicea. 'We'll call her Elizabeth Agnes then. You going to stay here, Aggie?'

'No. I'm going back. The old ladies are looking forward to the baby. And I like it there in a way. No Dribble Dibble.' She tried to laugh. In fact how she'd have managed without Mrs Dibble this week, goodness only knew. She'd done more for her than her own mother, who'd come in, crossed herself as though she were in the home of the devil, and prayed to the Lord not to damn the little baby. 'The Rector says you can stay here if you want, Jamie. Till you go back.'

'That's good.' He didn't mention his parents again and nor did she.

'And Rector says he'll christen the baby tomorrow, and yesterday I was churched to thank God for little Elizabeth Agnes. It was nice they gave you leave after all to see the baby.'

How could he tell her it wasn't leave to see the baby? It was home leave because the new 7th Battalion of the Royal Sussex was leaving Aldershot for Southampton at the end of the month. Bound for France.

Caroline snatched up the letter lying on the morning-room table. The familiar handwriting made her heart leap. When was it written? After or before the battle to capture Aubers Ridge on the ninth? She'd read that the 2nd Sussex were involved in it, and that there had been heavy casualties. She tried not to think of the stark figure she had read. Over 450 officers fallen. Fallen – or shelled to bits? Please, *please,* let the date be after the battle. Her waves of panic stopped as she read: 14th May.

She ran up to her bedroom, shutting the door firmly. Quickly, she scanned the letter for important news. Usually Reggie wrote about the men in his battalion, or the village *estaminets*, and commented upon trench life – the kind of things she read about in the *Courier*. But this time there was no mention of battle at all. In fact it was very brief.

'My darling, the best news. I can snatch a twenty-four hour leave – not long enough for me to come to Ashden, but time for you to meet me in London. Will you? I know you will. May 21st. Victoria Station. No point in saying we'll meet under the clock. I'll see you anyway. For us there will be no one there but you and I.'

In two days she would see Reggie again.

Isabel answered the door herself as Mrs Bugle had been given the evening off to visit her bereaved sister in Hartfield. This suited Isabel. After all, she needed to get those hopgarden schedules sorted out for June or Caroline would be furious. The evenings were so long too. This hadn't been what she expected when she married; nor, she thought, had Robert. Robert had been fun, good-looking, a wonderful dancer. But now he had decided to be a soldier, although there was absolutely no need. He had a perfectly good job in the brewery and, if he'd stayed, he'd have had one in the munitions factory too. It was too bad. Her youth was being wasted; here she was, mouldering in an uncomfortable house which she virtually had to herself. She glanced in the ghastly mirror in the hall, smoothed away the frown, adjusted the rather low neck of her dinner gown and, fully satisfied, opened the door to Frank Eliot.

'Good evening. Thank you for coming so promptly.'

She ushered him into their drawing room. 'I'm so busy with my committees and – and – lots of things, I rarely have a chance to tackle this farm work before the evening.' She laughed lightly. 'You will take a sherry?'

Amused, Frank Eliot entered into her game – if it could be called a game. He owed little to the Swinford-Brownes now. Silly Billy, as he privately termed him, had made it quite plain he intended to sell up the hopgardens at the first opportunity, if not this year then next. As for Robert, he was a nice enough chap but being in the army in Norfolk was hardly like the Western Front – he was near enough to home to be responsible for his own marital affairs.

'You're too kind.' He disliked sherry, but sipped it politely.

'The evenings are very long. I am glad to have something so rewarding to do as the hopgarden rotas.'

'What is it you wished to see me about, Mrs Swinford-Browne?'

'The rota for June. Will there still be clearing to do? And can I offer the women work during the hop-picking season as well?' Isabel was pleased with her businesslike tone.

'I can take all you can offer, Mrs Swinford-Browne.' Frank's tone was bland, but Isabel looked at him uncertainly. 'Your sister is doing sterling work in the fields,' he continued. 'Will you be following her example and hop picking?'

Isabel was taken aback. 'I'm not quite so strong as Caroline, but perhaps.'

'I shall look forward to it.'

'Will you? It is nice to think I have a friend here.' Her voice grew soft.

He rose from his chair, joined her on the sofa, removed the sherry glass she was clutching defensively, turned her to him, and kissed her.

Her first thought was that his moustache tickled but his lips were warm and confident. She struggled a little, then as his hands soothed her and stroked her face, her hair, she relaxed and her mouth opened under his. Some minutes later she was aware that she was almost lying on the sofa and that his hands were no longer on her hair but on her breasts, pushing aside the dinner gown.

Panic-stricken, she pulled herself free. 'Mr Eliot, I am a married woman.' The indignation in her voice was not feigned.

He seemed to be breathing heavily but he released her. Then she realised he was shaking with laughter.

'So you are, Isabel, so you are.' He made as if to rearrange her bodice but she pushed his hands away. 'Come to me, Isabel, when you're ready.'

'I don't know what you mean,' she replied haughtily.

'For the picking of the ripe hops, of course. What else?'

'Victoria Station. No one but you and I.' Caroline was just one of hundreds of people waiting for the Channel train to steam in. She felt sick with excitement, anticipation and tension, and there were a hundred questions she wanted to ask but knew she would never dare. The feeling that seemed to fill her up and stop somewhere just under her chin could all be translated into one glorious word: Reggie. In a few moments she would see him. All the letters, all the words, all the emotions they had exchanged would be behind them and they would be together, if only for a few hours. What price chaperones now, she thought. Less than a year ago it would have been impossible for her to have met Reggie alone, even if they were engaged, but now that world was over and done with!

There was a stirring in the crowd and she saw the smoke of an approaching train. The train. The signal was down, and everyone surged round the platform barrier. Doors opened with the help of khaki-clad arms. She jumped down from the bench she was standing on, changed her mind and climbed back, then jumped down again and surged forward with the rest.

Reggie was right. There were only the two of them. As she saw him, the crowd seemed to part as easily as the Red Sea. But was it him? He seemed smaller somehow, despite the uniform and cap. How ridiculous. Of course it was Reggie! The same good-looking, almost classical features, the same easy walk, and smile. She wanted to laugh, to cry; gasping 'I love you' she hurled herself into his arms.

As they reached the cab line, she noticed with anxiety that he looked almost bewildered. The lightness she remembered in his eyes had gone and, now their greeting was over, even the smile had vanished. She had to steer him into the cab herself, and was surprised when he gave an unfamiliar address in Westminster to the driver. It was his father's flat, he explained, after they had arrived and been shown into the first floor apartment. Reggie threw himself into an armchair.

'How long?' she asked, watching him.

'I have to leave at four. I came overnight.'

'Did you sleep?' Were these pointless time-wasting words all she could think of when what she really wanted to burst out with was how much she loved him?

'Some of the time.'

'You don't look like it. Shall I make some coffee to wake you up?'

'I'll ring for some.' He forced a laugh. 'You're looking splendid, Caroline.'

Appalled, she faltered: 'Reggie, this is *me*.'

He hid his face in his hands. 'I'm sorry, darling. It's so different.'

'To how things were in Ashden?' Oh, how she remembered the carefree ecstasy of last summer.

'To over there. This time yesterday I woke up in a

105

muddy trench dug-out, with a plate of lumpy fatty meat thrust under my nose. This morning, I climb into a cab, see the old crossing sweeper outside the station, the girl who sells lavender on the corner, people strolling around as though they haven't a care in the world.'

Illusion, Caroline thought bitterly. They had cares, oh they had. But not the same ones.

She sat down and put her arms round him. He wasn't shorter, that was an illusion too. He seemed further away, that was all. Surely she could bridge that gap with the right words? So she began to talk of Ashden, of Agnes, of the rota she and her mother were organising, of all the things they had once shared. Gradually she sensed that he was beginning to listen.

'Do you want to talk about the war?' she asked when she had exhausted her news.

'No. Let's have lunch at Romano's, shall we?'

She was disappointed. She wanted these precious few hours to be theirs alone. But she would not argue with him when time was so short.

It was not the Romano's of pre-war days. As a great treat, Aunt Tilly had taken her there, when it was crowded with theatre actors and actresses, and chorus girls with their escorts. Now all she could see was uniforms. But to her surprise, Reggie seemed to relax at last, laughing and joking with the other officers. Her heart ached. She seemed to be sitting opposite a stranger, a casual friend, not the man she loved, and was going to marry. She was even reduced to talking about the new coalition government Mr Asquith had been forced to accept.

Then suddenly Reggie put his hand over hers. 'Do you still love me, Caroline?' he asked.

She felt ridiculously happy. It was going to be all right after all.

Once back in the flat she could not restrain herself any longer. 'Reggie, I can't stand life without you. When can we be married?'

'When I see whole bodies around me again, not mangled or yellow with gas. When men can be husbands and fathers again, not cannon fodder. If only you knew—' He stopped.

'Tell me. Please.'

'I can't.' But his lips did the telling, as he kissed her.

'If we can't marry,' she whispered, 'then let us at least love.'

He buried his face in her hair, then kissed her again, his hands moving over her, her legs, her breasts. His body felt firm and alive. She closed her eyes with happiness, hoping that at last they would be one.

Then he pulled back. 'Shall I take my dress off?' she asked uncertainly.

'No.' His voice was harsh. 'Reggie, what have I done?'

'Nothing. Nothing. I just can't. Not with you, Caroline.'

'*Why* not with me?'

'Because I—'

'Don't you love me any more?' She felt utterly humiliated and confused, her only thought being that he did not want her.

He kissed her gently on the mouth. 'I love you, Caroline, as much – no, more than ever. I just want to save my pudding for later.'

She began to feel better as she remembered how, when Reggie was little, he had insisted on Mrs Dibble's pond pudding every time he lunched at the Rectory. On one occasion he had been caught shovelling it from the plate into an old biscuit tin so that he could enjoy it all the more later on. Old times, old ways, and now they were changing.

She struggled to understand what he was going through. 'Don't worry, Reggie. I am fighting at your side. Really. You should see me working. Boots, trousers—'

'Please don't,' he interrupted hoarsely. 'Do your rotas if you wish, but don't work in the fields.'

She sat still with shock. 'You can't mean that. I am staying in Ashden like you wished. Why don't you approve of my work in the fields?'

'I don't care about boots and trousers. What I mind about is the hell over there and my need to think of Ashden at peace. And Ashden to me means you and my family.'

But which, Caroline wondered as she waved him goodbye an hour later at Victoria, was the stronger loyalty? Then a terrible thought occurred to her: was it a coincidence that Reggie's brief leave had come so quickly after her quarrel with his mother? Or could Lady Hunney have ordered her son home? The Reggie Caroline loved would have disregarded such an order. Or would he? Back to haunt her came his words of last year: 'As soon as the old man dies, I'm lord of the Manor whether I like it or not. Just once in a while I feel like cutting loose.' But she knew he never would. Not Reggie.

She was certain of something else too: there could be no peace in Ashden while she and Lady Hunney remained in the village together without Reggie's restraining presence.

Chapter Five

'If you please, ma'am, Percy says when's the tennis match to be? He needs to start rolling.' Mrs Dibble pursed her lips challengingly.

On the point of hurrying out to settle a dispute as to whether Mrs Stone or Mrs Dodds was on the rota tomorrow for hoeing the flax, Elizabeth was startled by the question. 'Here?'

'Where else, ma'am? The Rectory always holds a tennis match in June.'

'But there's no one here to play, except Phoebe and George, and in any case now the—'

'It's always been done.' Mrs Dibble was not going to accept war for an answer.

'Not this year, I'm afraid.'

'If you say so, ma'am.' Mrs Dibble started the long march of disapproval back to the kitchen.

Elizabeth sighed. 'I can see you are not convinced.'

The rigid back turned round briefly. 'To my mind, ma'am, it's a wicked shame to let the Kaiser beat us.' Mrs Dibble disappeared into one domain that the Kaiser would never dare claim.

'What is the wicked shame?' Laurence came in through the front door from Matins in time to hear the dispute. 'Why is Mrs Dibble upset?'

'She was asking when the tennis match is to be, Laurence,' Elizabeth explained. 'Of course it's out of the question, now that Caroline and Felicia have left, *and* so many young men.'

Laurence thought for a moment. 'But Eleanor's still here, so is Janie Marden; there is Phoebe, George, Dr Cuss, perhaps Philip Ryde, and I'll ask Pickering if he knows how to use a racket. Why don't we invite the wounded officers from Ashden to be spectators?'

Elizabeth felt torn. One half of her begrudged the precious time, so badly needed on farm organisation now that Caroline had left so suddenly, the other half – well, the other half pointed out that her first duty was to support Laurence. She realised, to her dismay, that she had not done much of this lately. Parish work had never been her forte, and she disliked committees, arguments, even her role as village peacemaker. But war work was quite different. Why, she was *enjoying* what she was doing!

'Would sick men want to watch such an active sport knowing they might never play again? And –' Elizabeth exclaimed as a terrible thought hit her – 'what about

112

Daniel? Just think how he would feel as a spectator at a match he's always played in before.'

'We can't *not* hold the tournament because of Daniel,' Laurence said firmly. 'But do you have the time?'

'Mrs Dibble will—' Elizabeth broke off, ashamed of her instinctive reaction. Of course she must organise it. 'Yes, Laurence, I do.'

Laurence smiled. 'Good. And there's our new lady doctor. Another recruit.' He went into the morning room to consult the huge diary that always lay open on the table. 'We'll hold it on Saturday the nineteenth. Perhaps Caroline will come down for it.'

'I'm sure she will.' Elizabeth knew how hard Laurence had found Caroline's unexpected departure, and she resolved to write to her daughter. Then she went into the kitchen to tell Mrs Dibble. 'What about the food, Mrs Dibble? What will you do without the girls' help? I could ask Mrs Isabel—'

'Thank you, Mrs Lilley. I'll manage with Harriet and Myrtle.' Her wooden expression did not change, but Elizabeth detected some relaxation in the ramrod straight body. 'Managing' was, after all, Mrs Dibble's way of doing her bit for England.

'Even if we have, say, fifteen or so officers from Ashden as spectators?'

This time the eyes glinted. 'Nanny can give me some of her eggs, seeing it's for the war.' Mrs Dibble's pleasure could only be judged by the alacrity with which she burst into song as Elizabeth left: 'Fight the good fight . . .'

* * *

The Rectory tennis match. Caroline nearly cried at the absurdity and wonder of it. She had assumed it would not take place, but here was the invitation, in Mother's own distinctive black copperplate. Of course she'd go.

Caroline had been in London for nearly a week, at the WSPU headquarters in Lincoln's Inn House, and was finding it a totally different city to the one she had known from visits to the theatre and shopping in Regent Street. Now the streets were crowded with men in strange uniforms, most of whom seemed keen to enjoy the delights of London's night life, the dancing, theatres, and the new nightclubs.

But the night after she had arrived, on Sunday, the last day of May, Zeppelin bombers had attacked the East End of London. Seven people had been killed, and another thirty-five injured, and thousands of pounds worth of damage done. A general feeling of anger directed at anyone thought to have German links quickly spread through the whole of the capital, adding fuel to the bitterness still rippling through the country over the sinking of the *Lusitania*.

To Caroline's relief Lord Banning's town house, in Norland Square, Holland Park, was one step removed from the daily reminders of war. On her arrival she found she was not the only temporary lodger. To her amazement, her cousin Angela had arrived two weeks earlier to work as a VAD at the newly opened Women's Hospital Corps hospital in Endell Street, run by Dr Louisa Garrett Anderson. Caroline had no idea that Angela even knew Lord Banning or Penelope but it turned out she was a friend of Penelope's brother James.

Caroline had always liked her cousin, but had little in

common with her. Angela was thirty-one to her twenty-two and was, in her family's view, an old sobersides, stolid to look at and in disposition. Caroline's surprise had been all the greater at finding her in London, since it had been assumed at the Rectory that Angela would be stepping into Aunt Tilly's place as companion to their formidable and highly capable grandmother.

'What did Grandmother say to your leaving?' Caroline asked.

'I'm afraid she was not pleased. But as I said I was going anyway, and since I'm well over age, there was little she could say except—'

'Except?' Caroline prompted.

'That she'd withdraw my allowance,' Angela finished awkwardly. 'Fortunately Father came to the rescue, on condition Mother doesn't know.' She looked meaningfully at Caroline. 'Anyway, I'm earning now,' she pointed out with some pride.

Despite her conviction as to its value, Caroline was finding her new work distinctly dull. Her excitement in hearing of Mrs Pankhurst's plans for the July demonstration was quickly dissipated by the mountain of letters she had to answer, as she sorted volunteers into their designated roles and described the white dress and flowers that each member should wear. The ancient typewriting machine allotted to her seemed to be in conspiracy with Mr Asquith to interfere with the WSPU's smooth running and her fingers spent much of each day covered in black ink.

It had been decided that every Allied nation was to be represented by one of its countrywomen, and Caroline's particular task was to select a suitable candidate for Belgium. So far she had put forward six names, none of whom had found favour with Mrs Pankhurst's right-hand woman, Annie Kenney, who was in overall charge of this part of the procession. Caroline was a little downcast, but she reminded herself she had only been working there for a week.

She had also been disappointed to see little of either Mrs Pankhurst or her fiery daughter Christabel. They tended to descend at intervals like goddesses, and then disappear again in a flash of lightning. Countless stories circulated about them, both admiring and not so admiring, and Caroline was beginning to realise that there were as many undercurrents and rifts in the office as there were in Ashden.

Tonight, Caroline was dressing reluctantly to go out to dinner. Penelope, who was still convalescing, had telephoned to say that she didn't feel well and asked her to accompany her father. Much as Caroline liked Simon Banning, the prospect of a diplomatic dinner on an early June evening did not appeal when London had so much else to offer. She had suggested to Angela that she might like to go, but her cousin had informed her that she disliked most social events. Still, Caroline consoled herself, she'd be going to the Carlton, and the food would be excellent. She had never been there before, and was curious to see the famous Palm Court. Her old blue gown would have to be good enough for it, simply because she didn't have anything else. Thank goodness it was now fashionable to look neat and unostentatious rather than like a model from Vogue magazine. She inspected her image in the mirror, stuck a few more pins in her hair, perched her evening hat on top, and decided she was ready.

By the time their cab arrived at the Carlton, Caroline found she was beginning to look forward to the evening, diplomats or no diplomats. But when she emerged from the cloakroom to rejoin Lord Banning, he appeared to have vanished. After waiting for a few minutes, she took a deep breath and plunged into the Palm Court, already crowded with dinner suits, uniforms, evening dresses and huge waving fans. She glimpsed Lord Banning talking to a small group of people. Shock hit her. She was lightheaded. She must be. For a moment she could have sworn he was talking to Aunt Tilly. And wasn't that—

'Felicia!'

Heads turned as Caroline rushed to embrace her sister, and then Aunt Tilly. Felicia was thinner than when Caroline had last seen her, and was wearing a black evening dress which suited her dark hair and eyes magnificently, but highlighted the signs of strain on her pale face. Something looked different though; and it took Caroline a moment or two to realise it was the cut of her dress, and her hair which was twisted on top of her head in a severe style without the curls that Caroline was used to.

Caroline hugged Felicia again. 'What are you both doing here?' she demanded. 'Are you back for good?'

'Two days, I'm afraid,' Tilly said ruefully. 'This is a FANY effort to raise money for the Belgian Hospital

117

Lamarck at Calais. Felicia and I were only asked to come at the last moment, so Simon thought he'd surprise you.'

'He certainly did that.' Caroline gave her darling, unpredictable aunt a second hug. She looked thinner too. She was a tall woman, and had a face that commanded attention. A lived-in face, Caroline decided, delighted to see Tilly was still ignoring any call to fashion. Surely that purple monstrosity used to appear regularly at Ashden long before the war? Both of them, here and *safe*. Oh, life was so wonderful.

'How's Mother, Caroline? And everyone else?' Felicia asked eagerly. 'And Reggie?'

'I saw him recently on a brief leave.' It was too much to hope her careless tone would deceive Aunt Tilly.

'Still in love?' she rapped.

'Of course.' More, more.

'Then pray explain what you are doing in London. I'm delighted you're working for the WSPU, but what happened to the agricultural rota you wrote to me about so enthusiastically?'

'Mother said she could manage alone. Didn't you get my letter?' Caroline was surprised, for her post to Reggie rarely took longer than a week.

Even the excellent dinner now took a lower priority in her enjoyment of the evening. Their party was sitting at the head table, and she was delighted that, contrary to the 'rules', she had been placed next to her sister. She suspected Simon might have had something to do with this.

'How's Daniel?' Felicia asked when Caroline had run out of Ashden news. 'Is the paralysis lifting?'

'Not yet. But they're still hopeful. Doesn't he write to you?'

'No.'

Quickly, Caroline changed the subject. 'Tell me about your work, Felicia. I do remember what it's like.'

'It's similar to what you did in Dover. Tilly drives the ambulance,' Felicia replied immediately, 'and I stay inside with the men.'

Caroline was dissatisfied with her answer. It sounded too prepared. 'How near do your ambulances go to the front line?'

'Not near at all. Casualty clearing stations are miles away from action, and we drive the men back to the base hospitals, or straight to the hospital trains.'

Caroline glanced at her sharply, but decided not to press further.

After the dinner was concluded, the speeches began. Caroline listened enviously to the Hon Secretary of the FANY describing the work its teams were doing overseas, but the words 'advanced dressing stations' reminded her of Reggie, and her mind drifted off. She came to with a jump as she heard the words, 'and His Majesty King Albert has graciously offered the decoration of the order of Leopold II to two remarkable women, Lady Matilda and Miss Felicia Lilley, for their courageous front-line work with the wounded.'

Caroline nudged her sister accusingly. 'Front-line work?' she whispered. Felicia and Tilly looked as stunned as she did.

'We thought it best to keep our work quiet.' Tilly leant

across the table. 'We weren't the first – the credit goes to Elsie Knocker and Mairi Chisholm – the Two Women of Pervyse, as the newspapers call them. And we won't be the last.' She looked at Simon suspiciously. 'Did you know about this?'

'No.' He held up his hands in supplication. 'I swear it. I wouldn't have had the courage to keep it from you.'

'You, Simon, are like the hat you gave me. Steel within, and soft felt on top. Courage, indeed.' She almost snorted her indignation.

'I want to know all about it. From both of you,' Caroline intervened.

'After Tilly's had a dance with me,' Simon said.

Left alone, Caroline and a much shaken Felicia managed to retreat to the Palm Court.

'Well?' demanded Caroline, having secured two seats ensuring reasonable privacy.

'There's nothing much to it,' Felicia said defensively. 'The Belgians need heroines to advance their cause. They want to hand out decorations. I'm young—'

'Yes. You're only nineteen.'

'Mairi Chisholm is eighteen. You can't understand what it's like out there, Caroline. The Red Cross won't officially let anyone serve till they're twenty-three, but there is such a crying need for willing hands that if you have qualifications and determination, no one is going to turn you away – particularly,' she added, 'if Aunt Tilly has anything to do with it.'

'But why did she take you with her into the front line, when FANY's work – according to the secretary this evening – usually operates well back?'

Felicia was indignant. 'Do you think I am such a fragile flower that I can't make my own decisions? Tilly did all she could to dissuade me. I simply stowed away in her ambulance the first time I knew she was visiting a regimental aid post – that's the one nearest the front. It was at Neuve Chapelle. There was a bombardment, we were ordered back, but we refused to go because men were dying and wounded all around us. During the battle for Ypres we did the same, but we found shelter in a half destroyed farm and made that our base. Does that answer your question?'

'Yes, but I have another.'

'You're going to ask me why I do it?'

It was Caroline's turn for anger. 'Now you're underestimating me. Oh, Felicia, are we so driven apart by war?'

Appalled, Felicia took her hands. 'You're right. We mustn't let it divide us. It can so easily happen.'

So easily. Was that what was happening between her and Reggie? Now it was happening with Felicia too, and she realised it was up to her to bridge the gap between them. 'What is it like?' she asked. 'Please tell me.'

Felicia took a deep breath. 'It's a new kind of war, Caroline. War has always been terrible, but this is an apocalypse. Men with blue faces, gasping out their lungs for the breath to live, the smell of gas gangrene, bits of bodies lying like pieces of a jigsaw puzzle, blood and pain everywhere. On the field, in the ambulances, in the aid posts, doing your best to give first aid to dying men, seeing

121

others fighting to live. It's all pain, Caroline, *pain*.'

Caroline was silent for a moment, then said urgently: 'You mustn't leave us, Felicia. Not in your heart at any rate.'

'I'll try. Sometimes though, out there, the heart has to be sealed off in order to survive.'

'You mentioned the hat I gave you.' Simon steered Tilly round a couple who were dancing ragtime rather too energetically.

'Certainly. I am known to the troops as the Lady of the Blue Hat.'

'I'd rather offer you greater protection.'

'Simon!' There was a warning note in Tilly's voice.

'I suppose,' he continued, 'if I kissed you – not here of course, but perhaps discreetly behind a palm tree – you would refuse to speak to me again?'

'Of course.'

'Then I won't. Instead you will lunch with me tomorrow. There's a little restaurant I know in Soho, where Mama does the cooking, and Papa serves it. I am known to them as *il signore degli ravioli*, owing to my fondness for the dish. We shall forget we are peers of this realm and cogs in the effort to win a war, and become a man and a woman. You will be called *la signora del gelato*.'

'*Gelato?*'

'Ice cream. Hard outside but given time, will melt.'

Tilly hesitated.

'Are you evading my bombardment?'

'Does it matter? You seem to be an expert in trench warfare.'

He laughed. 'My expertise lies in the timing of the offensive.'

'Suppose the enemy has crept away in the meantime?'

'She won't.'

'You're very sure of yourself.'

'Ah.' His hand held hers a little tighter. 'One of the many advantages of maturity.'

Chapter Six

Mrs Manning had passed Father's test; Phoebe was permitted to work in the recreation hut on condition that she conduct herself like a lady. Seated beside Private Harry Darling in the darkened cinema, she wondered both at her own daring and whether this was violating her promise. Not only was she out unchaperoned with a private soldier, but she was at a cinema showing an American film, *The Squaw Man*, with Indians and cowboys. Father had forbidden her to go to the Swinford-Browne picture palace in Ashden but, she consoled herself, he had said nothing about cinemas in Tunbridge Wells.

This was the first film she had ever been to and bore no relation to the old magic lantern shows they had enjoyed when they were young. It was fast and exciting, with a dashing hero played by Dustin Farnum and the music crashed out of the piano louder than had ever been permitted at the Rectory. And because it was about America, it was educational, so Father couldn't possibly object, even if he knew – which he wasn't going to.

As she came out into the sunshine afterwards, she blinked, and turned to Private Darling – Harry, as she now called him. 'I did enjoy that.'

He swelled with pride. 'I'm glad, miss.'

He'd never stepped out with someone like Miss Lilley before. Come to that, he hadn't stepped out with anyone much. Miss Lilley had been kind to him, and his mates assured him she was a stunner. He could see that. Full figure and a face like one of those roses he saw in the gardens in Crowborough. The only roses he saw back home grew in Victoria Park and they weren't like the ones down here in the country, sprawling everywhere like they owned the place. His mates had dared him to ask Miss Lilley out on her afternoon off, and to their surprise he had.

Phoebe was wondering whether he would kiss her. Half of her was enthusiastic at the prospect, the other half, remembering the fright she had had last year, was nervous. This, she reminded herself, was a soldier; a stranger. It wasn't like teasing Christopher Denis, Charles Pickering's predecessor as curate.

Harry did kiss her, but not on her lips, nor even on her cheek – he didn't dare. He kissed her hand instead.

Phoebe bicycled home, singing 'You are my honey-honey-suckle', feeling like a princess, and seeing herself as a beautiful mother to the soldiers. No, not mother, sweetheart. She avoided washing her hand that night, and kissed it against her pillow to re-capture her illicit pleasure.

Agnes Thorn hauled herself out of bed to feed Elizabeth. She'd been up six times during the night and now it was time to go downstairs to light the range and the living-room fire, no matter if it was June. Living room was an odd word for the enormous, bare baronial-type hall in which the old ladies spent their days, but they felt the cold. Jamie must be colder still in the mud of a trench in the front line. She hadn't heard a word since he left for France with the 7th Sussex at the end of May.

Elizabeth was her delight and her chief concern – the latter because once she had brought her downstairs, she was hardly allowed to see her save to feed her, and even then Miss Charlotte and Miss Emily wanted to watch. It embarrassed her. They were good with the baby and rocked her to sleep, but she couldn't help noticing that Elizabeth was always 'our' baby. It made her uneasy, somehow.

She should be glad, she supposed, for their help in looking after Elizabeth, for she grew very tired. Even though Mary from the village did the cleaning, she was on the go from six to eleven, with hardly a pause, seven days a week. And she was up at nights too. She never had a minute to herself even to visit the village unless she could think of a good excuse to run an errand.

She was lucky, she told herself, to have a roof over her head, and to be earning her own money. Well, not earning – the Miss Norvilles couldn't afford more than her keep. But at least she had her separation allowance now she was married.

Her only regular escape was on to Tillow Hill to scour the undergrowth and fields for young dandelion leaves, nettles for soup, wild garlic, and anything that could eke out their meagre diet. And all the while Elizabeth Agnes kicked her legs and cooed with her two elderly guardians.

> *Darling, darling Reggie,*
> *What do you think? The tennis match is to take place at the Rectory to cock a snook at the Kaiser! It's on the nineteenth. I shall go, but every moment I'm there I'll be thinking of you and of our glorious day last year, and be glad that soon you will return safe and sound to play there again. I can't even bear the smell of roses this year, not without you, but I shall go and help make sandwiches. Who was it 'went on cutting bread and butter' in life's adversities? My darling love, since I'm talking of butter, have I ever mentioned to you that you are the butter of my life, and the jam too—*

Caroline broke off. It was not easy to think what to say next. She could not ask what he was doing, for he could not, or would not, write much about that. But if she wrote of her own life all the time, she felt callous. She had told him in a previous letter about her move to London, explaining that this way she could oblige his mother by giving up her field work. For the moment, she had added – just in case. 'Oblige' Lady Hunney indeed. It was like obliging the Kaiser!

Reggie had not commented in his reply save to say he was glad she was enjoying her new job. She had informed him that she was working for the WSPU war effort, and if he chose to think this was the recruiting side rather than the advancement of women's role in the war, so much the better. Lady Hunney, she was well aware, was so violently opposed to the suffragist movement, whether militant or not, that it could only do harm to spell out exactly what she was doing.

George was engrossed in a newspaper story of how Flight Sub Lieutenant Warneford had won his VC shooting down a Zep over Belgium a week ago. He had reached the part where Warneford succeeded in wrestling his Morase Parasol back under control, but had to land to make repairs in enemy territory. How did he get off the ground again with no one to swing the prop? The chaps at Skinner's had been talking of little else all week. George still had six months to wait before he could join the Air Force. As soon as he was seventeen, he'd have a shot at it – and tell the Pater afterwards. He worried over how wrong it was to wish the war would continue till Christmas at least, and decided he would add an 'if' to his nightly prayer to the Almighty.

His father chose that moment to enter the morning room. 'Ah, George, have you finished the parish magazine yet?'

George had not.

His father looked at him quizzically. Guilt was written all over his son's face. 'Good. I've an item for you. A few words about young Jack Hallet. He's died from typhoid in Gallipoli.' He paused. 'So none of your cartoons, George. They would not be appropriate this month.'

'But my cartoons are serious, Father.' George was indignant. 'This one has a shell hole and the Kaiser and Sir John French meeting in it saying—'

'*Not* this month, if you please, George. We must think of the bereaved.'

George slumped in his chair after his father had left. Nothing, but *nothing* to do except swot for Oxford. Who wanted to go to Oxford anyway to study Julius Caesar's boring campaigns?' They offered little in comparison with what was going on now. Then he had a brilliant idea and seized his sketch pad, chuckling. Pa couldn't say this was a war cartoon. Now if he put the Kaiser in a toga . . .

Dr Beth Parry, clutching her bag, ran to Ashden school after a summons from Philip Ryde. One of the children, Ernie Thorn, had fallen and hurt his leg. When she arrived, Ernie was sitting on the grass supported by Philip, with a crowd of awed children surrounding them. Philip greeted her with relief as Ernie let out a wail.

'We'll have it sorted out in no time, young man.' Beth assessed the way the foot was lying. 'Can you raise your foot, Ernie? Just a little?'

Ernie tried. Nothing happened. He raised frightened eyes to Dr Parry. 'We're going to tuck you up nice and warm, Ernie, even though it's June. Do you have a blanket, Mr Ryde?'

'My sister's out,' Philip began, 'otherwise—'

'I'd like to telephone Ashden Manor Hospital. I think young Ernie has a fracture on the shaft of the leg, and I know Ashden has a new kind of splint – a Thomas splint – specially designed for this type of accident. But they need to apply it here before he's moved.'

Philip pointed to the telephone on the wall of the entrance hall to his quarters. He fetched the blanket while she made the call.

When they went back outside, however, Len Thorn was standing belligerently over his young cousin. 'Well, well.' He swaggered towards Beth, looking her up and down insolently, from the neat black hat to her boots. 'Our new lady doctor, isn't it?'

'Yes. Mr Thorn, isn't it?' she returned.

'My Uncle Len,' Ernie piped up.

'That's right, and I'd like to know just what you are doing to this poor little chap.'

'Looking after his broken leg, Mr Thorn. He needs a special splint and it's on its way.'

'One of those street-corner quacks, are you? Or a VAD? Virgins are Dangerous, that's what I call 'em.' Len sniggered.

Philip stepped forward. 'Go home, Len. I won't have that talk here.'

'And leave young Ernie with Florence Nightingale?'

'If you care to consult the British Medical Association—' Beth's voice suggested Len might not be capable of reading, 'you will find I am a fully qualified doctor. You need have no concern for your cousin.'

'No concern?' Indignation was written all over Len's

face. 'It's you oughta be concerned, Miss Call-Me-Doctor Parry. All our gallant men are in the trenches. What's going to happen to them when they come home and find women doing their jobs? You tell me that.'

'I really haven't the time to tell you anything, Mr Thorn. I'm here to look after Ernie.'

There was a wail from Ernie, who clearly thought it about time he received more attention and another humbug.

'Piss off, woman,' Len snarled, swinging a leg to stand astride the child, and hitting the injured limb by mistake. Ernie screamed in agony.

Red with anger, Philip grabbed his arm to frogmarch him from the premises, but a punch in the face from Len's other hand sent him staggering back: 'A pity you don't expend your fighting energy in the trenches, Len,' Philip retorted.

'Pity you can't, Mr Crippled Constable.' Losing interest in Ernie, Len went out of the gate laughing, just as the motor ambulance arrived, complete with Ashden doctor, a VAD and splint.

It took half an hour to despatch Ernie and notify his parents. When at last they had departed, Philip turned to Beth, who was repacking her bag. 'I'm sorry you should have been so insulted on school property, Dr Parry.'

'Len isn't the first, Mr Ryde. Neither, I fear, will he be the last.' Beth tried to sound cool, but did not completely succeed.

'It's not easy for the villagers. You're young and unmarried. In a place like Ashden where new ways come slowly, there is bound to be difficulty. May I offer you some tea?'

She hesitated for a moment, then said, 'I should like that, Mr Ryde. And perhaps,' she added wryly, 'I can give you some ointment for the black eye which will doubtless shortly be emerging on my account.'

Isabel was annoyed. Frank Eliot never seemed to be in, and she just had to get the rota organised for July. It was too demeaning to have to walk to the hopgardens to find him, so she compromised. She would call earlier in the evening and catch him as he left the farm to return home. This plan worked well: as she arrived at the front door of the cottage she saw him walking down the track from the hopgardens towards her.

Her heart seemed to flutter, but she tried to ignore it. He might be attractive but he was no gentleman and she was, after all, a married lady. He had behaved abominably to her on countless occasions and yet, she owned to herself, his face leapt before her in her dreams with far more alacrity than Robert's ever did.

She would not walk towards him, she would not – but he seemed in no hurry to rush towards her. So she prepared a speech, clutching her notepad in as businesslike a fashion as she could. She watched his feet crunching over the ground; it was less dangerous than watching his face. When should she speak? Now? When he doffed his hat?

She didn't say anything in the end; and he didn't bother to doff the panama. He simply removed the notepad from her hand, laid it on the shelf in the porch, put his arms round her and kissed her. Not harshly, not mockingly, but so sweetly she found herself responding. At last he disengaged himself, and stared at her with those strange eyes of his.

'You're very beautiful, Isabel. You need to be loved, you need to blossom and flourish like a rose.'

She clung to him, though a tiny part of her was annoyed that he dared to call her by her Christian name. She was a Swinford-Browne.

'Will you come in, Isabel?' He stepped indoors and stretched a hand to her.

It was dark in there for the ceilings were low and sunlight did not penetrate.

She swallowed. She wanted very much to go into the house, but the thought of what Father would say and the fear of crossing that threshold into the unknown held her back. 'No,' she finally blurted out.

Frank watched as she left, walking, then breaking into a run. Then he picked up her forgotten notebook and bore it into the house like a trophy.

In bed that night Isabel tossed and turned. If only she could just talk to Frank Eliot, even have him kiss her, but without any danger that he would take liberties like he had in Hop House – or even worse. The thought of the 'even worse' sent a thrill down her body. What was she to do?'

Then, in the small hours, when hope of sleep was lost, a brilliant idea came to her: the tennis match.

'I'm here, Mrs Dibble.' Caroline ran into the kitchen. 'I hope there are some sandwiches left for me to make.'

Harriet and Myrtle looked up. All morning they had

run back and forth at Mrs Dibble's command; the slightest objection being met with the retort that it was for the war effort. They couldn't see the connection.

'There are, Miss Caroline.' Mrs Dibble was determined not to betray how pleased she was to see her back. 'And crusts on this year, if you please. Bread's up to eight pence a loaf.'

'No soldiers for breakfast then?' Caroline joked. A boiled egg accompanied by Mrs Dibble's soldiers of newly baked bread cut into slivers, crustless, and buttered, had always been a special treat at the Rectory.

'The only soldiers round here now are those poor souls at the Manor, God bless them. Hoping to get a decent tea for once this afternoon – that's if you get on with that icing, Myrtle,' she snapped, seeing her minion staring at Miss Caroline's short skirt.

Caroline set to work. For all her brave words, she loathed these piles of sandwiches in the morning – but how she loved them at tea, filled with cucumber, cheese from the Sharpes' dairy farm, egg and cress, and cinnamon and sugar. None of that today, she realised, with sugar being so expensive. Even Mrs Dibble's secret stores couldn't last for ever.

'Where's my mother, Mrs Dibble?'

'At Home Farm to see if she could persuade their high and mighty highnesses, the Sharpes, to part with some more cream. They don't deliver now.'

'Why ever not?' Caroline was surprised – the Sharpes had always delivered.

'Young Joey ran off to join the Navy on his fifteenth

135

birthday, that's why not.' Things had come to a pretty pass when the Rector's wife had to go to plead for cream in person. The sooner this war was over and they could get back to normal living the better, in Mrs Dibble's view.

The players assembled in the early afternoon: Phoebe, agog with excitement, Eleanor, Beatrice Ryde, acutely conscious of the honour of playing at the Rectory, Patricia Swinford-Browne, home on leave from the police, Isabel, Janie Marden, Beth Parry, and Caroline herself. To Caroline's regret, Penelope had returned to Serbia to rejoin Lady Paget's unit.

The men had been rather more difficult to drum up, George explained. He was playing, as was Dr Cuss. Philip had volunteered to have a go, and Isabel had suggested Frank Eliot – it was decent of her to help. Charles Pickering was also here, although George doubted whether he knew the difference between a tennis racket and a cricket bat. Tim Marden was home on leave from the RNAS and Phoebe had offered to fill the gaps with a couple of soldiers from Crowborough. George had been doubtful and offered to find a couple of Skinner's chaps, but she seemed quite keen, so they compromised with a school chum of his and a soldier called Harry Darling – stupid name for a chap.

How different it all was from last year, Caroline thought. Then Daniel had been a player, not one of the fifteen officers watching round the court, together with two VADs. Last year Tilly and Felicia had been here, not under fire in the front line tending maimed bodies. Last year Robert had been playing and now he was in the 1st/ 4th Northamptons billeted in St Albans, waiting to go overseas. And last year, oh, last year, Reggie had been here too.

With an effort, she put him out of her mind and began to enjoy the afternoon. But at the toss she was awarded Charles as partner, and her heart sank. In her view, Charles was not only a stuffed shirt of a curate, but his habit of looking down his long nose at her reminded her of the Caterpillar in *Alice in Wonderland*. Bother, that made her think of Aunt Tilly, who used to read it to them when they were young.

'Sorry, Charles, you've drawn me.' She greeted him as cheerfully as she could. 'I'm renowned for being the only one in the family whose serve can *always* be returned.'

'In that case, Caroline,' he pushed his spectacles further up his nose, 'I suggest I cover centre court and rear court, and you take the net.'

Pompous ass, she thought, pointedly sitting next to Beth Parry while Patricia and George started to play.

Pit-pat, pit-pat, comforting familiar sounds. Was it wrong of her, she wondered, to enjoy being in the Rectory garden with roses and flowers spilling everywhere and wisteria tumbling over the walls? Was it wrong to enjoy this brief respite from war? The sky overhead was unbroken by cloud; no Zeps would come droning over the Rectory.

'Why did you come to Ashden?' she asked Beth, 'and not one of the London hospitals?'

'Where they are more used to women, you mean?' Beth replied levelly.

Taken aback, Caroline agreed that's probably what she had meant.

'I come from a small village in Suffolk. I know villages, I don't know London. I do what I can do best here. Surely that's what every woman should do?'

Caroline felt reproved. She wasn't sure what she thought of Beth Parry. 'If it's possible,' she replied coolly. A pause. 'Do you play much tennis, Dr Parry?'

'I believe, Miss Lilley, you're about to discover. We are being summoned on to the court.'

Infuriatingly Beth Parry was a very good player and so, remarkably, was Charles Pickering. If it hadn't been for the fact that Frank Eliot was almost as incompetent as she was, Caroline would have been outplayed all round. As it was their one-set match turned into a battle between Charles and Beth, taking the score to an exhausting fifteen-thirteen before Beth and Frank finally achieved victory. By this time, Caroline knew exactly what she thought of Dr Parry. She didn't like her.

Laurence was absorbed in watching the tennis match, which was rare for him for he had never been a player. In particular he realised he was watching Beth Parry, and wondering how she would fare in the larger game of life in Ashden. Dr Marden was enthusiastic about her gifts as a doctor, but even he could not persuade Ashden of this if the villagers decided against her. Laurence supposed it was almost fortunate that the Mutters and Thorns had chosen her as another prize to fight over. Len Thorn's loud and widely pronounced views on women doctors had set the

Mutters on the opposite track and he found himself hoping that the Mutters would win.

Dr Parry was a woman of unusual capability, and her handsome face was beginning to fascinate him.

Charles Pickering seemed to assume that their partnership in the match entitled him to her company throughout the dance on the Rectory terrace in the evening, Caroline realised ruefully. Phoebe was leaping around with her young soldier who had lost some of his shyness and was dancing to George's ragtime records with great enthusiasm. Philip, who usually made a beeline for Caroline, partnered Beth Parry, George kept trying to distract Eleanor from Dr Cuss, and Isabel was dancing with Frank Eliot. Surely she was rather close? Caroline hoped Father wasn't watching, and then saw that he wasn't. He was dancing with Mother, who was looking better than Caroline had seen her for a long time, eyes sparkling, and her full tall figure majestic in a dress made from green holland by Mrs Hazel. She was suddenly aware that Charles's hand felt warm on her back.

'Miss Lilley—'

'Caroline, please,' she said politely.

'Thank you, Caroline. This is very pleasant.'

He was trying to be nice to her, she thought, and did her best to respond. He couldn't be blamed for the ache inside her; for her feeling of resentment that she was dancing with him and not with Reggie.

'Isn't it?' she replied. And, suddenly happy, spun him round, much to his surprise.

* * *

'Shall I escort you back on the path past Lovel's Mill?' Frank suggested.

Isabel, looked at him demurely. 'What a good idea. I really can't be bothered to explain to my parents-in-law if they happen to see us walking together past the Towers. Do you have a torch?'

The night was warm, and somewhere a nightjar rattled. Isabel didn't hear it; she was too taken up with the sound of Frank Eliot's breathing at her side. How intriguing his face looked in the dim light of the torch. It did in the day too of course, but night invested it with romance and mystery. She was sure he would kiss her. The thought of his hand, holding the torch, on her body, made her deliciously alive. After all, Robert would never know . . .

But he didn't kiss her. Instead, as they reached Hop Cottage, he asked matter-of-factly, 'Will you come in, Isabel?' There could be no mistaking just what he was suggesting.

'What if I had a baby?' she asked, and was upset when he laughed.

'You won't. I'll make sure of that.' He held out his hand, with the fascination of the Devil tempting Faust.

She took it hesitatingly. 'I want to, I do, but I'm not brave enough, Frank.'

He stroked her hand, then kissed it quickly. 'Don't leave it too long, Isabel,' he said.

Outside the Rectory gate Phoebe waved goodbye to Harry as he set off to walk the six miles back to barracks. She felt exalted, on a cloud of happiness for, with great daring,

Harry had kissed her on her mouth, and on her neck and even where her low-cut evening dress allowed him to kiss. She'd stopped him then, like she should, and he'd been full of remorse, so she had kissed his lips this time. And oh, the bliss, for she knew now that this was not only romance; it was love.

Chapter Seven

My dear wife,
I have received your loving letter Agnes you have no
idea how much it means to me and the socks too to
know you knitted them for me. I am safe and cheery
now waiting for this war to be over so I can get home
to you and our lovely daughter. This war so far is not
what the recruiting sergeant said it would be all spit
and polish and three square meals a day but we keep
cheerful and so must you my darling Agnes.

Agnes refolded the letter for the twentieth time and blew
out the candle. She knew from the newspapers that the
Royal Sussex had been in action; she couldn't remember
where and she didn't care provided he was alive. And he
was.

The sound of a wail awakened her, with that sick feeling

she always got when woken from a deep sleep by Elizabeth Agnes. She rolled out of the bed, bleary-eyed, and then realised she'd overslept. It wasn't the middle of the night, the sun was out and birds were chirping on Tillow Hill. It was seven o'clock and to her surprise Elizabeth Agnes was sleeping peacefully.

Then she realised the wailing was still going on, a dull keening sound that chilled her far more than the cold breeze of early morning. Bravely, she put her coat on over her nightgown and summoned up courage to go and investigate. The noise was coming from the floor below, and she hurried downstairs in her slippers. The first sight that met her horrified eyes was Johnson, in full black evening attire and top hat, standing outside the door of the ladies' bedroom. *Like he was at a funeral* was her first thought.

'What's happened?' Agnes asked sharply. There was no love lost between herself and Johnson, and she sometimes feared he was willocky mad, so strange did he act.

He ignored her, so she pushed past him to the door. It was locked.

'*Tell* me what's happened.'

This time the fierceness of her tone made him answer. 'Miss Emily can't get Miss Charlotte to wake this morning. Miss Charlotte is not so well.' His pale blue rheumy eyes stared vacantly at her.

A stroke perhaps? Or a heart attack? Alarmed, she rapped at the door. 'Miss Emily, can you hear me? Let me in and I'll be able to help your sister.'

The wailing continued as if she had not spoken, so she

shouted out again. This time the noise inside paused for a moment, then restarted.

Agnes hesitated. Suppose Miss Charlotte were just asleep? No, it was much more likely she had died in her sleep or was ill and needed urgent help. She put all the authority she could muster into her voice. 'You must go for Dr Marden, Johnson, and –' she had a splendid idea – 'the Rector.' If Dr Marden could not persuade Miss Emily to open the door, the Rector might. The Norville ladies were Roman Catholic, but the nearest priest was in Hartfield, and that would take time.

Once again Johnson ignored her, and when Agnes insisted, shouted angrily, 'Get about your business, woman. It's time for my breakfast.' He raised his arm as if to strike her, and she backed away. She would have to go to fetch help herself.

'I'll go and get your breakfast immediately, Johnson,' she lied, hearing the waver in her voice.

He must be nearly eighty himself and as mad as the old ladies, she thought, as she threw on her print gown in her room, not even bothering with stockings. She glanced at Elizabeth Agnes, and realised that she could not leave her behind, so she picked her up and put her in the sling the countrywomen used. She could not wait to get into the clean fresh air. Her *and* her baby. As soon as she was outside the perimeter wire she began to sob, partly for herself and partly for the awfulness of life.

It took three-quarters of an hour before she, Dr Marden and the Rector were all back at Castle Tillow. To Agnes's relief, Mrs Lilley had insisted that she leave Elizabeth

Agnes in Mrs Dibble's care at the Rectory. She fed the baby as quickly as she could then hurried back to the castle. But when she arrived, she found to her anxiety that nothing had happened. The Rector and Dr Marden were standing outside the door, discussing what to do, and the awful wailing could still be heard within. At least Johnson had disappeared, either banished or voluntarily.

The Rector rattled the door knob in one last attempt. 'Miss Emily,' he called, 'won't you let me in? I do need to speak to you.'

This time the wailing stopped, and to Agnes's horror was replaced by a high-pitched giggle. 'I'll ask Charlotte if she wants to see you.' A pause, then a triumphant: 'Charlotte says *no*.'

'Is she ill? Can Miss Charlotte not tell us herself?' Dr Marden roared. He was a big man, and his voice boomed so much that Agnes had been scared of him when she was small.

'It's time for morning prayers,' the Rector supported him. 'Surely you wouldn't want Miss Charlotte to miss them?'

'The Devil is without,' came the reply.

'I am an ambassador from his Holiness the Pope,' the Rector announced firmly, 'with a message for Miss Charlotte.'

Sudden excitement. 'Did you hear that, Charlotte?' They heard the sound of a bolt being drawn back, and the Rector and Mr Marden rushed into the room.

Peeking in from the doorway Agnes was just in time to see Miss Emily clamber slowly back into the bed she was

146

still sharing with her obviously dead sister. As sickness welled up inside her, she found herself running down the stairs, away from this terrible scene, down to the kitchen in search of some semblance of normality. Light the stove, make some breakfast or at least tea for Johnson and herself. And the Rector would want a cup. He liked his tea.

She found Johnson sitting in his normal place at the kitchen table as though nothing unusual was happening, reading an old newspaper that had been wrapped round the meat Mary bought yesterday. Castle Tillow is a crazy house, Agnes told herself.

It was another hour before the Rector appeared in the kitchen. Johnson had had his breakfast and vanished once more, and Mary had been despatched to do the living-room fire. Agnes had poured herself another cup of tea and sat down, still feeling wobbly from shock. She looked up as the Rector came in.

'Agnes, Miss Emily would like some breakfast,' he said steadily.

'In *there*?' Agnes almost shrieked. Surely not in that bedroom?

'No. In their living room. Miss Charlotte is dead, Agnes, and I'm afraid Miss Emily still does not quite believe it, so instead of leaving the body here, Dr Marden is arranging for it to be removed to the village mortuary.'

The mortuary was a grand name for the brick shed behind Mutters the builders where the coffins were made. In last year's hot summer all the flowers and herbs in the world hadn't kept the bodies smelling sweet.

'I'd like you to stay with Miss Emily, Agnes,' the Rector continued. 'Do you feel you can?'

She stared at him, aghast. 'My baby,' she protested.

'My wife will bring the baby back to you, as soon as I get home.'

'But Miss Emily's out of her wits, Rector, and Johnson too.'

'You're scared of Johnson?' The Rector looked worried. 'I hadn't realised that. Of course you must not stay if so.'

'No, I don't think there's any harm in him, Rector, but it's a responsibility, isn't it?' She looked at him appealingly.

'Yes, and I wouldn't ask it of you if I didn't know you were capable of it, Agnes. There are no relations so far as we know. We will try to find her solicitor through the local Registrar, but that will take time and Miss Emily is in deep shock. Dr Marden will come every day for a little while and so will I. But she needs a woman and my wife cannot be here all the time.'

All Agnes's motherly instincts rose to the surface; she felt proud to be trusted. 'I'll stay, Rector,' she promised.

'Mr Swinford-Browne!'

Caroline spoke aloud in her surprise at seeing Isabel's father-in-law. The theatre performance had been fun, and when the companions she was with – three women from the office, two of their brothers and a fiancé – suggested they go on to one of the new nightclubs, she had agreed enthusiastically. The last person she expected to see sitting at a corner, his knees squeezed tight against his companion's as they watched the dancing, was somebody who should have been keeping his wife company at The Towers.

And, it occurred to her, who was his companion – a highly painted stranger whose plunging neckline and short empire-line dress would have made Ashden blink?

William Swinford-Browne's face turned a dull red of combined fury and embarrassment. He rose and, in bowing to Caroline, brought his head so close to hers that he was able to hiss: 'A business meeting, Caroline. Remember that, will you?'

She could not resist saying solemnly, 'The war effort, of course.'

He looked at her sharply. 'Like yours, with that Pankhurst crowd.' He said this with so much force that she thought perhaps it had some hidden meaning, though she could not imagine what. She dismissed the subject from her mind; poor Edith Swinford-Browne had enough to put up with without learning that Ruth Horner had had at least one successor.

Robert sipped his Earl Grey tea without enthusiasm. He couldn't understand why he wasn't revelling in the home leave to which he had so eagerly looked forward. He'd be going overseas at the end of the month, but the mingled excitement and apprehension inside him had evaporated, leaving only apprehension. His pals in the battalion told him that they were hailed as heroes when they went home on leave, yet it seemed to him that Isabel was studiedly avoiding any mention of the Army.

He looked at his wife's head bent over her post, and remembered how the way her curls tumbled over her temples had made him believe he was marrying the sweetest girl in all the world. 'Did I tell you they've issued us with khaki drill and pith helmets?'

'That sounds nice.' Isabel smiled.

'That means we're going somewhere hot. Very short odds on it being the Med and jolly old Gallipoli for me.' He forced a laugh.

'We should have been going to Monte Carlo this summer. People are still going there, despite the war.'

Robert felt he had failed her – yet how? He wasn't responsible for the war, and as far as he could see he'd done the right thing in volunteering. At least Father wasn't ignoring him now, damned rude though he was about him being a private. Mother had wept bucket loads of tears when he told her he was going overseas. There were tearful references to Rupert Brooke, who had died going out to the Dardanelles. Well, Robert intended to get there after all this training, not die of disease halfway across.

Over brandy and cigars one night, Father had said, 'Offered you a commission yet, have they?' And when he had replied no, had continued, 'Bally fool. You should have taken up my offer. I can always get you out, say the word. There's a job at the new factory.'

Robert had shuddered. He had lied to his father, in fact. He had been offered officer training but that would have delayed his getting into action. Besides, he'd grown to like being with the troops. He'd had a rough time at first; he didn't understand their language, or their accents; he didn't share the same interests. But when they had failed to get a rise out of him, they had simply ignored him. Now he was treated jocularly; he was a cuckoo in the nest, but he was there. Very soon, he'd be going to Gallipoli, and the wife he was leaving behind was as beautiful as ever, but as lifeless as a doll. He tried to tell himself she was a lady, a rector's daughter, and he shouldn't expect much in bed. But why was she always so tired? The house couldn't be occupying her, it must be the war work she constantly boasted of. She was as bad as Mother. He had even tried talking to her about it.

'Tell me about your work, Isabel.'

'I've been very busy,' she had said immediately.

'What with? Mother says she hardly sees you.'

'I've been helping my own mother with her agricultural work. I'm responsible for all the hop rotas. You've no idea how much work it involves.'

'Do you miss me?' he had dared to ask.

She had been startled. 'Of course I do, Robert. I miss you all the time. Marriage isn't at all exciting, though. You don't even want to see your friends, now you're home, let alone go dancing.'

He considered this. His friends? 'Do I have any in Ashden? Peter Jennings has joined up and I can't think of anyone else.'

'In London you have some, and in Tunbridge Wells. But all you want to do is stay here. It's not very exciting for me. I don't get leave from *my* war work.'

Robert's conscience was stirred. He hadn't thought of it from Isabel's point of view. Now he realised he had been selfish in wanting just to potter round the village. He had a sudden idea. 'How would you like to go to Father's picture palace this evening? They're showing a Charlie Chaplin – *Tillie's Punctured Romance*.' That was all about going off to the war too. Only in real life it wasn't all heroics, as the films made it out to be. It was fear, excitement, filthy language and songs all around you, and the knowledge you were being swept along like lemmings to a cliff edge. But he was still glad he'd volunteered as a private. He was one of them, one of those many thousands of men chanting:

Oh the moon shines bright
On Charlie Chaplin
His boots are cracking
For lack of blacking . . .
Before they send him
To the Dardanelles.

Harriet knocked on the door rather more peremptorily than she had intended. The Rector swung round as she entered the study, irritated at yet another interruption.

'If you please, sir. Mrs Lilley not being here, I want to tell you I'm leaving.'

Really, it was too bad. Where was Elizabeth? Then Laurence remembered that she had told him she needed to visit Grendel's farm to check the number of raspberry pickers required. All very well, but that left him to deal with the housemaid's tantrums. His anger subsided as he saw the humorous side of it. 'You'd better sit down, Harriet.' When she was sitting stiffly upright on the chair he used for Rector's Hour, he asked, 'Aren't you happy here?'

'Happy? Oh, yes, sir,' Harriet replied unconvincingly. Being happy was not a state she often thought about. 'But I'm a parlourmaid, and Mrs Dibble treats me like I was under her, ordering me to do this, that and the other just as if I was a tweeny like Myrtle. As a parlourmaid I'm answerable to you and Mrs Lilley. And I don't expect to have to look after babies, either.'

'But that was many weeks ago, and these are unusual times. It's hard to get staff, as you know, and Mrs Lilley would be most distressed if you left.'

'But it's the hours, you see, sir. And the pay, if you don't mind my saying so.' Evidently, Harriet thought she had been deeply wronged.

'We could review—'

'No, sir, it would be more of the same. I've quite decided.' She had, but only a minute ago.

'Have you anywhere to go?' the Rector asked. 'Yes, sir. Mr Swinford-Browne's munitions factory.'

Two-thirty, the official time for the gathering of the hordes on the Embankment, ready for the three-thirty start of the WSPU march. To everyone's disappointment the weather was far from kind. Not only was it raining, with lowering skies, but the rain was of the cold, driving type that chilled them to the marrow. Rain meant muddy roads, and there was no sign of it lifting. No matter, Caroline told herself, for if the sun did not shine, the colourful streamers in red, white and blue, the forest of umbrellas, not to mention all the flowers that covered everything and everyone, would compensate.

At two o'clock Ellen, her VAD friend from Dover days, had arrived. She took one look at the milling crowd of white-clad marchers, and commented, 'Like a load of blooming water lilies, ain't we?' She peered out from under a huge umbrella – a man's – which Caroline recognised as belonging to the home where they had boarded. She felt as if two old friends had joined her instead of one.

At the head of the procession, behind the band, was the main feature of the demonstration, the Pageant of the Allies, and Caroline's particular responsibility. Behind the band marched a girl dressed in a Grecian robe and carrying a trophy composed of all the flags of the nations at war with Germany and Austria. Then came a representative of each nation: first Belgium, for which a tall, slender lady in her thirties had been selected. Clad in black, with a purple veil round her head which streamed out behind her, she carried her country's torn and tattered flag. To Caroline's admiration, she had insisted on walking barefoot for greater effect, despite the mud on the roads. In contrast to Belgium's sad, expressive face, the girl representing France almost danced along, arrayed in the bright hues of the tricolour and a red cap; behind her came women representing Montenegro, Russia, Japan, Italy and Serbia. Bringing up the rear was Great Britain with a woman representing England dressed in white carrying roses. Three women surrounded her in the national costumes of Scotland, Wales and Ireland. Oh, how Caroline wished Reggie were here to see it. He would be so proud of her for being part of this great effort.

'This'll knock 'em in the Old Kent Road,' Ellen commented as, at three-thirty, the band struck up with the 'Marseillaise' and the whole procession moved off to coil itself round Bridge Street and prepare to march up Whitehall.

'I think it's me knocked in the Old Kent Road,' replied Caroline ruefully. Was it twenty-five thousand the WSPU had hoped for? There were more like fifty thousand, and helping to marshal the crowds into formation, Caroline felt exhausted. The excitement of the waving crowds dispersed her tiredness though, as they paraded through the London streets, up Park Lane, carrying banners declaring 'Shells made by a wife can save a husband's life' and 'Women's battle cry is work, work, work'. Nurses cheered from the windows of all the temporary hospitals in Park Lane's private houses, and recruiting officers took their opportunity to drum up candidates in the watching crowds.

Eventually they reached Whitehall again, where the elected deputation of leaders, led by Mrs Pankhurst, left to be received by Mr Lloyd George, for a private discussion. Then the main procession went back to the Embankment, to wait for him to address them. Caroline found herself wedged so tight in the waiting crowd that one umbrella served for four or five women. Were they just words, or did Mr Lloyd George mean what he was saying, she wondered, when finally he appeared to make his speech.

'Without women victory will tarry, and the victory which tarries means a victory whose footprints are footprints of blood,' he declared.

She, Angela and Ellen dined together that evening in the Hotel Cecil to celebrate the success of the day. By then news had circulated of the more solid proposals Lloyd George had put forward to Mrs Pankhurst and her delegation. Ellen was not convinced. Conservative attitudes to women could not be changed overnight, quoth Lloyd George, which she declared to be more Welsh soft soap. So far as munitions were concerned, the government was taking control of privately owned companies which meant no more sweated labour. Now that was something, Ellen agreed. There was enough of that kind of sweat where she grew up to grease the rifles of Fred Karno's entire army.

'We are Fred Karno's army
The ragtime infantry . . .'

Ellen loudly carolled the popular soldiers' song to the amusement of the officers at the next table, before pointing out that although from now on women would receive the same rate as men for piecework, despite all Mrs Pankhurst's arguments, Lloyd George could not guarantee the same for timework.

But Ellen must agree it was a start, Caroline argued. 'You're very quiet, Angela,' she added, seeing her cousin's abstracted look.

Angela jumped. 'I was just thinking that before the war we'd have been taken for women of the streets, dining here without gentlemen.'

Caroline laughed, more at the idea of the respectable Angela as a lady of the night than at what she had said.

'Much better than 'aving men along,' said Ellen approvingly. 'All the pleasure and none of the old gorblimey.'

'The what?' Angela's brow wrinkled.

'The gorblimey what's he doing now?' Ellen amplified.

'I don't understand.'

'Look at that terrible hat over there,' Caroline said hastily.

In a sudden wave of affection, Isabel wound her arms round Robert's neck as he leant from the train window. All that was safe and secure seemed to be steaming out of her life. Last year, marriage had taken her from the Rectory, with all its comforting shelter, and plunged her not into the life she had expected but into a dull routine of household problems. Now Robert himself was leaving yet again, and this time not just for St Albans for further training but to go abroad, where she could not reach him no matter what went wrong.

As the train puffed out of Ashden station, Isabel felt truly alone for the first time. She had to run the house with the sole help of Mrs Bugle. Even the butler had been purloined to work at The Towers. The only good aspect about Mrs Bugle was how terrible she was – at least The Towers wouldn't want to steal *her*.

She walked slowly along Station Road and turned past The Towers into the track towards Hop House. Towards home, towards the hopgardens. The hops would be ripe in another six weeks, perhaps less if the weather were favourable. Should she go to see Mr Eliot? Of course she should, she told herself: he needed all the help he could get this year. The bookings from the East End had not been up to usual levels, and there was a question-mark over the use of troops. They might be going overseas, for there were rumours of an offensive in the autumn.

Long days stretched out in front of her, imprisoned by the boundaries of duty: the daily battle with Mrs Bugle, the forbidding disapproval from The Towers for her failing to move in with them, the unspoken anxiety of her mother, the knowledge that after Robert's leave her mother-in-law would soon be eyeing her once more to see if a baby were on the way. It wouldn't be. To her relief, Robert still made sure of that on the grounds that it wasn't a world he wanted to bring children into. So if she was to have a baby while this war was on, it wouldn't be his . . .

Appalled, she said a prayer of apology. She was only a year married and here she was thinking of another man already. She tried hard to thank the Lord for all His gifts (even for Mrs Bugle, as many people had no servants at all now), for her loving family, and for Robert about to fight for his country in a foreign land. That night she stayed on her knees much longer than usual in the hope that her sinful thoughts would vanish. But they didn't. They nestled in one corner of her mind, while she battled with her conscience. She would go to help her mother-in-law with her gas masks, she decided. Surely that was sufficient a peace offering even for God.

The Rector tried not to laugh when he saw the Julius Caesar cartoon. George undoubtedly had a flair for drawing, and he had initiative. He had sold three cartoons this month to London newspapers and magazines, receiving in all £9 3s 6d. But, for the moment, he had more important matters to discuss with his son. He found him in the garden, slouching, hands in pockets, talking to Percy Dibble. One glance at the Rector's meaningful face and Percy decided the potting shed could do with a tidy-up.

'When are you breaking up for the summer, George?'

'The twenty-fourth, Father,' he answered cautiously.

'And what plans do you have for the holidays?'

'Chipping Major has asked me to stay.'

'When?'

'Late August. Over the Bank Holiday. I meant to mention it.' George was defensive, realising this was no casual enquiry after his welfare.

'And before that what plans have you?'

'Mother wants me to help out with harvesting.'

'Can she do without you for a few days?'

George looked wary; he hadn't the slightest idea what Father had in mind.

'I would like you and Phoebe to pay a visit to Grandmother Buckford with me.' Laurence winced as he saw the look of horror on George's face. 'Merely a few days. I am concerned about her. Your mother is worried about the Zeppelin threat in Dover, but since there have been no raids over London or the south-east since early June, I feel they must be waiting for the longer nights. I don't think we will be in any danger.'

'But Mother needs me here,' George argued. Surely Mother would support him since Grandmother Buckford disapproved of her son's marriage and still refused to meet Elizabeth. The abandonment of the annual visit to Dover had been one of the bonuses of the war so far as he and his sisters were concerned.

'I should be grateful, George.'

Put that way, George had no option. But Dover – ugh. Memories of childhood horrors and humiliations flooded back: Grandmother seizing him to point out the dirt behind his ears in front of cousin Robert, his hero; being sent to his room because he didn't like playing with regiments of toy soldiers – 'The Buckfords have always been an Army family, George.'

Suddenly an idea occurred to him and he beamed. 'All right, Father. It would be rather jolly to see Grandmother again—'

His father looked at him suspiciously but did not follow it up. George had remembered that Tim Marden was stationed at RNAS Dover, and had issued a vague invitation to 'take him up' in a 'trainer' if he were in the neighbourhood.

'I'd like to enquire what's a-happening, Mrs Lilley.' Mrs Dibble broke off relations with the pastry for the rabbit pie to seize this rare opportunity for A Discussion.

Elizabeth wilted under Mrs Dibble's accusing eye. 'I've still had no applicants, Mrs Dibble. I've asked around the village and I've pleaded with the *Courier* to put in an advertisement – they're refusing most now for lack of space. The only person who came from the Tunbridge Wells agency was most unsuitable.'

'I saw her, thank you, Mrs Lilley. I don't want no retired scarlet women here, even if it means doing without.'

'No one seems to want to do domestic work, I'm afraid. I thought I would get some response from the village, at least.'

'If you don't mind my pointing it out, ma'am,' Mrs Dibble picked up her rolling pin again, 'you've been asking them to work in the fields.'

'It's a job that needs doing. We all depend on our food supply being maintained.' Elizabeth felt even more guilty.

Mrs Dibble sniffed. 'No good will come of it, you mark my words. Percy said there was trouble at the Norville Arms last night. Them Thorns are spoiling for a fight and now it's got out that Miss Caroline helped organise that march in London, there was words spoken. It's that Len Thorn behind it all, you mark my words. He's a good for nothing scamp, and that new lady doctor don't help. Disgusting, I call it.'

Elizabeth was more perturbed at what Mrs Dibble had said than she felt it wise to reveal. Edith had mentioned the march to her in tones of marked disapproval, and now the whole village was talking of it. 'Women make very good doctors. Look at Dr Flora Murray and the Garrett Andersons,' she pointed out.

'Oh, in hospitals and over there, I daresay it's different. But this is Ashden and it's not decent.'

'That's enough, Mrs Dibble.' Elizabeth tried to keep the sharpness out of her voice, but did not entirely succeed.

'It's no different to men examining lady patients.'

'You know where you are with a man,' Mrs Dibble maintained cryptically, and to this, Elizabeth could find no reply.

Chapter Eight

Home; home for her birthday, or rather to *celebrate* her birthday. It fell on a Tuesday this year, so Caroline and Angela had marked the day by going to see Elsie Janis in revue at the Palace. Then, at the weekend, Caroline was going to Sussex for a 'dinner dance' Rectory-style; in other words, Mrs Dibble's special buffet, and a hop around the terrace to George's gramophone if weather permitted. Last year she had . . . No, she would not think of last year.

Reggie had remembered her birthday – he had sent a letter to join the others which she kept locked up in Grandmother Overton's box and, with it, an oil painting. It was not a Rembrandt exactly, but to her it was just as precious. He explained in the letter that it had been the idea of a local artist; a photograph of him was set side by side with one of her, pasted on to an oval-shaped piece of wood, and then the whole surface had been painted over, fitting the two of them into a garden scene with flowers and grass and trees. Reggie must have described Ashden to the artist for in the background was a house bearing a remarkable resemblance to the Manor. 'This is how it will be when this hiccup in our lives is all over. Just shut your eyes, darling, and imagine it. Or, rather, look at this . . .'

She obeyed his instructions but doing so brought more pain than pleasure. Such a future seemed a Shangri-La, beautiful but unattainable, and far removed from the busy life she was leading now. Since the demonstration, which had been supported by *over* fifty thousand women, the WSPU had been overwhelmed by the size of its postbag, and every letter had to be dealt with. Most were from women asking for work, although there were also occasionally letters of abuse which were ceremonially burnt. Then there were offers of jobs from factory owners and small traders, all of which had to be sorted out with the relevant Ministry. She'd even seen an application from William Swinford-Browne for women to work in his East Grinstead munitions factory, and with great satisfaction tucked it at the bottom of the pile.

She had been able to leave the office promptly this Friday afternoon. The walk down Station Road worked its usual magic on her, as she happily greeted each tree, saluted The Towers, and picked a wild scabious for her buttonhole. As she approached the corner, she said good evening to Mrs Thorn who was on her way to Bankside, and was a little puzzled that she did not appear to see her. She soon forgot it, however, in the pleasure of rushing into the Rectory.

On Saturday evening about twenty of her friends gathered for the 'dinner dance'. Mrs Dibble, despite dire prognostications of 'running short', had drummed up an excellent supper, and as for the dancing, well, she had brought some jazz records down from London in the hope that she could get away with anything on her birthday. She had slid them surreptitiously to George with the strict injunction he was to leave them till Father had had his supper. Eleanor and Dr Cuss wheeled Daniel round in his invalid chair, and Caroline sat beside him in the drawing room as the dancing began outside on the terrace.

'Do you mind watching, Daniel?'

He grinned. 'Not in the least, Caroline. Don't worry about me. Especially now.'

'Why now?' she asked curiously, as Eleanor joined them. 'Go on, tell her, Daniel.'

'I think, we think, *they* think, the paralysis is really lifting at last. We thought it was earlier, but nothing much seemed to happen. Now it hurts like hell – or, since it means I'm feeling things again, perhaps I should say it hurts like heaven.'

'Oh, that's wonderful,' Caroline cried. 'How long will it take, do you think?'

'No one knows. But if, if, *if* it lifts, they'll be able to fit me with a peg leg straight away, either at Queen Mary's Roehampton or in a Belgian hospital near Rouen which specialises in re-educational work.' His eyes were alive with hope.

'You'll be almost as good as new,' Caroline said. 'You'll be able to travel, and do all sorts of things.' His face clouded, and she realised she had blundered. She then compounded her mistake by putting her other foot right in it. 'Have you heard from Felicia?'

'No.'

'She can't have much opportunity to write. We only get a note now and again.'

'I asked her not to.'

'You're a prize idiot, Daniel,' Eleanor informed him. 'Talking of which' – she glanced at her brother – 'shall I tell her?'

'Tell me what?'

Daniel nodded, so Eleanor continued, 'We want to warn you Mother's got her warpaint on, and she's after your scalp, Caroline.'

'That's not unusual.'

'It was your London demonstration that set her off. Edith Swinford-Browne told her about it.'

Trust William Swinford-Browne to cause mischief where he could, Caroline raged. He must have rushed to discredit her in Edith's eyes by telling her of Caroline's work with the WSPU, in case she took it into her head to try to discredit *him*.

'But the press said how well organised it was. She can bathe in the reflected glory of her future daughter-in-law.'

'It's no joke.' Daniel added his note of warning to his sister's. 'You know how violently she's opposed to women having the vote—'

'The march was about work, not the vote.'

'Yes, but it involved the same people, the same principle,' Eleanor explained. 'I'm afraid that as far as Mother is

166

concerned, Eve was put on this world solely to tend to Adam's needs.'

'I seem to remember Eve rebelled,' Caroline muttered.

'But God won.'

'You're serious, aren't you?' Caroline looked in dismay at her friends.

'It pays to be where Mother's concerned,' Eleanor said ruefully.

'I'll remember not to talk about it any more,' she promised.

'Not even to Reggie,' Eleanor suggested, so quietly that Caroline hardly bothered to listen. In any case it was too late. She'd already written a full account of the demonstration and her part in it. 'And there's also been some feeling in the village about the march. Strong disapproval of the Rector's daughter being mixed up with such shenanigans.'

'But that's ridiculous. Ashden doesn't care what goes on in London and, in any case, why should they object to my helping women to find work, when I did just the same here?'

'Yes. But only half the village supported you.'

'The Thorns,' Caroline exclaimed, remembering Mrs Thorn's odd behaviour. 'They're stirring up trouble and using me as the battering ram. Ah well,' she tried to joke, 'I'd better raise an army of Mutters to escort me everywhere.'

'Until the weathercock changes,' Eleanor said pessimistically.

Phoebe was dancing with Charles Pickering. She hadn't dared invite Harry here again, in case it drew Father's attention to him, but although her feet were occupied in waltzing with the curate, her thoughts were still with yesterday.

She and Harry had gone to Ashdown Forest. Phoebe was not an enthusiastic walker, but with Harry it was different. At first, faced with what seemed impenetrable woodland, he had been nervous at the wildness and space around him and, trying to see it through his eyes, Phoebe had to admit he had a point.

'It's like an army,' she had told him. 'Taken all at once it's terrifying, but when you look at the trees one by one, you can see the wood is made up of individual soldiers.'

He'd laughed at that, tripped over a root and sworn. 'I don't go tripping over me mates' boots,' he told her.

'That's an oak tree,' she said, wanting to make him part of the life she'd always known.

'Like the Royal Oak?'

'The one where King Charles hid.'

'Did he hide in a pub?' He was perplexed and they had giggled when they disentangled their meanings.

When they emerged on to open moorland, he grew more interested. His sharp brown eyes were everywhere. 'What's that?' He pointed to a chaffinch. 'And what's *that*?'

Harebells in the grass were so common that Phoebe had hardly noticed before how delicate and beautiful they were. Then, reluctantly, she broke the terrible news to him. 'Father says I've got to go to Dover for a few days soon. My grandmother lives there. We hate her. She's a monster.' She wondered if God were listening, and added hastily, 'She's very generous of course. Just, well, you know.'

Harry didn't. His grandmother – the other was dead – had the foulest mouth and the warmest heart of any of his family. 'Why go then?'

'She's our grandmother and Father says we have to.'

'Like the Army, eh? All drill and duty. When do you leave?'

'Eighth August.'

He kicked a stone from his path. 'We might be going overseas around then.'

Why hadn't it occurred to her that soldiers were in camps only temporarily? Phoebe's face puckered up with distress. 'I don't want you to go,' she cried.

'I don't want to leave you either. Will you write to me, miss – Phoebe?'

'Every day,' she promised.

He smiled at the chaffinch, at the harebells, at the forest around him, and at Phoebe who was looking as lovely as the lady in that picture, 'April Love', his mother liked so much. He could see tears in her eyes, though. He'd seen them there in temper, when she quarrelled with old Ma Manning, but never before had there been tears for *him*. He found himself kissing her, although he had told himself he shouldn't. He ran his hands through the muslin over the curves of her body. He could see her ankles peeping out under her skirt; and the way her breast curved before it disappeared into the white prison of her underclothes. 'Let's lie down, Phoebe,' he said hoarsely.

Amid a torrent of emotions, Phoebe realised she was lying on the grass again with a man, and liking it. She wanted to be close to Harry. His cap was lying on the ground, and she loved being able to see every detail of his short gingery hair and the freckles on his face. As his hand rested hesitantly on the dress covering her legs, she tensed, then relaxed again. She felt his hand pushing up her skirts, warm on her thigh above the stockings, and the tingling where before she had known only harshness. His fingers went on touching her, but just when she thought she would burst, he stopped and sat up, white as a sheet.

'What's wrong?' She meant what was wrong with her.

'This is,' he replied after a moment. 'With you.'

'Why me?'

'You're a lady.'

'I'm me. I'm Phoebe.'

'I know, and that's why too. I love you. So it's wrong.' He was staring straight ahead, very red in the face.

Phoebe sat up beside him almost shyly, and smoothed down her skirts. 'I love you too.'

'Do you? *Do* you, Phoebe?'

'Yes!' With a joyful shout, she hugged him again. Laughing, they tumbled around like puppies, till he rolled over a sharp stone and swore once more. He kissed her on the nose and the cheek, and she closed her eyes. Love was wonderful, life was wonderful and this moment was what happiness meant.

Isabel had not dared invite Frank Eliot to Caroline's dance for the same reason as Phoebe. Consequently she had been forced to rely for dancing partners on Martin Cuss, when duty prised him away from Eleanor, and Charles Pickering, or George. Even Philip Ryde was preoccupied with someone else, in his case the new doctor. Eleanor had driven her home after the dance, but had not come in, so Isabel was left to face the silence and darkness of Hop House alone.

She woke up on Sunday morning and came to a decision. True, she then spent the morning wrestling with it, but while she was doing so she was changing into suitable attire. She dressed with care, choosing to wear an old voile dress, the only gown to accompany her from the Rectory to marriage. It suited her, was unostentatious, and presented the image she wished.

She knew Frank Eliot had a fine baritone voice, and could therefore contribute to the Entertainment for the Troops concerts. They could sing duets. *Why* hadn't she thought of that before? They'd need rehearsals of course, but she had a piano. That decided her. It was her duty to call at Hop Cottage this afternoon.

He attended church infrequently, and Isabel's heart leapt in confusion when she saw he was there. She avoided him after church, and chattered all the more gaily at lunch in the Rectory. When Caroline said she had to leave to return to London at three o'clock, Isabel made an excuse to leave with her, and they walked up Station Road together. She soothed her conscience by remaining to wave Caroline off, standing well back in case the smuts from the train smoke sullied the pale green gown, and then walked quickly back along the lane to Hop Cottage.

Frank Eliot was lazing in his garden in a hammock slung between two trees. A battered old straw hat lay over his face, one hand dangled over the hammock's edge, the other rested peacefully on his stomach. Hearing the small cough she gave to announce her arrival, he sat up with a start, the hat fell off, the hammock tipped perilously, and he slid to the ground.

'Isabel!' Pleasure was replaced by caution. 'Do sit down.' He brought up a deckchair. 'Have you brought me a rota?'

'No. Just myself.' Then, realising this might be too easily misunderstood, Isabel said hastily, 'This garden is lovely.' It was, and, she thought, surprisingly well tended.

'Yes.' His eyes wandered round. 'My wife taught me to love flowers and how to create a garden.'

'Your wife? But I thought—'

'She died ten years ago.'

An instant vision of herself and Frank singing 'The Ash Grove' together flitted through Isabel's mind. Or perhaps she would play the piano, while he sang at her side. 'That's very sad.'

It had changed his life for ever. Caution steadied hope, reality optimism, and cynicism love.

'You're a strange man. You look—' Isabel re-phrased what she had been going to say, 'you don't look as though you would be interested in flowers.'

'You'd like some tea?'

'Ginger beer would be nice.' Isabel felt pleased with herself. This afternoon she didn't want to be an elegant lady of fashion, but a simple country girl.

He disappeared inside the cottage and re-emerged with two glasses full of ginger beer. 'Why are you here, Isabel?' he asked.

She found herself speaking the truth. 'I was lonely.'

He got up from the grass beside her, pulled her to her

172

feet and kissed her. 'Lonely for me or for Robert?'

'For you – I think.'

'Isabel.' He held her close, so close she could feel the tenseness of his body and hear his breathing deepen. 'Come inside,' he said after a while.

This was what she'd expected, wasn't it? And he'd promised she wouldn't have a baby. He led her upstairs to a bedroom, as sweetly scented with lavender as the Rectory itself. Expertly unbuttoning her delicate dress, he brought it swiftly to the ground, and he embraced her again. Sudden panic seized her, and she drew back. She wanted to, oh how her body wanted to, but what would *Father* say?

'What's the matter, Isabel?' He kept his arm round her.

'I'm worried,' she began, and broke off because she did not know how to finish.

'About Robert? Because we're here and he's on his way to battle?' His hand cupped one of her breasts.

'Oh, no.' Preoccupied with the odd feelings he was arousing, she was startled at hearing her husband's name. 'He chose to go. *And* he chose to go as a private soldier. Not even as an officer. He could have stayed here longer if he'd accepted a commission.'

The hand was still. 'Isn't it rather admirable of him to go then?'

'Why?' she felt a sudden chill between them. 'What's the matter, Frank?' She was alarmed as he released her and walked over to the window.

'Do you care so little for him, Isabel?'

'Of course I care for him.'

'Then why are you here with me?'

'You knew he was going out to the Dardanelles. You encouraged me to come here. It's *your* fault.'

'Yes.' He passed a hand over his face. 'I'm sorry, Isabel.'

Isabel felt vulnerable, foolish, standing in her underclothes. 'What Robert means to me is my business,' she said shaking.

With an effort Frank turned round to face her. 'He may only be a private soldier but at least he has had the courage to volunteer to fight for his country, while a skunk like me seduces his wife.'

'I don't understand you,' she cried. 'I thought you loved me.'

He kissed her gently. 'It's not you, Isabel. It's my fault. Only mine.' He knelt down to pick up her dress and cover her.

'I hate you,' she screamed, pulling away from him. 'You've insulted me. You're not a gentleman.' She ran from the room, still endeavouring to button the dress, then fled from the house, the scene of such humiliation.

Shaken and concerned, Frank blamed himself for being a fool. For having let it get this far, for acting so callously, even for not making love to her the way she so obviously wanted. Then he remembered her indifference to her husband's plight, and the remnants of desire ebbed from him. He poured himself a whisky although it was only four o'clock, and then walked out into his garden to look at the flower borders he had created. He had believed he could find love again after Jennifer, but he couldn't. Only mutual need, and that for him seemed not to be enough.

* * *

Mrs Dibble burst into the study between callers for Rector's Hour, without so much as a knock. 'It's those Thorns, sir.'

'What *do* you mean, Mrs Dibble?' Laurence was becoming irritated at being called upon to solve every crisis. Spiritual problems, village welfare, servants' welfare – it was all laid at his door.

'The Thorns are marching to protest against that new lady doctor. I thought you'd want to know.'

Laurence was already out of the study and running for the front door, not even stopping to pull on his hat. As he raced to the gate he could see the Thorns and their supporters marching along the High Street from the Red Lion past the forge and ironmongery proudly bearing a banner: 'Ashden says get out lady doctors. Men's jobs for men.' Len Thorn was swaggering along at the column's head. Spilling down Bankside from the Norville Arms came the Mutters. As Laurence reached the Rectory gate, the two groups met; the shouting intensified and, after a struggle to seize the banner, fighting broke out.

To his horror, Beth Parry ran past him towards the fracas. As both sides saw her, there was a moment's pause, and Laurence heard her say, 'If men are to go to the front, women must do their jobs. And the front is where some of you should be.'

With a roar, Len Thorn dropped the banner and seized her by the arm, shaking her violently.

'Let that lady go, Len,' Laurence yelled, pushing his way through the fighting bodies. Two Mutters grabbed Len from behind and Beth was released.

'Isn't there enough war in the world, Len, without you

stirring up more?' He turned to Beth. 'Has he hurt you?'

'There was no need to intervene, Rector,' she replied stiffly. 'I can stand up for myself.'

As she stood rubbing her arm Len Thorn brushed the Rector aside and made for Beth again. Quickly Laurence interposed himself between the two of them. 'Come with me, Dr Parry. Into the Rectory. And don't you dare try to prevent us, Len Thorn.'

He hurried her into the Rectory kitchen. 'Mrs Dibble, kindly make some tea for Dr Parry, and I want a knife, a sharp knife—'

'What for?' Beth cried, aghast.

'You need have no concern, Dr Parry. I don't intend to become Ashden's Jack the Ripper.' Seizing the knife, Laurence rushed out once more.

By the time he reached the fracas, punches were being freely distributed, Len Thorn was using his banner to knock Harold Mutter senseless and more and more onlookers were threatening to join in. It was now or never if he were to remain Rector of Ashden. Laurence jumped on to the seat around the oak tree to gain height above the fighting mob.

'No sermons, Rector. We know what we want,' Len Thorn shouted.

'I don't want you to listen, I want you to watch. As Our Lord is most surely watching you.'

Reluctantly, they all paused as Laurence turned to the trunk of the oak tree and began to carve as high up as he could reach.

'There.' He pointed as he finished carving. 'The initials

T. H. Now I'm going to carve J. H. and then P. C. What for? T. H. stands for Tim Hubble, J. H. for Johnnie Hay and P. C. for Percy Combes. These men were here a year ago drinking in the Norville Arms and now they are dead. I'm going to carve the initials of all our fallen men here. They died fighting for peace in this land and you honour them by brawling in the place they loved. From now on, every man who volunteers can carve his initials here before he leaves to remind you what's happening overseas. Honour the dead by respecting the living – man *or* woman.'

Chapter Nine

Too impatient to wait to buy her own copy, Caroline snatched *The Times* from the morning-room table, and assuaged her guilty conscience by reminding it that Simon had not been to Norland Square for some days now. She had lain awake worrying much of the night. Why hadn't she heard from Reggie? There had been silence for three whole weeks. The last letter she received had been written on 10th July to thank her for her birthday present. It was now August 5th.

At first she had not worried greatly since he had explained that letters could be held up, or even blown up, if the Field Post received a direct hit. Now, however, after reading in the newspapers about the terrible attack last week at Hooge, she was deeply concerned. Not content with using gas in April, the Germans had not only continued their bombardments with Moaning Minnie heavy shells but brought in a new terror, spouts of petrol and flame called flame-throwers. The slaughter had been for nothing. And the tactical objective, a mine crater, had not even been won. That hole in the ground had been a château before this war began, peopled with human beings and surrounded by gardens. Not now.

Had Reggie been caught up in that battle? Had he *died* in it? Each day she turned fearfully to the officers' roll of honour, dreading to see the familiar name leap out at her. H – she ran her eye quickly down the list, aware of her thumping heart. There was no Hunney. Yes, there *was*. With relief she saw the name was not Reginald Hunney, but Gerald Hunney-Beresford, another branch of the family. She remembered Reggie talking of his cousin Gerald. She had even met him ages ago when they were all children. Now he was dead – just for a mine crater.

'All right?' Angela came up beside her.

'Yes, but why haven't I *heard*?' She lifted a stricken face to her cousin. Was Reggie one of the dead, but still unidentified for some reason? Carefully, she refolded the newspaper to as near a state of flat perfection as she could manage, and replaced it on the table.

'My brother, Robert, is there too,' Angela pointed out. 'And I'm even more worried about Registration Sunday on the fifteenth.' All men and women aged between fifty and sixty-five were to sign, stating their occupation and what they would be willing to do if called upon to serve the country. 'Father is convinced that it's the first step towards general conscription, and if so, what will happen to Willie?'

Caroline understood immediately. Angela's younger brother had refused to join the regular Army, saying he was more interested in preserving life than destroying it. His passion was flowers and he worked for the Royal Horticultural Society.

'He told Father he's prepared to go to war, but not to fight,' Angela added. 'Still, the war can't go on much longer, can it?'

Caroline said nothing. It seemed to her it could. Neither side was getting anywhere. Simon had said the only hope of breaking the stalemate on the Western Front was to attack elsewhere, in Turkey for instance, in order to join up with Russia on that front. But that brought another anxiety. Although she and Simon had both had cheerful letters from Penelope in Serbia assuring them all was peaceful and the hospital growing splendidly, Simon, through his Foreign Office contacts, was concerned that another invasion, this time by Germany and Bulgaria as well as Austria, was imminent. And Penelope refused to return to Britain.

'Isabel!' Elizabeth was surprised. Isabel rarely came to the Rectory now, save for Sunday luncheon after church and perhaps once during the week. 'Is anything wrong, darling?' The poultry quota must wait if her eldest lamb were in trouble. And to Elizabeth's eye, it was quite clear she was. Isabel looked strained and, worse, had that hurt look which her mother remembered from her childhood, when the world denied her what she wanted. It was not an attractive look and would one day plant bitter lines on her flawless complexion. But that was where mothers came in, in Elizabeth's view. My child, right or wrong, and alas, with Isabel—

'Tell,' she commanded.

'Oh, Mother,' Isabel burst into tears. 'I'm lonely. I miss Robert so much.'

Elizabeth held her in her arms to comfort her. 'Everyone is suffering because of this terrible war, Isabel. Now, *why* are you lonely? You have your friends in Tunbridge Wells and Forest Row. And here in Ashden you have Edith and William, besides us. And Janie of course.'

'No one likes me. Robert has disappointed everyone by refusing to be commissioned and his parents see as little of me as they can. I think it's wonderful of Robert to be a private soldier.' By now she had convinced herself that she did. 'But it means he'll be away for ever.'

'He's not missing, is he?' Elizabeth was alarmed.

'No, but he's on the other side of the world.' Isabel's misery broke out anew. 'Gallipoli – it's so far away. And he doesn't get home leave like the officers. Suppose I never see him again?'

'You will, pet.' Elizabeth had an idea. 'Would Robert mind if you came back to the Rectory for a little while?'

Isabel looked happier and plumped herself down on the old familiar sofa. 'Oh, Mother, I'd love to.'

'There's your Mrs Bugle to consider, of course, and the Swinford-Brownes. They'll have to be consulted.' Already Elizabeth was planning.

'None of them will care. I'll keep Mrs Bugle on and go up there once in a while.' Isabel dismissed that as a minor problem, now her own was solved. A deep wave of relief flooded over her. Mrs Dibble would replace Mrs Bugle's awfulness. Mother would replace Edith Swinford-Browne's carping comments and she, Isabel, would be safe again. Safe from the constant recollection of the humiliation of her treatment by Frank Eliot.

Phoebe fidgeted in the train. Father was reading, George was sketching. Da, da, da, *dee*, da, da, da, dee . . . In Dover for *tea*. How I hate to be me, I wish I were *free*, Phoebe thought crossly, as the monotonous rhythm drew her ever closer to Dover. Of the five of them she got on best with Grandmother, partly because she and Isabel had been the ones to appreciate her offer to send them to finishing school in Paris. Isabel had gone with great eagerness, Caroline had refused, for Felicia the experience had been a disaster, but Phoebe had been looking forward to it when war broke out and prevented her going. It was not the school that attracted her, of course, it was merely a means of escape from Ashden.

How long ago that time seemed! Now Phoebe wanted to stay in Ashden for ever, or at least until Harry returned. He might not, she thought with dismay. Here she was being dragged away to Dover, not even knowing when his battalion would be leaving, or from which port. It would probably be Southampton, but suppose it was Dover? How agonising to be in the same town as Harry and not even know he was there. And suppose, just suppose,

Harry were killed? Soldiers were daily. Lots of them. They marched off, leaving their girls behind them, and then never came back. Phoebe had a sudden inspiration. She would ask Uncle Charles, whose favourite she was, to find out. He had a home command in Dover. And he wouldn't tell Father.

George was sketching, but inside he was choked up with his secret. Tim had replied to his letter, and told him to come along to the RNAS station at Guston Road. Things were quiet, so he might be lucky, and Tim could take him up. If not he'd show him round the station. George decided not to tell Father. Not yet anyway.

In theory Laurence was reading *The Times* but in practice he was bracing himself for the coming ordeal. It was by no means easy for him to face his mother from whom he'd parted so bitterly when he married Elizabeth nearly thirty years ago. It said, he supposed, a lot for his mother's strength of character that she could maintain such a rigid disapproval over so long a period. In all that time she had never met Elizabeth, and so there was as little pleasure in this visit for him as there was for Phoebe and George. Nevertheless it had to be endured; his five children were part of the Buckford family and should therefore maintain contact.

It was at least an opportunity to see Charles, the present earl, though they had absolutely nothing in common. Laurence often hankered to visit his brother Gerald, to whom he had been closest as a child, and had occasionally toyed with the idea of visiting him in the United States if the Lord would provide him with the means to do so. So far He hadn't made it His priority.

Laurence's income was becoming an increasing problem. Before the war, his living had covered their essential needs and Elizabeth's small private income had topped it up. Even then there had been little left over for jaunts. Now, his finances were being squeezed by reduced tithes, as local farmers struggled with rising prices, and by increases in his own taxes and food bills. What with uncollectable tithes, income tax, local tax, and tenths (by which a tenth of his income was kept back by the church body, Queen Anne's Bounty, to top up the salaries of clergy in an even worse plight than he was), country rectors were amongst the hardest hit in the land. When Caroline was a child, she had asked him why, if Queen Anne was so generous, he couldn't ask Her Majesty for some more. If only it were that simple! Although Caroline and Isabel no longer had to be supported, and Felicia was away, this seemed to make little difference to the amounts flowing out of the Rectory on food and other living expenses. He was almost at the point of considering an appeal to his mother. But so far pride had always held him back.

'Laurence, I am glad to see you.' Black eyes, once the toast of London, snapped their attention back to Phoebe and George. 'You have grown, Phoebe.' Phoebe blushed, and tried to hold her chest in. 'George,' she continued, 'I am glad to see you take more and more after the Buckfords.'

George did not feel complimented. Who wanted to look

like Grandmother anyway? She may have been a beauty; well, so was Mother, and *she* still was. Grandmother Buckford sitting so erect in her straight-backed chair, dressed in royal blue, hair beautifully coiffured, looked like a gargoyle. He had never actually seen a gargoyle, apart from the small one on the rainspout at St Nicholas, but surely Grandmother must be like the horrors he had read about in *The Hunchback of Notre Dame*. Or perhaps she resembled She in Rider Haggard's novel, the beautiful, immortal woman who shrivelled up into an ancient crone when her power was gone. Unfortunately Grandmother's power had not, ancient crone though she was. 'You're looking well,' he faltered.

The eyes snapped back to him, as though she could read exactly what George was thinking. 'We shall have a long talk this evening, children. You may go to your rooms.'

The visit had begun.

Under the pretext of purchasing new gloves, Phoebe, sick with mingled excitement, fear and desperation, had found her way to Dover Priory, the town station. She had had difficulty because Dover town was a military area, but mention of Major Charles Buckford had acted like a charm. Uncle Charles had been ripping: he had found out that Harry's battalion of the London Regiment was leaving for the Western Front on the ninth from Dover, not Southampton, and since the Marine Station was in use for landing the wounded, Harry's train would be coming in to the town station. So here she was.

She had been waiting for an hour already and was relieved to see that others were there too, on what she assumed was the same mission. Then with a triumphant hoot of steam the train puffed in. From outside the station she could see troops beginning to pour along the bridge over the platforms and down on to the nearside. They were coming out, not through the booking hall but through the side gates, close to where she was standing, in order to assemble in the yard outside. She stood to one side, feeling vulnerable amid this crowd of khaki, despite her experience at the camp. At Crowborough she had been someone. Here she was just Phoebe Lilley, and the soldiers' whistles of approval flustered rather than amused her.

How could she hope to spot Harry amid these thousands of men? She was beginning to feel panicky at the sheer numbers milling around her. Suddenly, there he was, his familiarity startling her, as her dreams became fact.

'Harry!' Her voice came out as a croak but heads turned all the same as they lined up, packs on backs.

Private Harry Darling, jerked from one world into another, couldn't believe his eyes as he moved towards her uncertainly. They stood, looking at each other, until a stentorian shout recalled him to ranks. Boldly, he planted a kiss on her cheek, just missing her lips. Then another, only this time he found them. Another shout, roars of approval from his pals, and he was gone again. Leaving her happy, oh so happy.

Phoebe picked a wild rose from the hedgerow on her

way back from the station, determined to press it in a book, as she had a flower from Ashdown Forest. She'd never forget today, never, not even when they were old and had babies of their own.

George was sleeping peacefully. He was dreaming of Grandmother piloting a Fokker, flying further and further away from Dover, until she reached Gallipoli, whereupon she landed, took Uncle Charles's knobkerry from the Boer War, and began to smash all Nanny Oates' eggs. Only George could stop her. But where was he? 'George! George!' the cry went up.

His father rushed into the room and George jerked awake. He was being called. 'There's an air raid warning,' Laurence cried. 'I should never have brought you here. Quick. Into your dressing gown and downstairs to take shelter.'

Shelter? With a Zep around? Not likely, George thought. In five minutes he, Phoebe, Grandmother, helped down the stairs by Father, and the staff, were gathered by the cellar door. Grandmother's hair was all down her back, and she didn't look nearly so formidable in her dressing gown.

She struck her stick on the ground. 'I will not cower in my own cellar at the whim of Kaiser Wilhelm, Laurence,' she declared. 'You may all go, if you wish. I shall remain here.' She took a seat by the window.

'I'll go and see what's happening outside,' Laurence said, anxious about her proximity to the glass.

Seizing his chance, George rushed out after his father

into the cool of the night. It was nearly half past twelve, according to the longcase clock in the hallway.

'Look, Pa,' he screamed. Searchlights were weaving and beaming arcs across the sky, lighting it up. Tim had told him that in May the anti-aircraft gunners had prevented Dover from being bombed to smithereens; they had driven the Zep inland and she had to drop her bombload over open country. Now it was happening all over again. Oh glory be!

'Inside, George,' his father ordered.

'No fear,' George yelled, daringly. 'Look at that!'

An enormous black shape nosed its way through the beams, engines droning. Immediately the sound of guns could be heard as the anti-aircraft batteries went into action. George hopped up and down with excitement, almost sure he saw something dropping from the Zep. And wasn't that an aeroplane climbing in the sky as the beams moved again? Perhaps it was Tim? Even Father was so fascinated that he failed to order him inside.

Then the Zep disappeared from view and all was quiet. The searchlights stayed on for half an hour or so but to George's disappointment, they saw no more aeroplanes.

Next morning they learnt (from the postman, who had told the cook, who told the butler, who told them) that the Zep had been damaged by the guns and had limped home over the water. The gunners had holed her and she'd lost hydrogen. Good job too. And George had been right. An Avro had been sent up to finish the Zep off, but lost it.

Dozens of bombs had been dropped in the harbour and on Admiralty Pier.

'And some sailors feared dead,' Laurence reminded them quietly, after George's display of jubilation. 'Shall we pray for them and for their families?'

Ashamed, George shut his eyes, but a little part of him was still up there in the clouds. Earlier that day Tim had taken him up in a 'trainer'. The aircraft had *sung* as the wind whistled through the wires, stinging his cheeks. Now he knew how the chap in the Avro had felt as he soared up after the enemy.

'Where are you taking our baby?' Miss Emily was fretful today, as indeed she was on many days.

'Just to feed her, madam.' Agnes tried to speak soothingly. In fact, it wasn't nearly time to feed Elizabeth Agnes, but leaving her so long with a lady as old as Miss Emily didn't seem natural somehow.

Miss Emily had been very quiet since Miss Charlotte's funeral, with no sign of the craziness of that awful morning, and often told her how grateful she was for all Agnes was doing to help her. She never mentioned Miss Charlotte. Agnes and Mary had packed up Miss Charlotte's clothes and personal possessions, and had stored them in an unused room, just in case Miss Emily should ask for them. The clothes weren't good enough for Mrs Swinford-Browne's Belgian Relief Fund anyway. The Rectory had found a solicitor to sort out the legal complexities, and life at Castle Tillow was settling into a routine once more.

After an hour or so, Miss Emily hobbled into the kitchen herself, a rare occurrence. Agnes was at the table rolling pastry, and Mary was in the scullery pummelling clothes under the one cold water tap, which ran through to the well.

'Where is Elizabeth, Agnes?' Miss Emily demanded. 'You must have finished feeding her now.'

'I like to see her as I work,' Agnes replied truthfully.

'It takes your mind *off* your work, young woman. I'll take her. Besides, I want you and Johnson to go down to the village for me.'

'With Johnson?' Agnes was astounded; she hadn't been asked to go to the village for months, let alone with Johnson.

'He will explain to you why you are going,' Miss Emily informed her loftily. 'He's just leaving. Baby will be quite safe with me.'

Reluctantly and still puzzled, Agnes crossed the bridge, and caught Johnson up on the track leading to the village. Dressed in his usual black, he looked like a huge old crow walking between the hedges which were thick with rosebay willow-herb. A young thrush was banging a snail on the rough track, and flew up in alarm as Agnes reached Johnson's side. They reacted quickly, birds. They had to, to look after themselves. It was instinctive.

Instinct! Agnes stopped. 'I'm going back.'

Johnson stared at her. 'Missus says the stores.'

'I don't care.'

'The stores.' His voice rose in alarm.

'I'm going back, I tell you.' She turned and ran,

outstripping the old man who wavered, then started back after her.

What had sent her flying back in this sudden unreasoning panic? Was she being stupid, or was she out of her mind with the loneliness of living so far away from everyone? Agnes burst through the front door, and was relieved to hear the sound of Miss Emily crooning to Elizabeth Agnes. She hesitated then, risking her mistress's anger, followed the noise into the drawing room.

Fear seized her by the throat, paralysing her for a moment. Miss Emily *was* crooning. She was also bending over Elizabeth Agnes's cradle with a cushion in her hands. And that cushion was pressing down somewhere near where the baby's head would be.

With a shriek of terror, Agnes threw herself towards the cradle, pushing Miss Emily away and sending her toppling on to the sofa. She snatched her baby up; Elizabeth Agnes's face was congested and slightly blue. Was she breathing? Was she in time? Instinctively Agnes blew air into her baby's mouth to help her breathe, then staggered towards the door and freedom.

'Charlotte wants her, Charlotte *asked*.' Miss Emily struggled up in indignation. 'You can't take her away. I'm sending her to Charlotte, don't you understand?' The old lady's screeches pursued Agnes, resounding in her head. 'Stop her, Johnson. Miss Charlotte ordered it.'

Johnson standing in the doorway, realised he was being given an order and lunged towards Agnes and the baby as she ran past him. He was old, but he was determined, and his bony hands reached out to bar her way.

192

'Help!' Agnes shouted as he tried to tug the baby away. Miraculously, Mary appeared. Mary didn't like Agnes, but she decided the baby was coming to harm; there were babies at home and there were rules about babies. She heaved her considerable strength against Johnson and managed to push him over.

Gasping with relief, Agnes rushed from the castle into the fresh air. She would never return, never, *never*. Was Elizabeth Agnes dead? Once outside she stopped, full of terror. As Mary caught up with her, tears were streaming down her face, and she was incapable of looking at her baby for fear.

'I punched him. Went down like a ton of Mus Mutter's bricks. Now hold her out so I can get to her,' Mary commanded, coming into her own.

Agnes obeyed like an automaton. Mary examined the baby with surprising gentleness, arranging her head and mouth to allow more air in; the congestion had already subsided and the sound of gasping hoarse breath could be heard. 'Best get her to the doctor,' Mary said.

'No.' Agnes was beyond reason. 'The Rectory. I must get to the Rectory.'

Elizabeth was in the kitchen with Mrs Dibble when the tradesmen's door flew open and Agnes, wild-eyed and sobbing, hurtled in with Mary Tunstall behind her. 'My baby, Mrs Lilley,' she sobbed. 'She tried to kill my baby.' She held out Elizabeth Agnes. 'She's crazed. Is she alive?'

Elizabeth rushed to look at the wheezing child. First things first. 'She's breathing, Agnes, but we'll take her

193

straight to Dr Marden, shall we? Mary, who is Agnes talking about?' she asked gently. 'Not you, of course?'

'No. Johnson, ma'am?'

'No,' cried Agnes. Didn't anyone understand? 'Miss Emily. She's gone willocky.'

Horrified, Elizabeth thought through all the implications.

'Mary, go to fetch Mr Pickering. You'll find him in the church. Tell him I sent you. Ask him to call for PC Ifield at once and then both go up to the castle. I'll ask Dr Parry to join them.' Why, oh why did Laurence have to be away now? 'Do you understand?'

'No, ma'am.' Mary looked frightened at the responsibility.

'I'll go, madam,' Mrs Dibble announced firmly. 'You come along with me, Mary. You can tell 'em what happened.'

When Dr Parry, Joe Ifield and the Reverend Charles Pickering arrived at Castle Tillow they found Johnson sitting outside the door of the drawing room with an old sword in his hand. The room was bolted against them, and Joe had to break in through the window, leaving Johnson just where they had found him. Inside, they found Miss Emily, lying in a pool of blood, her father's old shotgun at her side.

'You must stay here tonight, Agnes, unless you want to go back to your mother.' Elizabeth sank into a chair. It had been a busy morning, telephoning Laurence, speaking to the solicitor, sitting in while the East Grinstead police talked to Agnes and conferring with Dr Marden about the baby.

'No, Mrs Lilley. I'd like to stay here if I may.' She was calmer now. Dr Marden said the baby was all right, and wouldn't accept any money for what he did. But she wasn't up to facing her mother, nor them Thorns. They'd say it was her fault. Oh, how they'd gloat. No, she wanted to stay here while she had a think about where to go. If only Jamie was here. But he was in a trench somewhere far away.

Mrs Dibble coughed. 'Begging your pardon, Mrs Lilley.'

Elizabeth misinterpreted the severe look on her face. 'I'm sure we can manage for a few days, Mrs Dibble.'

'I was going to say, seeing as how Agnes can't go back to that place, and seeing as how we have a vacancy—'

'How foolish of me,' Elizabeth exclaimed. They both looked at Agnes. 'I realise you might want to think it over, but how would you like to come back to the Rectory as parlourmaid?'

Frank Eliot strolled round the hopgarden, inspecting the hops, which were beginning to ripen. They'd be ready for picking in a week or so, in row upon row of leafy green tunnels strung over the avenues. He'd only had three seasons in Ashden, and it looked as if this would be his last. The hopgarden would be sold, or turned over to wheat. He'd signed up on Registration Sunday stating he'd be willing to serve, though at thirty-seven he was growing old by military standards. He doubted if even the trenches would have room for the likes of him.

As he straightened up from inspecting a bine, he saw a woman coming towards him: someone he'd seen before but couldn't quite place. She was in her twenties and simply dressed, a land-worker perhaps – her face had had the sun and rain and wind upon it.

'I heard you was looking for volunteers for hop-picking,' she said gruffly.

'That's right,' he replied. 'Mrs Lilley has the lists. Have you seen her yet?' Isabel, he had learnt, had passed the job back to her mother.

'No. I will though. I'm Lizzie Dibble.' She stumbled a little on the last name.

'Aren't you—?'

'That's right.' She nodded bitterly. 'I'm the Hunwife. It makes me as bad as the enemy.'

'I didn't mean to offend you. I'm sorry.'

'That's all right. I'm used to it.' She grinned.

He looked at her more closely and liked what he saw.

'My mother, she's housekeeper at the Rectory, wanted me to go there as parlourmaid, but I wouldn't. Go into service under my own mother? Anyway, I like the open air.'

'There's plenty of work here too before the picking, if you want some.'

'Is there?' Her eyes lit up. 'I'm mucking out stables at Ashden Manor at present. They've only got one horse left after requisitioning, so they'll be grateful if I leave. Her ladyship can do the mucking out herself.'

She laughed, and he with her.

* * *

At last! A letter from Reggie. She had heard nothing for nearly five weeks. Full of relief, she drew the paper from its envelope. Immediately she knew something was wrong – it consisted of a couple of short paragraphs only. Her mouth dry, she forced herself to read it.

Darling Caroline,
I am coming home on leave – a short one, next weekend, 21st August. This time I must go to Ashden. I hope you will have time to come.

Then followed a few sentences answering questions in her letter, and that was all. Surely this wasn't the Reggie she knew? Was he wounded? Ill? Hoped she'd have time to come. Of course she would. The war effort could wait. She'd stay until his leave was over. Why, Reggie *was* her war effort! She dashed off a letter in the hope it would reach him, assuring him she would be at the Rectory by the Friday evening.

The days dragged by until Friday finally arrived. Never had the Rectory seemed so welcoming. She arrived in time to join the family – including Isabel, who had lost no time in moving back home – for dinner. In such familiar surroundings she began to feel reassured. Of course nothing was wrong. But her father, perceptive as ever where she was concerned, questioned her after dinner and she realised her worry hadn't gone away after all.

'What's wrong, Caroline?'

'I don't know,' she burst out. 'I only know something is. Do you think he no longer loves me?'

'I doubt that very much. It's more likely to do with the war and the terrible scars it causes on the living as well as those it kills. Take heart, my love. Our Lord is with you.'

A little comforted, she went into the garden willing the hours to pass quickly until she could see Reggie again.

And suddenly there he was! He must have come through the side gate, straight from the railway station, for he still had his pack with him. His arrival had been so quick, so quiet, that she doubted her own eyes for a moment. 'Hello, Caroline,' he said.

She realised she'd been imagining all sorts of ridiculous things for nothing. She ran to him and the arms that held her tight were as loving and warm as those that had enclosed her in the orchard last summer.

'Oh, Reggie, I've been such a fool,' she said at last. 'Even though I know how hard it is for you to write letters, when I didn't hear for such a long time, I thought you didn't love me any more.'

He held her close. 'Never, *never* think that. I do love you, Caroline. Oh, I love you.'

She thought she heard a note of desperation in his voice, but perhaps that too was her imagination, for the hunger in his eyes for her was undoubted. He loved her still. Nothing could go wrong.

Next day, Caroline set forth into the mouth of Hell. She hadn't been to the Dower House since her last unfortunate meeting with Lady Hunney. This royal summons to luncheon had hardly been welcome, but as Reggie's fiancée she could hardly avoid it, especially as Sir John had come down from London for the occasion. To her surprise Eleanor was not present. Nor was Daniel. For a moment she regretted this for she needed allies. Then she realised she was being silly. Why should she need allies with Reggie there?

Lady Hunney was in an unusually gracious mood. Dressed in a blue linen coatee gown, as immaculately steamed of wrinkles as her face, her ladyship welcomed her as though no word of dissension had ever marred their meetings. Reggie seemed subdued but that was natural, Caroline told herself. After lunch was over they could walk together in the grounds and then she could reach his heart.

The luncheon began peaceably enough, the talk so general it would have been difficult to deduce a world war was currently being waged.

'Do tell us of your work in London, Caroline,' Sir John said quietly.

Surprised but pleased, she began to describe the WSPU's successes in opening up new jobs for women, and of her own association with the Board of Agriculture.

'And your work for the Women's Social and Political Union, Caroline. Do you propose to continue working for the Pankhursts? I hear from Mrs Swinford-Browne that you took part in the procession yourself,' Lady Hunney said.

Caroline glanced at Reggie, but he wasn't looking in her direction.

'Yes. It was splendid – apart from the rain. The response

has been tremendous, and I'm sure the National Register benefited from it.' She was beginning to feel more confident. After all, Sir John worked for the Army in Whitehall, so he was bound to be interested in the government-backed procession.

'And what was splendid about it?' persisted Lady Hunney.

'It was inspiring. Fifty thousand women dressed in white, marching for the right to work for the war effort. If only you had seen them—'

'I am not in the least sorry I did not.' Her ladyship smiled. 'I fear, Caroline, I hold to my concern that if women take men's jobs, who is to perform those of women?'

'But there will be plenty who cannot work,' Caroline explained. 'It's just that we want more women to work. Lloyd George said that the war cannot be won without us.' She remembered Swinford-Browne's reaction when he saw her at the nightclub and wondered uneasily just what he had said to his wife, and she to Lady Hunney, to provoke such an inquisition? She was beginning to feel like Daniel in the lions' den.

'*Mr* Lloyd George is not a person of whose views I approve. He panders to the masses, and great harm is consequently being done to society. Even Ashden is divided on the issue.'

'Not for much longer,' Caroline said. 'Don't you agree that times are changing, Sir John?'

'I believe circumstances are changing,' Sir John replied levelly. 'Times take a little longer, in my opinion.

I suggest, Maud, we adjourn to continue this discussion in the drawing room. We feel we should, Caroline.'

Caroline was aware that she had misinterpreted the situation. This was not a casual conversation. It was about her. She looked at Reggie in appeal, longing for some sign that he was with her. But none came. He wanted her to win this battle alone, she realised. Very well, she resolved. She would do it, and with a smile on her lips.

She positioned herself carefully in the drawing room next to Reggie and facing 'the enemy', sad though it was to include Sir John under that title.

'Caroline, my dear,' Lady Hunney began. 'I have expressed my views before on the need for a standard of conduct as Reggie's future wife. The squire's wife must be above involvement, yet here you are allying yourself with a political party that is very controversial in Ashden. You are even taking an active part to further this policy.' Her voice was gentle, even regretful. 'Do you not see how unfortunate this is?'

'No.' Caroline tried not to sound belligerent.

'We have asked you here today to request you give up this so-called *work* of yours in order to maintain a more dignified life in view of your future role. I'm afraid we feel strongly that it is most irresponsible of you to do otherwise.'

'Irresponsible?' Caroline was bewildered. 'But I'm working for the war effort and with the government, like you, Sir John.'

'My wife's reasons and mine differ somewhat, Caroline,

but in essence I too would like you to stop what you're doing.'

They meant it. They really did. And *still* Reggie was saying nothing.

'But when I was here earlier this year, I wasn't *allowed* to do anything,' she pointed out angrily.

'I agree with my wife that work on the land is highly unsuitable. There is plenty for you to do in other areas. My wife will advise you.'

'I can't, Sir John.' Caroline was appalled. 'Can I, Reggie? Do you agree with your parents?'

The silence hit her almost physically when he did not answer. At last he replied awkwardly: 'Partly.'

She felt suddenly sick. She needed fresh air, not this stifling den of unreason. Give up all she was doing when she believed in it? Could they not see the war was changing everything? Outside she might make sense of what was happening, and to blazes with convention. Abruptly she left the room.

As she breathed in the first gulps of garden air she remembered again her conversation with Reggie last year in which he told her that he could not escape being lord of the manor much as he'd like to. Everything had to be subordinated to this duty. And *everyone*, it now seemed. Even her. But he loved her; he'd told her so only last night.

'Caroline!' Reggie had followed her into the garden.

'Well?' She faced him, trembling.

'I'm sorry.'

'About what, Reggie?' The words came stiffly.

202

'That it has come to this.'

'To what? I don't understand.' She almost shouted at him.

His face was grey. 'I would like you to return to Ashden. But I don't want you running around planting potatoes and jollying women into Wellington boots. You're a VAD. Couldn't you work in the hospital?' he pleaded.

'I can't believe you mean this.'

'Mother has a point. As lady of the manor you have to set an example, or the system doesn't work, and if you're gallivanting—'

She interrupted furiously. '*Gallivanting*? Is that how you see it, Reggie? I wanted to work abroad at the front, you stopped that. I worked on the land here, you stopped that, and now you want to stop me even having beliefs of my own, and acting in accordance with them. Why?'

'Women have one role, men another.' He sounded as though he were trotting out a textbook reply.

'You're right. I do have a role. In London. And I won't give it up.'

'Won't you?' He looked so sad, her heart ached.

'Would you have any respect for me if I walked out of something I believed in passionately?'

'I don't know. I don't care. All that matters is getting through from day to day.' He was shouting now.

She put her arms round him and rocked him to and fro. 'Then let me do the deciding for you, and go on being strong,' she whispered.

He remained still and presently she released him.

'It can't go on like this, Caroline. Mother—'

'She's not involved in this,' Caroline interrupted fiercely.

'But she is. Marriage is a social contract as well as a private one, and in the Hunneys' case it's hundreds of years and generation after generation of that society. *That's* what we are fighting to retain and here you are beavering away trying to create a new society.'

'I can't give it up, Reggie.' She was close to tears.

There was a pause, and then came the worst words she could ever have imagined. 'Mother and Father think we should suspend our engagement until the war is over.'

'You mean break it, don't you?'

'Yes.'

'But you said you loved me.' She thought he would come to her, such was the anguish in her voice, but he did not. Instead he seemed almost annoyed.

'I'm so tired, Caroline, I just can't think of anything save what's happening over there. Nothing else seems important. I want you still, but I want you here. I really can't take any more of those endless letters from Mother. My brain is so muddled I can't see anything but trenches and mud and blood.'

She watched him, knowing she could not share this experience. Felicia could share it, and so could Aunt Tilly, but not her. Because he had forbidden it and shut her out.

She took the engagement ring off her finger; it was an

old one belonging to the Hunney family and she had loved it. 'You'd better take this now.' She held out her hand with the ring on its palm.

For a moment she thought he would refuse, and a wild hope flared up inside her. Then, as he reached out and took it, the flame died.

Chapter Ten

Caroline walked back to the Rectory, clicking the side gate home by removing the tendrils of ivy that were reaching out from the wall to block its passage. She marched through the kitchen door, greeting Mrs Dibble as she had done thousands of times before. Then she ran upstairs to wash, before joining her parents and George for tea. She asked George when he was leaving for his visit to his school friend; asked Mother if she had gathered enough support to cover the harvesting requirements; asked Father how the baptism of Myrtle's new baby brother Horatio (after Lord Kitchener) had gone; and agreed how terrible this summer's strikes had been.

All as if life were normal. But it wasn't, and never would be again. Once her mother would have noticed that she was upset, but now only Father gave her a curious glance from time to time. Fortunately there was no need for her to contribute more to the conversation; George took care of that. He'd just had another cartoon accepted by *Bystander* and was full of his own importance. He would soon be as well-known as Bairnsfather and Tom Browne, he boasted.

After tea, she tried to make her escape but her father stopped her as she turned to go up the stairs. Her first thought was that he'd seen something was wrong, but it appeared he had not. 'Caroline, are you meeting Reggie again?'

'No.'

'Then I would be grateful if you would come with me to see Nanny. She is fretting because her lumbago is worse and she isn't able to collect as many eggs as usual.'

Caroline was appalled. She wanted to shut herself away and nurse the pain that was filling her from top to toe, and then to leave Ashden as soon as she could, and go back to London.

'I should be grateful,' her father repeated patiently when she did not reply.

Taking her sun bonnet from the hat-stand, she went out to join her father in the porch. It was five o'clock but the sun still shone brightly and with warmth. How *dare* it, on such a day?

'I take it,' Laurence said quietly, as he turned out of the drive not for Bankside where Nanny lived but towards Pook's Way, the track that led to the forest, 'that Lady Hunney has finally succeeded in driving a wedge between you and Reggie.'

So he had seen something was wrong. And how easy it would be to say yes, and blame everything on her old enemy. Her lips took a long time to frame the words. 'Reggie's views are very similar to his mother's. I had not realised that.'

'So he has been persuaded to break off your engagement?'

'No. Because to some extent he agrees with her.' Her voice sounded normal to her, and she felt quite calm. That was splendid, wasn't it? No tears, no tantrums, no grieving for a love that was past.

'And you cannot adapt to his way of thinking?'

Why did Father have to go on chipping away to get the whole story? 'How can I give up what I am doing for something I don't think I'm fitted for?'

'Being Reggie's wife?'

'Being the squire's wife.'

'It has been an honourable calling for hundreds of years.'

'Perhaps. But will it continue to be?'

'Why should it change? The men who have volunteered must have jobs to return to after the war ends. Munitions factories will no longer be required; they will close and girls come back into service again. Guidance from the Manor will be needed all the more, while things settle down. Ashden will resume its old way of life – it will take time but it will happen. As Britain will continue to be the hub of her Empire, so will the Manor be necessary to drive the village.'

'But I want to help win this war in my own way,' Caroline said hopelessly. 'Not Lady Hunney's – and not Reggie's.'

'Then let's turn round and go to see Nanny Oates. She is pursuing her own war effort too.'

Seeing Nanny was not the ordeal she had feared. Apart from a sharp comment that Caroline wasn't feeding herself properly in London, and was looking as sour as a gazel (her native Kentish name for a blackcurrant), she talked of her hens and eggs, and Caroline was left in peace.

Not for long. As soon as she was home, the second inquisition began.

'Where's your ring?' Isabel asked curiously, as they crossed in the entrance hall.

'Back with its owner.' Families! Normally Isabel wouldn't have noticed if Caroline dyed her hair pink, but today she was as observant as a blackbird after worms.

Isabel frowned. 'You mean you've broken off your engagement?'

Caroline was tempted to say yes, but it took too much emotional energy to lie. 'No. Lady Hunney and Reggie have broken it off for me.'

'How could Maud do it?' Isabel was bewildered.

Something snapped. 'I don't want to *talk* about it!' Caroline yelled, pushing past her and rushing upstairs to her bedroom, where she slammed the door. A closed door in the Rectory meant no callers please.

Isabel broke all the rules by coming in after her and hugging her. 'I'm so sorry, Caroline. Men are *horrible*, aren't they? How could Reggie do it to you?'

'It's the war,' Caroline answered, trying to respond to Isabel's warm affection but failing. 'It changes everything.' Did it? Had it? Or might it have happened anyway?

'I know, darling. I never thought when I married Robert that he would leave me. Now he's in Gallipoli, and I don't know whether he's alive or dead. Marriage isn't so wonderful,' she informed her sister earnestly. 'You haven't missed anything.'

By the time she returned to London on Sunday evening, Caroline had managed to paper over the wound of her unhappiness, though she still seemed to be dragging a heavy load around with her, like Marley's ghost with his chains of penance. In the office it was easier to behave as though everything were normal. 'If only they don't notice the ring's gone,' she told herself. 'I'll be all right.' She found that the huge piles of letters reassured her. There were obviously thousands of women who felt as she did that work was an answer to the problems of war. So why did she feel so desolate?

'Where's your ring?' Angela asked on her next free day at Norland Square. 'You haven't lost it, have you?'

Like Isabel, Angela was not renowned for tact. 'No.' Caroline spoke through gritted teeth. She had to tell the whole story again; the only comfort being that it was becoming so familiar, at least inside her head, that it was beginning to hurt a little less.

'I suppose it was inevitable,' said Angela when she'd finished.

'Why?' Caroline was stung.

'Well.' Angela looked surprised. 'I've only met Reggie once but he struck me as a stickler for tradition. He'll turn into a regular Jorrocks in middle age.'

'I'm a traditionalist too,' Caroline countered, somewhat disarmed by the thought of Reggie as a pot-bellied fox-hunting man.

'Then what are you doing working in London? It's different for me, of course. I'm a VAD so when the war is over I'll go back to Dover and take up where I left off, but you're rushing around on a crusade like Josephine Butler, except that you're organising work for women, not saving them from sin. When the war's over, and the men come marching home, you'll have to decide whether you're going to go on crusading for women to continue to do men's jobs, or for the vote.'

Caroline stared at her. This was an aspect she had not considered; to her the present need was so urgent that she had ignored the wider implications.

'Father thinks,' Angela continued, 'it's secret of course – that when the harvest is over in France in September there'll be a big British offensive. Really big, not just limited objectives.'

Once this news would have filled Caroline with terror. Now it had the ring of remorseless inevitability.

'There's a war of words on at present between the government and the Imperial General Staff. The brass hats don't think the Army is up to it after the awfulness of the spring, and the new troops going out there haven't had enough training.'

'What training do you need to be slaughtered?'

'That's not like you, Caroline.' Angela was shocked. 'Words like that don't win wars.'

'War, war, *war*!' Caroline shouted, goaded beyond endurance. 'I'm *sick* of it.'

'Perhaps Reggie is too.'

Furious, because she knew Angela was in the right,

Caroline stamped off to her room, aching with self-pity.

Despite her work, and despite filling her evenings with visits to concerts and theatres, her days dragged. Once she would have revelled in the new freedom; now she was beginning to take it for granted. Even George Grossmith in *Tonight's the Night* at the Gaiety, singing 'They Didn't Believe Me' with Madge Saunders, failed to enchant her; for at night she returned to face Angela's words in the loneliness of her room. Perhaps Reggie was too.

Why had pride kept her from making the first overture? She would write to him, bridge the gap, make it easy for him to heal the break; she would tell him how much she loved him and that she would wait for him. On the Saturday, she could hold back no longer. She rose early and ran down to the morning-room desk, her fingers trembling with emotion as she seized pen and paper.

Darling Reggie,

I must write, I must reach you before you're as far away in heart as in fact. I know it's just the war that is doing this to us, and that we are seeing each other as through a glass darkly because of it. When it is over, you will return and we shall meet in our apple orchard as though all this had never happened. Please, please tell me you realise this too.

If only you knew how I long for you—

She hesitated for a moment, then plunged on. She had to pour out her heart no matter what the pain, to prevent

213

further misunderstandings – for, surely, that was what had caused their rift?

. . . how I long to take your poor tired body in my arms and lull it into peace with mine. All that matters is that we love each other and, if we cling to that, then love will clear a path for us. Oh my darling, shall we try? Your whirling dervish will be waiting, O Lord Kitchener!

Her eyes misted as their childhood game stabbed her with poignancy. Far-off days, those days of summer. But they would come again. They must, no matter how hard she found it to make this appeal.

Seized with conviction that she was doing the right thing, she signed her name with a dash, then stared in dismay at the ink blob which the nib had deposited on her name and blotted it quickly. Not carefully enough; it smudged. She couldn't write it again, she couldn't. Anyway, the blob would remind him so much of the old Caroline that it would make Reggie laugh. She would send it, blots and all.

Elizabeth did a little skip as soon as she was far enough along the footpath not to be seen. She felt like a girl again, hurrying to her father's hopgarden.

Hop-picking time in Kent had been the major event of the year in her village. On a certain day towards the end of August the main contingent of pickers would arrive in their hundreds from the railway station, children and luggage spilling everywhere, down from the East End of

London for what was for them their summer holiday. Not all the pickers were East-Enders of course; in Kent, as here in Sussex, local women picked and helped repair pokes and baskets. Gypsies too, and waygoers, would arrive faithfully every year for six weeks' sure money. With probably selective memory she remembered the long balmy evenings, as families sat outside primitive huts cooking over a fire. And she recalled lovers' meetings in the cool of the day sheltered by unpicked bines. On such a night she and Laurence had sat, talking, laughing, loving.

It was in the hopgarden she had first met him. Staying nearby with his brother Gerald, he had come to pick at her father's farm, dressed in rough labourer's clothes, both boys pretending to be casual waygoers. She had been strictly forbidden by her parents to enter the hopgarden but, after one illicit visit, she had been so beguiled by this handsome 'labourer' that night after night she found herself sitting on his jacket at his side on the grass. And then, one evening he kissed her and that was that. Her life was decided.

As the soporific smell of the hops hit her nose, the illusion that she had stepped back in time was complete. Temporarily released from her Ashden role, she looked at the familiar scene before her and wondered why in all her years as Laurence's wife she had never thought to come here at hop-picking time.

She wandered down the rows of bines, delighted that she was all but anonymous; strangers were plucking hops brought down by the binman's hook and dropping them into the waiting bin. Shouts, yells, wads, snatches of music hall and popular war marching songs filled her ears; the buzz of conversation around her, 'It's a long way to Tipperary' roaring out from the next row. Then she realised that an altercation was going on in the row on the opposite side from 'Tipperary'. Abusive shouts and angry voices were so loud she wondered why the binman had not intervened, and she went to see what was going on. At first she could not make it out. Just a crowd of men and women with something – no, someone – in the centre of them. She caught a brief glimpse and realised to her horror it was not only a woman but someone whose face she knew.

'Leave me alone,' Lizzie was shrieking.

A particularly vicious swipe with a stripped bine caught her round the face and she staggered back into the yelling crowd behind her.

'Stop this at once,' Elizabeth shouted. She had a strong voice and the workers stopped for a moment in surprise, giving her the chance to push towards Lizzie. It was no surprise to see that a Thorn was taking a leading part – George, Ernie's elder brother – but most were strangers to her, East-Enders, no doubt still so incensed at Zeppelin bombs that they needed little incentive to attack anything and anyone German, even if only by association.

By the time she reached Lizzie the girl was screaming in pain, her arms twisted behind her. Then, just as Elizabeth began to fear for her own safety, the crowd fell to one side as Frank Eliot appeared, threatening to pack the lot of them back where they came from and bar them from the hopgardens for ever. With a last cry of 'German whore' from an unidentifiable source the brawlers melted away, leaving the three of them together: Lizzie tear-stained and marked with red weals from the bines, Elizabeth, her heart thumping now danger was past, and a grim-faced Frank.

'I didn't start it,' Lizzie cried. 'I can't help having a German husband. It doesn't make me a German, does it? I didn't sink the bloody *Lusitania*, or drop no bombs.'

'Is that what it was about? Then I'm ashamed this has happened in my hopgarden,' Frank replied.

Lizzie shrugged. 'It's happened before and will likely happen again.'

'Happened before?'

'In my cottage which the Rector got me.'

'Have you told Police Constable Ifield?' Elizabeth was appalled.

'What's the use? The whole village is against me just because I'm married to a German.'

'You can't go back to your cottage on the Ashden estate after this,' Frank said. 'Many of this mob were from the East End, but some were local.'

'What else do you suggest?' Lizzie sneered. 'Buckingham Palace?'

'The Rectory,' offered Elizabeth immediately.

Lizzie hesitated, taken aback by kindness. 'Thank you, Mrs Lilley, but no. I get on with Ma fine when we're apart, but not under the same roof. I'd rather take my chances in the cottage.'

'But it's so isolated,' Elizabeth worried. 'My husband told me it's almost as far as the Manor's forest boundary.'

'I could find you a small house on this estate when hop-picking's over, if you're prepared to go to the Rectory in the meantime,' Frank offered. 'No one would dare harm you here. The Swinford-Browne estate is guarded.'

'Could you?' Lizzie's face was suspicious, but hopeful.

'But—' Elizabeth stopped, remembering that Lizzie was no longer a Dibble but Lizzie Stein, a married woman, and she had no jurisdiction over her, whatever she chose to do.

Agnes stretched contentedly. Her old room at the Rectory was luxury compared with Castle Tillow, even though it now contained Elizabeth Agnes's cradle as well as her. It was funny being back; it was as though nothing had changed and she was still Agnes Pilbeam, the new parlourmaid at the Rectory. But she wasn't, she reminded herself. She was Agnes Thorn. Apart from its association with Jamie she hated the name Thorn. Jamie's mother wouldn't even speak to her now she'd refused yet again to work in the ironmongery. And not even Len would dare try to force her because of the Rectory. Yes, she was safe – and so for the moment was Jamie. Under her pillow was a letter which arrived yesterday, dated 7th September. 'We are being rested for a week or two.'

She didn't like the sound of that. Rested for what? Something important was going to happen, and Jamie would be in it. At least she'd seen him in May. That was another reason Mrs Thorn didn't like her. He hadn't gone to see his mother, or anyone else come to that. Only her. Nor had he at Christmas when they were wed. 'Why not, Jamie?' she'd asked.

'Because I ain't going back until I've got a medal, Agnes, that's why.'

'A *medal*? But that's daft, Jamie. You've shown 'em all what you're made of by volunteering, you don't have to have a special medal too.'

'Daft or not, that's what I decided. They didn't—'

He stopped, but she guessed what he was going to say. 'They didn't believe me last year' – but nor had she for a while. Oh, how she'd make it up to him when he came marching home for good.

Quickly she washed, fed Elizabeth Agnes, and hurried downstairs. 'Morning, Mrs Dibble.'

'Good morning, Miss P – Mrs Thorn. Late, aren't you?'

Agnes laughed. 'No. You're early. As always, Mrs Dibble.' Nothing and no one had the power to upset her now she was back in the Rectory. Mrs Dibble had once been a terrifying monster. Now she was a flesh and blood cantankerous old biddy.

'Myrtle says we're out of glove-cleaning paste.'

'I'll mix some up.'

'I'll do it myself. That way it gets done. *And* the mangle rollers is getting hollow again.' Mrs Dibble sniffed.

'What's wrong?' Agnes realised that even Mrs Dibble wasn't usually so pernickety over mere trifles.

'Nothing, Mrs Thorn.' The reply was quick and sharp. 'Why should it be, save that I'm all behind?'

'Something is.'

'Mayhap. We're going to have a guest.' Mrs Dibble looked defiantly at Agnes.

'The family, you mean? Miss Tilly?'

'No, us. The servants' hall. Only a guest, mark you. Too la-di-da to do honest work for her living.'

'Who are you talking about?'

'My Lizzie.'

'But I thought—'

'What you thought and what is are as different as lardy cakes and latten bells,' Mrs Dibble snapped. 'She should never have married that German. I was against it all along. Just because someone's banging out jolly songs on a drum doesn't mean they don't have evil hearts.'

'She seemed very happy with him,' Agnes ventured.

To her horror, the impossible happened. Mrs Dibble, she saw, was crying. Her face was wrinkling up and she was screwing it up in an effort to stop the tears.

'You sit down, Mrs D,' Agnes commanded. 'I'm going to make the tea, and you can tell me all about it. It can't be as bad as you think.'

'Joe out there fighting them Germans. Lizzie attacked here for being wed to one,' Mrs Dibble whispered. 'I don't know what the world's coming to. And her not wanting to live here even though Mrs Lilley asked her for the second time. Not live with her own mother, indeed. Why not, I ask you?'

Agnes knew the answer to this one. She poured the water into the teapot. 'Sometimes,' she explained, 'mothers and daughters love each other but can't live together. I couldn't go home no more than Lizzie can. And Lizzie's been a married lady longer than me.'

'Miss Isabel's come home. She ain't so hard-hearted.' Mrs Dibble sniffed.

'If you ask me,' Agnes remarked companionably, 'Miss Isabel only comes home so she doesn't have to go on thinking for herself at Hop House. That Mrs Bugle, so I hear, isn't a patch on you. Why, if she were even a hundredth as good as you are, that Mrs Swinford-Browne would have had her at The Towers. What we would do without you, I don't know.'

Mrs Dibble's chest swelled infinitesimally as she watched the tea being poured into her cup, nice and strong. 'Always was a self-centred little thing, Miss Isabel, for all she can twist you round her little finger in a moment. She's not like Miss Caroline.'

'I miss Miss Caroline.' Agnes was wistful. They were the same age, twenty-three, and she felt a proprietorial interest in her.

'We'll be missing her a lot more, you mark my words,' announced Mrs Dibble darkly.

'When she marries Mr Reginald, you mean?'

'I do hear Mr Reginald and she aren't engaged any more. Have you seen that ring? I ain't.' Mrs Dibble reflected on the oddities of life. Here she was swapping stories with Miss Pilbeam, of whom she used to disapprove so strongly. Still, Agnes was a married woman now, *mature*.

'She's never broken it off?' Agnes exclaimed.

'Him more like. That Lady Hunney can be a tartar.'

Agnes gave due consideration to this, remembering how scared she had been as a child when Lady Hunney sailed through their cottage door without so much as a by your leave bearing a basket of fruit from Ashden's greenhouses for her mother who was sick. Her presence had seemed to fill the whole room. 'She is that,' she agreed.

'Say what you like,' Mrs Dibble declared. 'The Rectory's not the same without Miss Caroline or Miss Felicia.'

For the second time this week Laurence was holding Matins alone. It was September now and the corn harvest was still claiming many of his regular flock. Even the war respected the harvest, and the news from the front in France at least was quiet, waiting – just as the Zeppelins too had been waiting. There had only been three raids in the whole of August, but now by mid-September there had been a further five, in two cases on successive nights. There had also been a daylight raid on Margate – a sinister development. Hitherto such attentions as they had had in Kent had probably been the unintentional results of raids on London or the East Coast. It did not bode well for Dover – or Buckford House. Stray thoughts went through his mind which he tried to push out on the grounds that Matins and the Lord's Word must have priority.

'Almighty and most merciful Father, we have erred and strayed from thy ways like lost sheep . . . We have left undone those things which we ought to have done . . .' But those unwelcome thoughts lingered.

He did not mind being alone this morning with God. Here, in the peace of St Nicholas, surrounded by the ornaments and symbols of his calling, war could be distanced. But still it inched its way insidiously towards him, claiming all that was most dear. When Caroline first left home it had seemed of no more importance than her taking a long holiday. The Rectory was her home, whether the holiday was of weeks or months. But how could he be sure of this now? The rift between her and Reggie might drive her away for ever. She was establishing a new kind of life in London; would she ever be content to return to Ashden now that her future was no longer tied to it?

And what would happen to Felicia? Her shyness had always set her apart from her sisters. He remembered the disaster of the finishing school, when he had rushed to Paris and found her ill through unhappiness. Her large dark eyes seemed to him full of reproach for his having endorsed his mother's insistence that she come to this place. He knew he had made the wrong decision, and it had haunted him in his dealings with her ever since, making him acquiesce with scarcely a word when, with equal determination, she had announced her intention of going abroad. He had never truly known what Felicia was like, for shyness hid or had developed an inner strength he had never suspected. Though neither Caroline nor the press had been specific about what her work entailed, the distraught girl who could not face a group of girls her own age had marched off to the war front and won an award for gallantry.

At least Phoebe seemed to have settled down, even though he could wish it were elsewhere than in an Army camp. She was docile, polite, and enthusiastic about her job, and if her tidiness had not improved, her manners had. He could not ask for more. Isabel was home, George seemed to be devoting himself to his studies. And that left Elizabeth.

'O Lord, in Thee I have trusted. Let me never be confounded.'

It was he who had begged her to fight the war at his side when, confused that her brood of children had been

223

suddenly weaned from her control, she had lost her way. As a result she seemed to be becoming independent of him – though not necessarily by her choosing. She still brought some of the village problems to him for she heard much that might not necessarily reach his ears. This, he acknowledged, was good for Ashden, and perhaps some day he would see it as good for them, but for the moment he wondered where the world he had known all his life was taking him.

After Matins he left the church, intending to visit the post office before beginning his parish visiting. Before the war, there would have been breakfast to look forward to, with Elizabeth calmly reading her post. Now it had been agreed that family prayers and breakfast should be held *before* Matins so that Elizabeth could make an earlier start to her day.

Glancing up Station Road as he walked by the corner, he saw Fred walking to the station with a basket of eggs, and Len Thorn swaggering up behind him. To his horror, Len jumped up behind the lad, shouting and waving his arms, obviously with the intention of frightening him. He succeeded for Fred yelled, turned round, and head-butted Len in self-defence.

Laurence was not in time to stop Len's retaliation. As he ran up shouting for him to stop, the basket of eggs was torn from Fred's hand and thrown to the ground.

'Is this your way of winning the war, Len?' Laurence shouted as he reached them.

Len stared at him insolently. 'Accident, Rector.'

'Then you will apologise to Fred for it.'

'Suppose I won't?'

Laurence's anger rose. 'Blessed are the meek, Len Thorn. God didn't send you into this world to bully others.'

'That's right. Rector. Meek little babies like my niece you're keeping from her rightful kin.'

What was he doing bandying words with this hooligan, Laurence thought impatiently. 'Come to me when you want to make your peace with God, Len. Now help me pick up these eggs.

'Sorry to disappoint you, but I'm a working man.' Laughing, Len marched off towards the station, leaving Laurence to console Fred who was standing at his side, tears running down his face.

'There's a good dozen here not broken, Fred,' Laurence said, picking up an envelope which had tumbled from the bottom of the basket. To his surprise he recognised Phoebe's handwriting. 'How did you get this?'

''Tis a secret,' Fred informed him proudly, still gulping.

'Then you must keep it, of course.' With growing perturbation, Laurence looked to see to whom it was addressed. He should have guessed, he should have known. It was to Private Harry Darling, the young man at the tennis party. 'Don't worry, Fred. I'll take care of this now.'

Laurence felt immensely depressed. Never in the old days would a young man of Len's age have dared speak in such a fashion to the Rector. And never would his own daughter have so blatantly ignored his authority. He thought for a long time over what he should do, and finally decided he had no alternative.

* * *

Phoebe looked at her father warily when he put his head out of the door after Rector's Hour and asked her to come into his study.

'Can you explain this?' He handed her the letter, keeping his voice neutral.

'Where did you get that?'

'Through no fault of Fred's. I take it this is not the first time he has taken your letters to Tunbridge Wells for posting?'

'No.'

'And why is that, Phoebe?'

'Because I knew you'd make a fuss about it.'

'And why should I do that?'

Phoebe did not reply.

'I take it this is merely a letter written in friendship?' Laurence continued.

'Yes,' she stammered.

'More than friendship?' he asked inexorably.

'Yes,' she cried again, cornered. 'I love him, Father. Just like Caroline does Reggie, and Isabel Robert. What's wrong about that?'

'A great deal,' he replied, even more horrified now at how blind he had been. 'This young soldier seemed nice enough, but he has been brought up in an entirely different background to yourself. How could there be more than friendship involved?'

'Background isn't important.'

'Background is very important when it differs.'

'You married Mother; she wasn't from your background.'

'That's enough,' he said sharply. 'There is no comparison. Your mother came from an established country family. This soldier is uneducated—'

'He's not. He was at school till he was fourteen.'

'And from the East End of London. There is nothing wrong in that. But what have you in common? Nothing. How could there ever be a marriage between you, if that is what is in your mind? How could he support you?'

'East-Enders *marry*.'

'Yes, and they expect a wife who can run their home. Could you? Of course not. Would you scrub steps and wash clothes? Of course, if you had been used to doing so. But you have not. Phoebe, it grieves me to tell you this, but you must not continue to write to him or have anything more to do with him. If you do not agree I shall be forced to write myself and explain the situation.'

'You can't,' she cried. 'You *mustn't*.' She ran at him, pummelling him with her fists, screaming, till he was forced to sit her down. He wished he had consulted Elizabeth before speaking to her.

At that moment he heard the front door and, hurrying out of his study, he found Elizabeth had returned. 'Before you go upstairs, my love, Phoebe needs you.'

Alarmed, Elizabeth rushed straight into the study.

Much later that evening, after a strained dinner, Phoebe opened Laurence's study door. 'I've come to say that I'll tell Harry that we mustn't be in love any more. On one condition.'

'And that is?'

'That I can write once a month as a friend.'

227

Laurence hesitated. Eventually he said, 'God and your conscience will watch you, Phoebe.'

In their bedroom that night he took his wife in his arms, burying his head on her breast. 'What magic have you wrought with Phoebe, Elizabeth?'

'Nothing,' came the muffled reply against his hair. 'Only sense . . .

Caroline realised she could delay visiting the Rectory no longer. She usually spent every other weekend in Sussex, but had invented a reason for not going last Saturday. It would be an ordeal, even though Reggie would not be there. In London she was busy discussing moving to new premises to save money, attending meetings at the Board of Agriculture now Women's Agricultural Committees were to be fact, not just a proposal, and helping on the WSPU newspaper the *Suffragette*. She had been prominent in a move to get the title changed and next month, for the October issue, it would be renamed the *Britannia*. They were also extra busy with Mrs Pankhurst's plans to hold a series of meetings on 'How to Win the War', beginning on 5th October at the London Pavilion where Dame Clara Butt would be singing again. It all helped take her mind off Reggie.

As she boarded the train at Victoria she felt tension rising for, at Ashden, she would have to be Caroline Lilley again instead of the bright London face she had invented. She was glad that Ellen, who it had been planned should accompany her this weekend while hop-picking was on, had had to cancel because her duty rota had been changed.

Ellen's friendly observant eye would have been the last straw. Even so, she would have to face yet more sympathy from her family.

As she began the walk down Station Road she wondered if she should stroll up to Hop House, but remembered Isabel had moved back to the Rectory. Then she saw a familiar figure walking towards her. She laughed in pleasure: Isabel wasn't at the Rectory, she was here. Oh, how wonderful! Caroline hugged her. Of course it was wonderful to be home.

'I thought you might like company.' Isabel seemed pleased with herself.

'Provided you don't want to dash into The Towers as we pass.'

'No,' Isabel assured her. 'And we'd better duck as we go by in case they're weeding the front border.'

Caroline laughed again, not so much at the idea of Edith and William ever stooping to remove a weed from their immaculately kept gardens, but because Isabel had actually made a joke. She was obviously feeling much happier than she had done on Caroline's last visit.

'How are you?' Isabel gave her arm an affectionate squeeze. 'Busy,' declared Caroline, 'I'm glad to say.'

'It will get better. I know.'

Caroline watched a blackbeetle inch its way to safety in the hedgerow. How could it get better? And how could Isabel know? 'I expect so,' she replied lightly.

Isabel glanced at her and did not comment.

'What's new at home?' Caroline continued.

'Nothing much. George is busy sketching cartoons, and

229

only mentions aeroplanes fifty times a day – to me, that is, not to Father – and Phoebe has suddenly settled down. She's growing up at last. You'd never know her.'

So nothing had changed in the Rectory in a month or more, although everything had for her. Life was still a great wall to be climbed and even God didn't seem to be offering a helping hand to haul her up.

Later that night Isabel crept into her room with a candle. 'You don't think I'm very sympathetic, do you?' she whispered. 'But I *am*.'

Caroline lit her candle again. 'You've no idea how hard it is. Every time I think of Reggie a great pain hits me. Just here.' She indicated her stomach and chest. 'I can't believe it's true. I'll never love anyone else, and I know he loves me still, and yet he hasn't replied to the letter I wrote.' The misery came pouring out. 'Oh Isabel, I abased myself, and he hasn't even replied.'

Isabel clung to her. 'I know, I do know.'

Next morning Caroline felt stronger. Family prayers and breakfast, albeit earlier than they used to be, made everything seem normal again. 'How's Poppy?' she asked, helping herself to one of Mrs Dibble's specially made muffins.

There was a sudden silence, and she looked up. 'I thought I'd insist she took me out this morning.'

'Darling, I'm afraid—' Elizabeth began gently.

'She's dead, isn't she?'

'She was very old, darling, and she died peacefully. We had Eleanor come and, knowing Poppy of old, that was nice. There was nothing we could do for her any more.'

Caroline stared at her muffin which suddenly required a great deal of chewing. Poppy had come as a foal from Ashden Manor. Poppy had been with her all her life, and now she was gone. 'Where is she? Did you—'

'George and Father took her to the pets' cemetery in the Manor Park.'

'Oh.' She tried to eat the muffin again. So that's what she must do this morning, after seeing Nanny. She would force herself to go to Poppy's grave.

The park looked frighteningly familiar yet now Caroline felt a stranger. She and Reggie had spent their childhood here: there was the wild garden where they played at being Mowgli, from *The Jungle Book*, and there the folly where last summer Reggie had declared his mother could never prevent their marriage.

Stop this, she told herself. At once. And she did try. Sneaking across the path that led to the Dower House, she hurried to the rhododendron woods at the far side of the park where the pets' cemetery lay in a specially cleared enclosure. Here General Gordon, Reggie's first gundog, and her pet rabbit Ezekiel were buried, as well as their sheepdog Ahab's predecessor. And here was Poppy's newly dug grave, withered flowers still on it, and a headstone carved by Fred, reading 'Dear Poppy, Faithful Friend, 1894-1915'.

Suddenly it was all too much. She choked, and the tears that she had not shed over Reggie came in a rush for Poppy.

* * *

231

'Caroline!'

She stopped at Daniel's shout, hesitated and reluctantly walked back to him. He was being pushed in his invalid chair by a nurse. Caroline didn't feel like talking to anybody, but talking to Daniel was preferable to conversation at the Rectory today. In the dining room her parents lamented the 40% rise in income tax announced in last Tuesday's budget; and, if she went into the kitchen, Mrs Dibble would be lamenting the yet heavier duty on sugar.

'It'll be donkey tea and kettle bender for us, you mark my words,' Mrs Dibble had warned Mother gloomily, a familiar threat in times of hardship, though they had never yet descended to boiling water poured over burnt toast crumbs to drink or over bread, pepper and salt to eat.

'And now you can push me back,' Daniel announced some time later.

'Shall I go to find Meg?' Caroline suggested. Daniel had dismissed the nurse on Caroline's arrival. 'She's a better driver.' How could she say she did not want to risk seeing Lady Hunney?

'Please do it, Caroline.'

Just as she had feared. Lady Hunney opened the side windows herself, as these were easier for invalid chairs. Caroline braced herself for the ordeal, then saw it was unnecessary. Lady Hunney's face was grey, and she seemed smaller than she remembered.

'Thank you for bringing Daniel back, Caroline.'

'It's wonderful news that he's able to walk again.' He had given her a brief demonstration on his crutches.

'Not exactly the Olympics yet,' he joked, 'but wait till I

get the tin leg.' Then he too saw his mother's face. 'What's wrong?' he asked sharply.

'Your father has just telephoned. The offensive has begun. Near a small hamlet called Loos. The 2nd Royal Sussex – Reginald – is there.'

'The offensive started on Saturday.' Laurence put down *The Times*. 'It wasn't the harvest we were waiting for, it was for the French armies to re-arm with new, bigger howitzers; they are nicknamed the Conquerors. Let us pray they are right, and that they put an end to the need for further battles. We've attacked from Arras to Ypres, and apparently have had some success. Loos has been taken already. No word of the casualties.'

'All those young boys,' murmured Elizabeth.

'You must be relieved, Isabel.' Her father smiled at her.

'What about?' Isabel asked.

'That Robert is in Gallipoli, and not the Western Front. Though there's severe fighting there too, of course.'

'Of course I'm relieved.' In truth Isabel was rather enjoying her new life at the Rectory. The status of honoured guest, instead of merely eldest unmarried daughter, was extremely pleasant.

In the kitchen Aggie stared at her *Daily Sketch*. A new offensive. And Jamie might be in it. Somehow she was sure he was, if only because of the hints he'd dropped about the rest period. The censor would have cut out any mention of where he was. She would have to wait for another letter, or some clue to the 7th Sussex being in action. She felt sick.

'What's it say, Agnes?'

The use of her Christian name alerted her to the fact that Mrs Dibble had something on her mind. Of course, Joe – a territorial in the 5th Sussex.

'A new offensive, Mrs D.' It was a compromise since she had never been invited to call her Margaret. 'But no mention of who's involved,' she added quickly.

'A big one?' Mrs Dibble sat down heavily.

'Sounds like it.' They looked at each other, sharing a common worry.

Phoebe, having had breakfast earlier, had not dared touch *The Times*, though the thought of Harry preyed on her constantly. All she could see on the front page was the personal column and the advertisements from the shipping companies, just as if everyone was still enjoying holidays. It wasn't till she got to work that she heard the news. She didn't care about the offensive itself. All she could think about was whether the London Division was in it.

Chapter Eleven

Laurence's day had been busy, even by present standards, and it was not until mid-afternoon that he found his mother's letter awaiting him. Usually these arrived on the first day of each month, plopping like cuckoo's eggs into the Rectory nest. To receive one written on Saturday 9th October, only a few days after its predecessor, and received today, Monday, was disturbing.

The morning's events had drained his resistance. His village calls were now far more numerous than his daily Rector's Hour could cope with, or too personal for people to wish to be seen attending the Rectory. Attendance at church had risen too, as villagers turned to God for support in times of crisis. Not everyone saw it that way, however – not Mrs Barton, Alfred Thorn's sister, whom he'd just been to see. Yesterday she had received the dreaded yellow envelope denoting a government telegram. She had shown it to him: 'We deeply regret to inform you that Private John Barton was killed in action on 4th October. Lord Kitchener expresses his sympathy.' He had suggested they pray together. She had done so until they reached 'But deliver us from evil', when she burst out, 'Well, He *hasn't*, has He, Rector? Not my John.'

'He has gone before you into the life everlasting, Mrs Barton.'

'Begging your pardon, Rector, I want him here.' She burst into loud sobs. 'How can He let it all happen, you tell me that.'

Of what use were theological arguments about moral freedom and God's plan for the world, to a woman whose son lay dead? There, with a black ribbon round it, was John's photograph taken before he left for France, so proud to be one of Kitchener's First Hundred Thousand. And only weeks after his arrival he was dead. Shortly his few possessions would be sent back with typical Army efficiency – and lack of compassion. Portraits of the King and Queen hung over the mantelpiece torn from a magazine and carefully framed. Mrs Barton followed Laurence's gaze. 'God bless them, they do their bit.'

'And so does Our Lord, but His ways are more difficult to comprehend. And John has done his bit too. He went to war because he wanted to make a stand against evil. Now he has given his life for that cause. He would want you to be proud of him, even in your grief.'

'Will you carve his initials on your tree, Rector? He'd be

valiant proud. But it don't make no difference. I'll not be coming to church again.'

As he left the cottage, he saw Beth Parry dismounting from her bicycle and leaning it against the fence. 'Is Mrs Barton ill?' he asked.

'I heard her son had been killed. I thought I would call to see her.'

'I'm afraid she is too grief-stricken to listen to our words at the moment.'

Beth hesitated. 'I had not been intending to encroach on your prerogative, Rector. But as a woman, I can sit in silence with her. That may accomplish something at least.'

His respect for her grew even higher. 'Do bear in mind she's Alfred Thorn's sister. She may be hostile to you,' he advised.

'That seems unimportant. Good-day, Rector.' Beth walked past him up the cottage garden path, still bright with nasturtiums and a few unpicked tomatoes, and the door closed behind her.

Humbled by his failure, Laurence waited a moment or two to see if it would re-open but it did not. The new doctor, he realised, was a remarkable character. He had already noticed with some amusement that both Philip Ryde and his curate Charles Pickering not only spoke of her approvingly but were vying for her attentions after church service. According to Elizabeth, Philip had been spotted at her side at one of Maud Hunney's concerts in Tunbridge Wells, and Charles had been seen with her boarding the London train. The same informant had added, a little regretfully, that they had both returned later the same evening. A village like Ashden had a thousand eyes, as Laurence knew only too well, and none of them needed sleep.

The Rectory entrance hall felt as empty as it looked when he came in. George would not be back from school yet, nor Phoebe from work. From the kitchen he could hear Mrs Dibble singing loudly, 'Do no sinful action, speak no angry word—' Normally, however many times he told himself that the voice lifted in song was a prayer to God, the sound of her singing intruding as he worked in his study was an interruption. But today, he found it comforting to hear the children's hymn ringing through the Rectory. 'Ye belong to Jesus, Children of the Lord.' It had been Caroline's favourite, and her familiar accompaniment to her performance of Rectory household chores. 'Ye are newborn Christians, Ye must learn to fight.' Each line took two energetic pushes with the polishing duster on Granny Overton's desk in the drawing room, Caroline had explained to him one day . . . 'With the bad within you, *And* to do the right.'

And he had tried. Yet often, as with Mrs Barton, he failed. Then he noticed the letter from his mother, and opened it in the seclusion of his study.

My dear Laurence,
I am displeased with Charles. He has offered Buckford House to the military for the duration of the war. Officers, he has stipulated; one presumes therefore the silver will be safe. He is proposing to move his family to Wiltshire while he remains at his

command in Dover. Naturally I have refused to go
with them. My home is here. In the circumstances
I am considering whether to move into the Dower
House, as Charles wishes, or to stay with you in the
Rectory. I will inform you of my decision shortly.
  Your affectionate Mother.

Laurence read the letter again to ensure he had not
misunderstood. How could she even consider coming to
Sussex when she had refused to visit them, or even to meet
Elizabeth? It was out of the question. Mother must move
into the Dower House. He would tell Elizabeth so. Where
was she? He went through to the kitchen to ask Mrs Dibble
and, as he entered, Agnes's baby woke up and began to
cry. Mrs Dibble looked at him reproachfully, but he had no
time to waste.

'Mrs Lilley's at Owlers Farm today, sir, this being the
last of the corn harvest.'

As he entered Silly Lane, Laurence told himself that
outings such as this were good for him. Before the war he
had sat in his study, expecting the village and his family
to come to him. Now he seemed to be rushing around
perpetually in search of them.

Reaching the Roffeys' market garden, he could hear
cries and laughter further down the lane. Shading his
eyes against the late sun, he saw a horse-drawn corn
wagon with a crowd of people running at its side,
cheering it on. Of course, they were bringing in the last
of the corn up the lane to the barn. It was an ancient
fertility rite which still persisted, the Church having long

since elected to have the last word by holding a harvest supper and festival.

As the wagon drew closer he looked to see if Elizabeth were among them. A few doffed their hats to the Rector, but many did not notice him. The wagon was loaded with corn sheaves packed high at the front to make a throne; on it sat Elizabeth, her black hair beneath a crown of corn, a sceptre of corn in one hand and the ritual corn dolly in the other. She did not see her husband standing on the hedge bank, clinging for support to a hazel bush. She was smiling and her eyes were bright. She seemed the same girl he had met in the hopgardens all those years ago: alive, vibrant and hopeful, so different from the rigid darkness of life at Buckford House. Laurence wanted to cry out to her, to stop the wagon, to climb on it and claim her as his wife. But he could say nothing for it had passed and she was already out of his reach and far away.

Beth returned from her rounds exhausted. She had taken Dr Marden's motor car to visit his outlying patients this afternoon, for he was in East Grinstead for the day, and she found driving tiring. She disliked his precious Wolseley, but Dr Marden's horse had been requisitioned by the Army, and arrival on bicycle was not what Ashden expected of its doctors. She compromised by using both means of transport.

As she went into Tillow House she found Dr Marden was not yet back, although it was past surgery time. There was only one person waiting, she saw to her relief – until she realised it was Len Thorn. She hardly recognised him. He had a rapidly emerging black eye and his face was puffy with bruising and brown with dried blood from a deep cut. A dirty handkerchief had been tied round his hand. 'Come into the surgery, Mr Thorn,' she said.

He scowled but, rather to her surprise, followed her in.

'How did this happen?' she asked as she cleaned him up.

'Mutters,' he growled, wincing.

'Did they have a reason?'

'Young Barton. If it's any business of yours.'

'I see.'

'It were ten of them against nine of us,' he continued, 'so I let that Mus Cyril have it, I did.'

It looked more as if Master Cyril had let Len have it, but Beth held her peace. Dr Marden's daughter, Janie, had told her that the Mutters and the Thorns were now running a competition as to how many Thorn and Mutter initials were carved on the oak tree. Woe betide anyone who passed after the Norville Arms or Red Lion closed their doors, the favourite time for assessment as to who counted as a Thorn or Mutter and who did not.

'I still don't hold with women doctors. T'ain't natural. They didn't ought to be wearing trousers,' Len grumbled as he rose to leave.

Beth was amused. It wasn't much of a thank you, but it was a move in the right direction. 'That will be one shilling, Mr Thorn,' she told him.

He paid in silence.

* * *

241

'No!' The word exploded from Elizabeth. Now she knew why Laurence had been so quiet all evening.

'Mother must move to the Dower House,' he agreed, 'and I will tell Charles so quite firmly.'

'The woman is mad. To insult me all my life, and then inform me she is considering coming to live under my roof, in my home. It is insupportable.'

'It cost her a lot to ask.'

'She hasn't asked,' Elizabeth pointed out. 'You cannot seriously be contemplating her living here?'

'I felt it right to warn you that we may, despite all Charles can do, be faced with the possibility.'

'Well, you have warned me, and my answer is no.'

Once, Laurence felt, Elizabeth might have been less intransigent. The Rectory had always been open house for their family and friends; with her warm heart she gathered around her all those in pain. He had hoped that she might see his mother's request, if request it could be termed, as some sort of triumph. Now he realised how mistaken he had been.

He tried again. 'Despite our shared feelings about her, we are a Christian household. We have more rooms here than we can possibly use.'

'But your mother is not homeless. There is the Dower House; she can easily rent another property. She can move with Charles's family to Wiltshire.'

'She grows old, Elizabeth.'

'But not helpless. I beg you not to ask me to do this, Laurence.'

'I will speak to Charles and we will advise her to move to the Dower House.'

There was a pause as if he waited for her response. Before the war, she would have done anything to relieve the sad look in Laurence's eyes. Now she could not. Not God, not her conscience, nothing, could make her believe her duty lay in looking after Laurence's mother.

The news from the front line depressed Caroline so much that she had tried postponing reading the newspapers until the evening, but it proved impossible. The assault round Loos was still continuing and the news was full of something called the Hohenzollern Redoubt. But what mattered to her and to thousands of other families much much more was the ever lengthier Roll of Honour lists of the fallen. Of course, she would have heard from Ashden if anything had happened to Reggie before it appeared in the newspapers, but she felt she had to read the lists anyway, just in case.

The news in England was not much better. There had been no less than six Zep raids during September, one of them so severe that over twenty people were killed and nearly a hundred injured after bombs fell in Golders Green, Euston and Liverpool Street. Babies had been killed, and a bus driver. The most dangerous bomb had fallen by the beautiful old church of St Bartholomew the Great. She had gone along after work next day to see the damage, and had been intrigued to see that the explosion had ripped the plasterwork off the entrance to the church to reveal an old Tudor frontage.

Recently, however, the raids seemed to have stopped, probably because the government had organised proper anti-aircraft defences round London. Everyone felt much safer, and Caroline felt pleased she was going out this evening to dine with Simon at Rules. London's theatre land and restaurants were full of life even though all the windows had to be blacked out by heavy curtains. Outside the streets were dark, with only the odd dimmed street light to illuminate the pavements. Like everyone else, Caroline was forever falling down kerbstones, and she took Simon's arm as they came out of Rules after dinner.

'We'll walk to the Aldwych. We might find a cab at the stand,' he suggested.

As they reached the Aldwych, the Gaiety Theatre was suddenly lit up by the crisscrossing beams of searchlights moving across the dark sky. Inside Leslie Henson and George Grossmith were still playing in the highly successful *Tonight's the Night*, and at the stage door Caroline recognised Jupp, the well-known ex-sergeant-major doorkeeper. Two young boys came out of the stage door and crossed the road towards them.

'Marconi House is next door to the theatre,' Simon joked. 'We always say in Whitehall that Jupp gets the news from France about a Zep raid before we—'

His words were blotted out by a terrible wailing and the crack of anti-aircraft guns, followed by two horrific booms somewhere nearby. Caroline saw him reach out to draw her to safety, then everything spun round her. Noise enclosed her in an exploding box and a giant hand picked her up, threw her into a doorway, dragged her back again, then knocked her to the pavement. There was a roaring in her ears and all around her she could hear falling stone and crashing glass, screams, and then more wailing followed by dull thuds. When she opened her eyes, she was alone. Simon had vanished and everywhere – in front, to the left, and right to the Strand there was the noise of people running.

Cautiously she tried to move, aware even in this darkness that there was blood on her. Everything seemed to be working. No broken bones. She sat up as two men loomed above her, carrying a theatre board as an improvised stretcher. She shook her head, and pointed to one of the two Gaiety lads who was lying inert a few yards away. There was no sign of the other boy. Nor of Simon. Only bodies and – pieces of bodies. She started to feel sick, and concentrated on the fact she was a VAD with first-aid training.

Caroline staggered along the side street where the first thuds had occurred towards the corner of Exeter Street and Wellington Street. There were bodies everywhere. Vomit rose again in her throat, and she swallowed hard as she saw Nell Gwynn, as she and Simon called the orange seller who sat outside the Lyceum every night. Caroline picked her way over to her in the dark. The hand still clutched an orange, but a quick inspection told her that she was dead. Then, near the crater that the bomb had made, she heard a groan and fell to her knees to see if she could do anything to help. She felt the stickiness of blood, welling out of a shattered arm. It needed immediate attention.

A man stumbled into her and, seeing what she was doing, knelt down beside her. 'Tourniquet,' she said briefly, hitching up her skirts to pull off her petticoat. The buttons resisted, and his hands ripped off a strip from the bottom. She snatched it from him. 'Help me,' she said.

In the darkness, illumined only by occasional glimmers of a dim torch or light from the theatre, she could only see his hands, manoeuvring, then holding the shattered arm in position. She concentrated on those hands as she tied on the tourniquet. If she tried to memorise every single line and angle of them, she wouldn't have to think about the horror in front of her, or what she had just realised was half a woman's torso lying near them. Hands, that was all she needed to look at. Those hands.

As she finished, stretcher-bearers arrived, and began to put the seriously wounded into ambulances. She ran over to the pub on the corner of the street which had obviously had many casualties for its walls were shattered and victims were being carried outside. Then minutes later, the pub was cleared, because of a shattered gas main. She was only a little distance away when the hissing gas caught fire, exploded and sent flames roaring into the air. Soon fire engines added their presence and noise to the pandemonium. Dazed, she hurried to offer her services to the Strand Theatre where casualties were still being treated.

An hour later, when there was no more she could do, she rode in one of the ambulances to the Charing Cross hospital. There was no sign of Simon, and he might well be there, she reasoned. On arrival, however, she was too weak to protest when she was whisked off for treatment herself.

'I'm not hurt,' she tried to explain. 'I'm looking for someone, that's all.'

'But have you looked at yourself recently?' the nurse asked in concern.

Wearily she did so. She did not recognise the face in the mirror. There was blood all over her and she was covered in scratches; her hair was like a bush. 'It's not my blood,' she said.

As her cuts were dressed feeling began to return to her. There was a heavy pain in her chest, and the whole of her body seemed one massive bruise. They insisted on her staying in for the night. 'Simon. Lord Banning,' Caroline said again. 'Is he here?'

'Tomorrow,' the nurse replied. 'We'll know tomorrow.'

When Caroline awoke next morning, she wondered where she was. Then she remembered; instantly, the horror returned.

'How do you feel?'

She turned her head and found Angela sitting at her side. Never had she been so glad to see her. She stretched out her hand and Angela squeezed it. 'Simon?' she asked anxiously.

'He's here. Hurt, but not dangerously. I remembered you were going to be in the area, so when I heard the news about the bomb, I telephoned Norland Square, and was told you weren't back. So here I am. And I've told your parents that you're safe. One of the Zeps bombed near Tunbridge Wells, so they were doubly alarmed when they read the newspaper this morning.'

'Was Ashden hit?' Caroline asked. Bombs in Sussex. She felt too weak to contemplate the uproar at home.

'No. But your mother says everyone saw the Zep.'

'George must have been beside himself with excitement.' Caroline tried to smile. 'But have you seen Simon?'

'Yes. I've told him you're safe and he said he'd give you audience later this morning. Was he joking, do you think?'

Caroline looked at Angela's serious face and wanted to hug her, but she couldn't, her bruises hurt too much. They arranged that Angela should take her back to Norland Square after she came off duty that evening. Then, as soon as she had had breakfast and dressed in the spare clothes Angela had thoughtfully brought with her, she made her way to Simon.

She found him sitting up in bed reading *The Times*, a bandage round his head.

'And there's one round my middle you can't see,' he informed her. 'Shrapnel. Honourable war wound in the Strand front line.'

'You should have given yourself a tin-lined topper, like the hat you gave Aunt Tilly.'

'Do you think she'll come rushing to my bedside?'

'Far more likely she'll send you a comforter knitted by her own fair hands,' Caroline joked. Both knew Tilly would never leave her post now the Germans were counter-attacking so heavily on the Hohenzollern Redoubt.

'I'd even settle for that.' He paused. 'Do you realise how lucky we've been? I got blown towards the Strand and all I could think of was what had happened to you. We have merited a short report on page eight of *The Times*. "A certain number of incendiary devices and explosives were dropped", it says, "eight killed and thirty-four injured, but little material damage done". I rather think we'll be reading amended figures tomorrow.' He smiled at her. 'Stay with Angela as much as you can. Don't be on your own, Caroline. They say I can go home tomorrow.'

From the talk in the hospital during the day, Caroline learnt that there had been far more bombs dropped than the ones she had been aware of. In the Aldwych, a home for Belgian refugees had been hit, and the headquarters of the Belgian Relief Committee, Lincoln's Inn, Old Square, Holborn, and Gray's Inn, had all been bombed with high explosive or incendiaries. All rained down from one Zeppelin. His companions had bombed other areas, including Dover and Tunbridge Wells. It was by far the worst raid so far. So far? She tried to put out of her head the niggling thought that if London were so well defended, as she had always believed it to be, how had just one Zep managed to wreak such carnage?

Next morning, back at Norland Square, Caroline telephoned the Rectory. She had been putting it off, unwilling to relive her experience even to her family. Today's *Times* revealed that at least fifty-six people had been killed and well over a hundred injured, a figure which Simon predicted would rise when the final tally was known.

'Darling.' Her mother's relief was obvious, even though she knew already she was safe. Caroline could hear the tears in her voice. 'You're really all right?'

'Just bruised.' Mentally, Caroline thought, as well as physically.

'I'm coming up to town immediately.'

'Why? What's wrong?' Caroline asked sharply. 'The Zep didn't bomb you?' Fearful images of Nanny Oates lying like the orange-seller filled her mind, of Phoebe or George mutilated, or the Rectory's walls blasted.

'Nothing like that. It's Reggie, darling. He's been wounded, and his mother is insisting he comes back to Ashden to recuperate.'

Elizabeth returned to the breakfast room to tell Laurence about Caroline's call, but before she could do so the telephone rang again. This time Laurence answered it and was gone a long time. When he came back into the room he looked grey with worry.

'That was Charles,' he told her. 'One of Wednesday night's Zeppelin bombs fell in the grounds of Buckford House. The Dower House was hit and is uninhabitable. Mother has therefore decided to come here next month when the military take possession of the main house.'

'No!' Elizabeth's answer was almost a shout.

'I cannot refuse her.'

'Laurence, if you value our home, do not do this. You are the one who cannot bear disturbance in the Rectory. Now you are throwing open the door to trouble.'

'But the alternative is slamming it when my mother most needs us.'

'You will allow her to insult me here?'

Laurence flushed. 'Of course not,' he answered. 'I shall explain to her that you are the mistress of this household and that she must treat you with respect.'

For the first time in their married life, Elizabeth walked

out of the room and slammed the door behind her. Ahab, ambling from the kitchen in search of a favourite stick, barked a chorus of reproach. Laurence, left alone, wondered what further ordeals might lie in God's plan.

Chapter Twelve

Isabel put down Robert's letter, reflecting that Gallipoli sounded almost as boring as Sussex. All Robert could find to write about was that nothing much was happening, and there were signs that winter was on the way. The biggest excitement since he arrived had been the flocks of birds passing over migrating from Russia; birds, apparently, were not seen in Gallipoli often. Father had talked about fighting at Suvla Bay, but if Robert had been involved, he hadn't mentioned it.

Anyway, Robert was alive, and that was good news. But so, she reminded herself, was she – though sometimes it was hard to remember. Life at the Rectory was pleasant enough, she admitted. Every week she visited Hop House to keep an eye on Mrs Bugle, though in fact it was unnecessary, since Mrs Bugle was quite appalling, eye or no eye. But at least her visits kept Mother Swinford-Browne content. And she rarely saw her father-in-law, who was always busy at the factory. Deprived of the social benefits both of marriage and of being single, she found herself at a loss. She was twenty-six, at the height of her beauty, and the years were passing with no one to appreciate it.

Isabel dressed carefully in the shade of blue she knew flattered her most, glad that Agnes was back. Harriet had never learnt how to iron properly, but even linen obeyed Agnes's calm, competent hand which banished all wrinkles. Today, she decided she would do some war work. She would visit the wounded, more particularly Reggie, who was now in the Manor Hospital. She had always got on well with him, whereas Daniel had always teased her unmercifully. Luckily, he was living at the Dower House, so she could avoid him except when she went to see Aunt Maud. Isabel got on well with Lady Hunney and could never understand why Caroline should have such difficulty in doing so.

She found Reggie sitting up in bed reading the *Illustrated London News*.

His eyes lit up when he saw her and he dropped the magazine. 'This is good of you, Isabel.'

Feeling virtuous, she leant over and gave him a sisterly kiss on the cheek. 'How are you?'

'Much better, thanks.'

But I heard you'd shattered your leg and, oh Reggie, you're wincing. Your arm—'

'It's nothing, Isabel.' He spoke harshly, then explained, 'Compared with the other chaps, I'm lucky, you see. I should be *there,* not here being fed grapes and tucked in at night by Mother.'

'But aren't you pleased to be out of it?' She was puzzled by the anger in his voice.

He supposed he was – in a way. But how with honour could he be? The fighting this autumn had deprived his battalion of almost all its officers from the old regular army, and here, in this bed, he felt isolated, as if he were betraying his men. All 1st Division had had to do was take the Hohenzollern Redoubt and one small village, Loos. They had been taken, but not by his battalion, for the flower of the Royal Sussex lay dead in No Man's Land. If he closed his eyes, he'd be back there: the gas, suffocating through the masks, the noise, the Moaning Minnies, the bodies, the fog, the desolation of death, and the occasional image – of one sergeant in particular who was to be recommended for the Victoria Cross, dashing for the wire, leading the tattered remnants of the platoon. He had been dead in seconds.

'How long will you be here?' Isabel asked brightly.

'About three months, they think.'

'Oh good, you'll be here for Christmas. That will be fun.' Too late, Isabel remembered the rift between Reggie and Caroline. How could the Hunneys all come to the Rectory as usual, if Caroline were home? Robert wouldn't be back of course, but she had been looking forward to a Rectory Christmas, and perhaps even a dance for all their friends. She smiled at him, in the way that had won Robert's heart. 'And in the meantime we shall have fun here too. I'll cheer you up. Just like Felicia used to look after Daniel.'

'Felicia was one of the staff.'

'I can still wheel you around.' Isabel felt hurt and showed it.

'That's very kind of you. Especially when,' Reggie added awkwardly, 'you must all think me a prize rotter.'

Isabel was surprised, and belatedly realised he must be thinking of Caroline. 'Of course not,' she said warmly.

He hesitated. 'How is Caroline?'

'Very well, she says,' Isabel replied offhandedly. 'Having a wonderful time in London. She goes to all the shows and restaurants. They're packed with servicemen. And she can go with girlfriends; she doesn't have to have an escort even. It's exciting.'

'Oh.'

Isabel's conscience smote her as she remembered Caroline's haggard face when she last saw her and how unhappy she had been that Reggie had not answered her letter. 'She misses you.'

'Does she?' Reggie's handsome face looked strained. 'It's easy over there, Isabel,' he said after a moment, 'but here it's not. Tell her that.'

She didn't understand what he was talking about. 'Of course,' she agreed. 'But I'll help. I'm missing Robert awfully.'

Reggie looked guilty. 'I haven't asked you about him, I'm sorry.'

'He's safe. God has looked after him.' The words came out as a whisper. 'We'll have to help each other, won't we? Be good companions in distress.'

She put out her hands to clasp his, and he took them. 'Good companions, Isabel.'

* * *

'He's safe, Mrs Dibble.' Agnes beamed. 'Do you hear that, Elizabeth Agnes? Your daddy's safe. This letter is dated the eighteenth and, do you know what, I don't think 7th Battalion can be doing any fighting at all at Loos, or anywhere else, because all he's doing is marching up and down practising. But,' she frowned, 'even that is dangerous. He says one of his mates got killed when he lit a detonator on a new weapon thinking it was a cigarette.'

'But it wasn't your Jamie. You look on the bright side, my girl.'

'And how's Joe?' Agnes remembered to ask.

'Muriel reckons he's not in the action either. The 5th did their bit at Aubers Ridge in May. She tells me that he's doing woodwork.'

'What?' Agnes stared.

'Sussex men are good at that,' Mrs Dibble announced. 'And our Joe's the best. Muriel says he's been moved to do special work somewhere. Perhaps he'll come home at Christmas and tell us,' she added wistfully.

'Wouldn't that be wonderful, Margaret, if all our men came home?' The forbidden name slipped out, but Mrs Dibble didn't seem to mind.

'Why don't we have a bit of a celebration tonight, both of them being safe? I've got a nice chicken in the larder – Mrs Lilley won't mind – and I'll ask Percy to get a bottle of his home-made wine out. I might even have a glass myself.'

Agnes laughed.

'And what's so amusing, if I might ask?' Mrs Dibble adopted her usual forbidding face.

'I thought you belonged to the Band of Hope, Mrs D.'

'So I do. And hoping is what we'll do tonight. Hoping our menfolk come home safe and sound. Now, since the Rectory can't be allowed to starve, I'll get Myrtle to give me a hand with the minced beef turnovers.'

It was on the tip of Agnes's tongue to point out that Myrtle was her exclusive property in the mornings, but today she could afford to be gracious. What was a bit of soda and chloride of lime on the steps compared with the wonderful news that Jamie and Joe were alive?

By the weekend of 23rd October, Caroline decided she could delay no longer. She missed the Rectory intolerably. Reggie or no Reggie, she must go home. She had not heard from him since her mother told her the news over a week ago. Should she visit him? Would he want her to? Surely it was the natural thing to do, even though Eleanor had warned her that he was unlikely to change his mind about their future.

'Not judging from the conversations I've overheard,' she qualified. 'Mother is still adamant.'

To Hades with Mother, Caroline thought angrily. 'What about you and Martin?' she had asked when Eleanor visited her in London. 'Has she turned her attention to you?'

Her friend laughed. 'I'm biding my time to break the news. Don't dare tell anyone will you? Martin says we're still young, so we've all the time in the world to wait for the right moment to tell her we want to get married.'

Oh, the heartache of walking along the familiar path to the Rectory and seeing St Nicholas, just the same as ever, waiting for her – and by its side the drive to Ashden Manor.

A few minutes' walk, a knock on the door and she could see Reggie. How easy it would be.

She turned in to the Rectory where Isabel immediately pounced on her. 'Darling, tell me all about London. Oh, and that terrible bomb. You still look black and blue. You poor thing.'

Caroline tried to oblige her sister. She described the clothes, the uniforms, the crowded pavements, the night life, even the odd characters like the famous Australian Old Robertson who wandered the Strand with a card in his hat reading: 'Please do not give me money. I am searching for my errant daughter.' She told her about the famous Trocadero, she even told her about Rules. But she didn't tell her about the bombing, the dead, the injured, or the battlefield that was London, and Isabel did not ask again.

'And how about you? Are you raising money for this Gallipoli Plum Pudding Fund of Lady Davies's?' The idea of soldiers eating Christmas puddings out in Turkey amused her when she saw the appeals in the newspapers.

Isabel looked blank. 'No.'

A pause. Caroline desperately wanted to ask about Reggie. 'How's Daniel?' she compromised.

'Going to St Mary's Roehampton soon to be fitted with his artificial leg.'

'That's splendid. And Felicia – have you heard from her?'

'Father had a short note last week to say they were still busy at Loos but it was slackening off and she hoped to write more soon. Reggie says—' Isabel grew red and broke off.

'Reggie?' Caroline asked sharply.

'I didn't want to upset you by mentioning his name but I went to see him once. Someone had to,' Isabel added virtuously.

The wound tore open again. 'How is he?'

'Getting on well. He'll be here till the New Year.'

'Should I go to see him? Did he ask after me? Mention me?' Caroline couldn't help it, she had to ask.

'Darling, I'm sorry, no, he didn't. Don't blame him too much. He's been through so much recently.'

Not even to ask after her. Caroline felt numb. 'I shall go to see him; he would think badly of me if I did not.'

'If you like,' Isabel replied carelessly. 'But don't go while the young fair-haired nurse is on duty.'

'Why not?'

'They seemed to be getting on rather well when I called. Reggie was joking with her and she was blushing, you know how he is. He needs someone to take his mind off this terrible war.'

No mention of her, and laughing with a nurse? Caroline left Isabel and hurried to her room where she curled up in a ball of misery.

There was nothing she could do. Reggie had not even answered her letter. She'd written again, to the hospital this time, just a short note saying how sorry she was to hear he was wounded. He had not replied. She toyed with the idea that Lady Hunney might have intercepted the letter, but rejected it. Reggie did not want her, and there was nothing whatsoever she could do about it.

* * *

Frank Eliot walked home from the station, still slightly shocked by the decision he had just taken. At the end of this week, on 29th October, the new Derby Scheme would come into operation. The new Director of Recruiting, Lord Derby, was asking men between the ages of nineteen and forty-two to attest that they would be willing to serve if called upon. Rather than wait goodness knows how long for the canvassers to come banging on his door with their little blue and white cards, Frank had taken the train to East Grinstead and insisted on registering immediately. Of course he couldn't join up right away; he had to sort out the hop yield first. But as an unmarried man, he knew he would be called upon before too long. What had he to lose but his life? He could see no future here.

As he approached his house, he saw someone waiting for him on the step and recognised Lizzie Stein, or rather Dibble, for she had taken to using her single name. He quickened his pace, for they had grown friendly in the last few weeks, since she'd moved into a cottage nearby on the Swinford-Browne estate.

'Mangle stuck again, is it?' he called teasingly. She had hated coming to him for help.

'I'll have to go back to Ashden,' she said flatly. 'That's what I came to tell you.'

'But you'll not be safe there.' He frowned. 'You might be attacked again.'

'I'll not be safe here much longer. Them Thorns started again last night now Mrs Swinford-Browne's taken the guards off the hopgarden. One of them killed in action – and it's all Rudolf's fault apparently. And mine. I signalled

261

to that Zep to come over too, they reckon. I don't fancy being out here all through the winter. I'll be nearer my folks in Ashden.'

Frank was surprised to realise how much he'd miss her. She was not as attractive as his Jennifer, but she was warm-hearted. He opened the front door and ushered her in. 'There's another alternative,' he said, as she stood awkwardly in the doorway of his parlour.

'And what's that?'

'You could move in here – as my housekeeper,' he added quickly, not wanting to offend.

She looked surprised. 'Good of you, Mr Eliot, but what would folks say?'

'They'd say a lot, but they'd get used to it. Then when the war's over and Rudolf comes back—'

'*If* he comes back.' She hesitated. 'If I moved in here, housekeeping's all you'd want?'

'As you want, Lizzie.' Their eyes met. He liked her directness. 'Do you trust me?'

'No, but Rudolf taught me how to defend myself,' she replied.

He laughed. 'You won't have to do that,' he promised.

Phoebe threw off her coat and ran straight to her room. Fred had brought the letter home from Tunbridge Wells as usual, but it wasn't Harry's writing. Terrified, she ripped it open. It was from an address in East London and it read: 'Dear miss this is to inform you that my son Harry is in hospital here in England wounded in the big battle for his country – he got gassed and is very poorly yours truly Mrs Edna Darling.' It didn't even say where he was.

What was she to do? She had worried and worried these last two weeks when she hadn't heard from Harry. And now she knew why. What did very poorly mean? It meant he was dying, she realised, and he wanted her at his side. But Father would never understand, never let her go to see him. She could, she supposed, appeal to Caroline. Caroline worked in London and would surely go to see Mrs Darling. But suppose Caroline came over all big-sisterish and told Father? No, she could not risk it.

If she was to get to see Harry, as he wanted, she must plan this very carefully.

'Mr Dibble!'

Percy, who was about to go into the Rectory vegetable garden, stopped in amazement. He hadn't seen Daisy – his pet name for his wife – running since he chased her round that hayrick before they were wed. Then he became scared. 'Joe?' he asked.

'No, no. Percy, you've got to go up there and hit him.'

'Who?' Percy was bewildered. He wasn't much given to hitting.

'The Rector?'

'No! That, that . . .' Mrs Dibble choked, 'hop man. He's seduced our Lizzie.'

'He's what?' Percy tried to take this in.

'Had his way with her. Seduced her.'

'Did he tell you?'

'No, you daft lummocks. *She* did.'

'He's hurt our Lizzie?' Slow anger began to rise in him.

'Not hurt,' Mrs Dibble admitted with some reluctance. 'She's moved in with him.'

'You said he'd seduced her.'

'She's a married woman, living in sin with an unmarried man. What do you call that?'

'What does *she* call it?' Percy was still cautious.

'She says she's his housekeeper. A likely story,' Mrs Dibble snorted. 'My Lizzie's been ruined. You've got to go and hit him, Percy.'

Percy thought about it. 'I don't think I can do that.'

'You're going, Percy. You're going.' She burst out crying. 'Oh, the shame of it. I'll never live it down, and she coming from a good Christian home. Poor, poor Rudolf.'

He patted her awkwardly. 'Maybe it's not what you think, Daisy.'

'Then you go and find out what it is, Percy Dibble. *Now*.'

In the hospital conservatory, Reggie looked up as Daniel was wheeled in by their mother. 'I'm off to say goodbye, old chap.'

'Roehampton?'

'By ambulance tomorrow.' Daniel turned to his mother. 'Ma, leave us alone, will you?'

No one else would have the nerve to order Mother out, Reggie thought.

'By Christmas I'll be able to push *you* around in one of these,' Daniel continued.

'That's the best reason for getting back on my feet I've heard yet,' Reggie said promptly.

Daniel laughed. 'And then you'll go back to the front?'

'Of course.'

'I wish—' Daniel broke off. Did he wish he could go back with Reggie? Half of him told him he might as well; the other, that when he had a peg leg he might be able to get on a boat and travel. Perhaps even ride a horse, or fix a car so that he could drive it one-legged. And even if not, he could study. Go back to Oxford. Anything to get away from Ashden, away from himself, anywhere where he would not have to think of Felicia and whether he'd been right to send her away. Every day he scoured the newspapers for mention of the 'Two Lilies of the Field' as they were now known. He still couldn't connect the stories he read with the calm, contained girl whom he had rejected.

'I saw Felicia—' Reggie began, as if reading his thoughts.

'Where?' Daniel's voice was harsh.

'In the casualty clearing station. She'd heard I was there and came to see me. She asked how you were.'

'Good of her.'

Reggie's patience snapped. 'Don't you have any feeling for her? She's doing this because of you, you oaf.'

'Do you think I don't know that?' Daniel whipped back.

'Why, for heaven's sake? You'll only have an artificial leg, now the paralysis is passing.'

Daniel did not answer him. Pride would not let him tell his brother what only he, his doctor, his mother – and Felicia – knew. 'And what about you, Reggie?' he retaliated.

'Me?'

'And Caroline. I knew she wrote to you. Why let Mother ruin everything? Don't you love her?'

'Of course I damn well love her,' Reggie said angrily. 'I love her here. But over there – I'm too damned punch-drunk when we're out of the trenches after our stint to think of anything save the nearest brothel. And now, I'm forgetting wonderfully. Thanks to Isabel. She's a dear.' It was true. When he was with her he could forget all about Caroline; but as soon as she went, back came the memories.

'That's bally selfish.'

'All right.' Reggie came to a decision. 'If the war ended tomorrow I'd heave myself out of this chair, hop to the station, rush up to London and drag Caroline to the nearest church. But it won't end tomorrow. It's going to go on and on. This battle is over, it will be quiet while we regroup over the winter, and then we'll start again. And again. And again. And by the time it's over she will have a life of her own and she'll fret at being a squire's wife. I can't throw the old place up and adapt to what she wants.'

'Then marry her now.'

'And be blown up in the next push forward? No.'

'You might not be.'

'But I might, and it could be worse. I could be incurably maimed and she would be stuck with me. No children, a eunuch for a husband.' He caught sight of Daniel's face, and put his head in his hands. 'Dear God, is that it? Is that why—?'

'Yes.'

'Does Felicia know?'

'Yes.'

'Daniel—' He put out his hand.

266

'Don't pity me,' Daniel jerked out, pulling backwards in his chair.

Reggie swallowed. What he said now would affect the rest of their lives. 'You can't afford – we can't afford for me not to pity you,' he replied. 'You'll take my hand, Daniel.'

Daniel glared at him, and Reggie thought he would refuse. But after a moment a hand came out to clasp his.

'Hello, Pa.' Lizzie did not look surprised to see him as she opened the door of Hop House.

Percy cleared his throat nervously. 'Your mother's not happy, Lizzie.'

'I am, though.' She grinned.

'With a single gentleman?' Percy was shocked.

'I'm housekeeper, Pa,' she proclaimed loudly. 'Just like Ma to the Rector. No one says things if she and the Rector are alone in the house, do they?'

'No,' Percy agreed doubtfully.

'Well then.' She looked as if she were about to close the door, but Percy got his foot in it.

'I'd best have a word with Mr Eliot,' he muttered.

'It's not called for.'

'It is by your mother, Lizzie.'

At that moment, attracted by the noise, Frank Eliot came down the stairs.

'This is my Pa, Mr Eliot,' Lizzie said resignedly.

'My wife thinks we ought to have a talk.' Percy said miserably.

'Certainly.' There was a glint of amusement in Frank's

face. 'Come in, won't you? Lizzie, you too.' He led them into his parlour.

Half an hour later Percy walked down through the fields and past the mill to the Rectory. He had had two glasses of an excellent port which the Rector would have appreciated. He was also convinced that Frank Eliot was a good man and that Lizzie could not have found a better place to work. All he was uncertain about was what he was going to tell Daisy.

As he walked in the kitchen door, however, Daisy flew at him. 'Haven't seen Miss Phoebe, have you?'

'No, why?'

'We're that worried. She hasn't come home from work. PC Ifield is out looking for her, the Rector's had Dr Marden drive him to Crowborough camp, and not a word. She's missing.'

Chapter Thirteen

Elizabeth paced round the drawing room, fiddling with magazines, adjusting the framed photographs and running to the doorway at every slight noise from the entrance hall. Laurence had been gone for two whole hours, and there had not even been a telephone call. This afternoon she had been helping with the preparations for the harvest supper which was due to begin in thirty minutes, and she had come home to hear the news about Phoebe. 'Why didn't your father come to find me?' Elizabeth had moaned.

'Because he knew you were busy,' Isabel soothed. 'He expected to be back before you came home.'

'Then why isn't he? He has to bless the harvest in an hour's time. I shall have to ask Charles Pickering to do it. Shall I telephone him? Or should I walk round to see him?' Elizabeth's eye fell on a new cause for concern: the corn crown and regalia for her role as Harvest Queen.

She made up her mind. 'I shall telephone PC Ifield. Then Charles.'

Isabel too was anxious. She had never been as close to Phoebe as Caroline but, now that her sister was missing, she felt panic-stricken. Had she been attacked while bicycling home? Surely not. Of course, there was Old Harry, a waygoer who often appeared on the Withyham road and hurled abuse at passers-by, but he'd never been known to attack anyone. It was far more likely to be one of those rough, common soldiers at the camp. She'd warned Mother it was dangerous for Phoebe to work there; she was hardly more than a child and very naive. But if they'd found her bicycle on the road, Father and PC Ifield would be here by now with the bad news.

Therefore, she reasoned, they were still at the camp searching for her.

Elizabeth returned from her calls. 'PC Ifield isn't back either. Oh, I do wish Mrs Ifield wouldn't bawl down the telephone as if she were marshalling a herd of cattle. I've been in touch with Crowborough police and Tunbridge Wells and they've no news. Should I contact the hospitals, do you think?'

'No.' Isabel was practical. 'If she were in hospital, PC Ifield would be told and Father would have telephoned us.'

'I suppose you're right. But what if there's a message waiting for Joe Ifield and he's not—'

'You must go to Harvest Supper,' Isabel cut in quickly and firmly. 'You can't miss it.'

Elizabeth stared at her. 'How could I sit there as Queen of the Harvest, smiling as if nothing were wrong, when Phoebe might be –' She broke off and then added – 'missing? Of course I'm not going.'

'Then why don't I go as queen in your place? Everyone would understand.'

'Don't tell anyone the reason. Say your father and I have been called out suddenly and may not be back in time.' Elizabeth hesitated. 'Are you sure?' Unlike Caroline Isabel had always been so dismissive about church festivals. But Caroline, alas, was far away.

Isabel looked noble. 'I'll go to change into something more, well, queenly.' As Robert's wife, it was only right she should be seen at village events. Moreover, it was probable that Frank Eliot would be there. The news that Lizzie Dibble had moved in as his housekeeper had filled her with disgust. If it were true, she told herself, she had had a narrow escape. She ran up to her bedroom and selected a full-skirted white voile summer dress, decorated with hand-painted roses and cornflowers. She tried to ignore the fact that it had been exceptionally cold all week, and that today temperatures were even lower.

'Will I do?' she asked, reappearing twenty minutes later in the drawing room.

'You look lovely.' Elizabeth's mind was elsewhere.

Slightly disappointed, Isabel picked up the regalia, kissed her mother, told her not to worry, and went to find a torch to light her down Silly Lane.

Elizabeth flicked through the *Illustrated London News* but saw nothing of the pages. Phoebe danced before her eyes: the duckling of her brood, the one most resembling her physically, the one she understood least.

A long half-hour later she heard the front door open. She rushed out into the hall. 'Well?' she cried.

She had hardly needed to ask. One look at Laurence's grey face told her there was no news. Laurence put his arm round her in silence, and led her back into the drawing room.

'It is not as bad as it might be,' he began. Elizabeth looked at him in sudden hope. 'There was no sign of her bicycle along the road to Crowborough. The entire camp has been searched, and Mrs Manning tells us that Phoebe left work at four o'clock at the end of her shift, though she admits she didn't actually see her leave the camp. I think we may be reasonably certain she has disappeared of her own accord.'

'But where?' Elizabeth's cry was one of despair.

'Mr Chappell hasn't seen her at the railway station. Nor have either of the carriers. I went to The Towers since Patricia is home but they have not seen her either. There will be an announcement in the recreation hall this evening for anyone with any information, and Joe Ifield is continuing local enquiries.'

Elizabeth buried her head in his shoulder, and he held her tight.

'Laurence,' she managed to say after a moment, 'Isabel has gone in my place, I cannot, but perhaps you should go.'

'Go where, my darling?'

'To the harvest supper. If you hurry you can be there in time, though I've asked Charles to stand in for you in case.'

'Let him do it. My place is here with you tonight.'

* * *

272

Isabel sat in state at the head table with Charles Pickering on one side and Philip Ryde on the other. She was enjoying herself. Of course, there had been general disappointment that Mother was not there, and a certain amount of initial suspicion of her as a Swinford-Browne, but after the first glass or two of elder and small beer, the villagers, packed into the tithe barn at long tables, forgot about her marriage and remembered only that she was the Rector's daughter. Everyone said what a lovely queen she made. The barn, even with the help of some paraffin heaters was very chilly and Isabel shivered in her thin dress; but it was worth it, she told herself, her goose pimples would disappear when the dancing began.

The timbered barn sprouted produce from every niche: hops curled from the beams and down the supporting timbers, cereals, vegetables and fruit decorated every corner and alcove, filling the air with a fresh rich smell which was dissipating now pipes and cigarettes were being lit. Charles had led the procession of several hundred farmers, workers and families into the barn and round the produce in a blessing ceremony, and then had come the Hollering Pot. Strictly, this custom should be honoured when the last hay was safely home, but if William Swinford-Browne wanted to abide by the custom and provide a pint of ale for every man in the village then no one had any objection. Even Isabel could see that it had been a good harvest. She remembered Mother gloating over the Board of Agriculture's statement that it was well up on the previous six years, and saying that this was due to Caroline's and her hard work.

After the Hollering Pot, the serious business of supper had got underway. Isabel was not used to meals of sausages, bread, potatoes and cheese, accompanied by ginger beer, cider or small beer, but pretended she enjoyed it greatly. Indeed, she almost did. It was such a change to be in a large gathering, especially one of which she was the queen. For the first time for over a year, she felt like one.

Usually, Sir John put in an appearance during the evening as squire, but now he was away most of the time in London. Or was he here after all? Isabel saw that the group round the door was falling back to make way for someone. Aunt Maud probably, or Father. No, it was Reggie, she realised with delight, in an invalid chair pushed by a nurse. She jumped up from the table and made her way over to him.

'How splendid, Reggie. Now you can sit beside me.' He grinned. 'Honoured, ma'am.'

The tables were being cleared and the village band began to take their places. Isabel longed to dance; the 'Lambeth Walk', a few fast waltzes and 'Sir Roger de Coverley' would at least warm her up. Nevertheless she was prepared to sacrifice all this for Reggie's sake. He needed a companion, and as king of the village to her queen, she should be it.

Late that evening the sound of the telephone bell shattered the silence. Laurence raced to answer it with Elizabeth hard at his heels. Mrs Dibble came to the kitchen door, hovering, trying not to overstep her place in her anxiety.

'Yes . . . What?'

Elizabeth waited in agony until he hung up. 'Good

and bad, my love. Her bicycle may have been found at Crowborough railway station.'

'*May?*'

'One has been discovered. And the stationmaster recalls a young lady who took a ticket to Uckfield late this afternoon, carrying a suitcase.'

'But she doesn't know anyone in Uckfield,' Elizabeth wailed. 'It can't be her. And if it was, oh, Laurence, was she on her own?'

'Apparently, yes. Surely Phoebe will telephone to tell us she is safe. You are certain she left no note here?'

'I've searched her room twice and there's nothing downstairs either. Only the missing clothes I told you about – a skirt, a blouse and jacket, and a nightgown. Enough for a night. So perhaps she'll be back tomorrow.' Phoebe would have told them if she had planned to spend the night with a friend, or had she simply forgotten? It would be just like Phoebe . . .

'And you're sure she has no friends in Uckfield?'

'Yes.'

Uckfield, which lay on the far side of the forest towards the Downs, was almost alien territory to the inhabitants of Ashden. It was a charabanc stop for the Sunday School treat to Eastbourne, but did not otherwise enter into their lives.

'Tomorrow I will go there and make enquiries. In the meantime we can only wait.'

Wait! Was there a more terrible word in the English language?

* * *

Frank Eliot and Lizzie Dibble walked home together after the harvest supper with only the aid of dim torches to guide them. Ashden was completely dark at night now for, in a burst of patriotism, it had elected to follow London's example and extinguish its one street light in case that Zep came looking for the village again. Frank had restrained himself from taking Lizzie's arm to help her along, until a stumble over a stone hidden in the undergrowth by the stile brought an immediate reflex action from him to save her. After that, he kept his hand there. It was strange having a woman on his arm again, especially one so much shorter than he. Jennifer, his lovely Jennifer, had been tall and slender.

Frank unlocked the door to his cottage, then listened to the sound of Lizzie's feet climbing the stairs to the second-floor attic room. He poured himself a brandy to warm himself up. It was cold outside and the fire here had long since died. Had he made a mistake in bringing Lizzie here? No, he couldn't accept that; if Ashden wanted to believe the worst about them both, so be it. Lizzie was a married woman, and his housekeeper, whatever the village chose to think. He'd soon be gone anyway, when they began to call on his age group of unmarried men under the Derby Scheme.

As he got into bed he reflected how odd it was that he now hated Ashden for the very things he'd loved about it when he first came: its insularity, its own set of judgements, its blind obstinacy to see farther than the limits of Seb Grendel's farm astride the parish boundary. Look what had happened when the Rector's sister came to stay, militant suffragette that she was. Dr Parry was another 'foreigner' fighting her way into some kind of acknowledgement that she breathed the same air as the other Ashden villagers. What was going to happen when soldiers who had experienced different countries and different ways of life came marching home? Now, that would be interesting—

'Frank.'

He sat up. The door opened and Lizzie's dark shape, lit only by a candle, stood on the threshold.

'Miss Florence Nightingale, I presume,' he said carefully.

'Only if you want her. I don't mind.' Lizzie sounded defensive.

'Don't you, Lizzie?' He jumped from the bed, took her into his arms and kissed her lightly. Not too close, just in case. 'Are you *sure*?'

'Yes, I am sure.' Her voice shook. 'I'm tired of being alone. I think you are too.'

He undid the cord round the neck of her thick nightgown and gently slid it off. He looked at the full heavy breasts and sturdy hips; it was a body made for loving. He reached out a hand and touched her breast.

For a moment he thought he had been mistaken as she caught it and took it away. 'But I mustn't—'

'Be in the family way,' he finished for her, understanding now.

'No.'

No child of Jennifer, he would have none of Lizzie either. He'd settle for love, a privilege he'd thought would be denied him for ever after Jennifer's death. Now it might have come again, he was deeply grateful.

* * *

George was walking on air. He had taken the parish magazine into Tunbridge Wells to be printed, because Jacob Timms was ill and couldn't manage it this month. But this printer was not wizened or grey like the lead of his type-setting characters, and he wasn't a man; it was a woman. At first he'd assumed she was an assistant, but it turned out she was Mrs Wilkins (of Wilkins and Son) who was taking over while her husband was at the front. He was an NCO, she explained, and a pound a week separation allowance didn't go far with four children nowadays, so she had to keep the business going. She was a brisk lady, with sharp eyes, rather like Mrs Dibble only sturdier, almost plump.

'This cartoon, young man,' she said, turning the pages over, smearing smudgy ink everywhere. 'You've been copying them from "Sergeant Trench's" in *Bystander* and the *Sunday Pictorial*, haven't you?'

'No.' George was indignant. 'Sergeant Trench is my *nom de plume*.' Father hadn't forbidden him to submit cartoons to the general press, only the parish magazine. However, it had occurred to him that Father might well notice the number of aeroplanes and RFC personnel appearing amongst his drawings and he had decided to pre-empt trouble by adopting a pen name.

'Good,' she replied, not a whit abashed. 'Any more?'

'Any more what?'

'Cartoons, young man. I'm looking for something to print on postcards for our lads at the front to send home at Christmas. My hubby out there says all they can get is sentimental English ones and naughty French ones –

want something like Bairnsfather. Like yours.'

'Like—' George blinked. At last he was being compared to Bairnsfather.

'You can have a royalty or an outright payment.'

George hesitated. 'Which suits you best?' he asked cautiously.

'The outright payment, of course.'

'You mean you make more money that way?'

'Suppose I make a loss?' she pointed out. 'You wouldn't get any royalties.'

'You can't think that likely or you wouldn't offer it,' George reasoned.

Mrs Wilkins saw the funny side. 'And you a rector's son! I hope he puts you in charge of the collection. So it's a royalty you want then.'

'No.' George decided to follow instinct. 'This first one you can have for a small outright payment; if you want to do more, we'll do it on a royalty. I want you to do more, you see,' he added, seeing her look of surprise.

'Partners, eh?'

'Yes.' Should he tell Father, George wondered on the way home. No, not yet. He'd leave it till next time. Hop, skip and jumping down Station Road, he threw his hat in the air, then fingered the crisp ten pound note in his pocket. This was riches, this was fame. This was some compensation for the RFC having meanly raised their minimum age to eighteen. A whole year to wait!

Then, guiltily, he remembered Phoebe was missing. They'd given him a grilling about her last night when he came in from Scouts, and today Father had gone to

Uckfield. He summed up his courage and went into the drawing room where he could hear Father and Mother talking.

'Any news?'

'None, I'm afraid, George. The Stationmaster and porters at Uckfield couldn't remember her.'

George felt sorry for the old folks; they both looked so worried – as he was, though he had confidence in Phoebe's ability to look after herself. He tried to think what he would do if he wanted to throw Ma and Pa off the scent of where he was going.

'What about Buxted?' he found himself saying. It wasn't splitting because she hadn't told him.

'Buxted? But her ticket was to Uckfield, the next station.'

'I know.' Really, parents were dim. 'But I'd get off at Buxted, walk round for a while, and then get a ticket to wherever I wanted to go.'

'But where would Phoebe want to go?' Elizabeth asked.

'Well, London of course.'

It was their turn to be puzzled. 'Caroline hasn't seen her,' Father answered.

George couldn't believe his father's lack of comprehension. Of course Caroline wouldn't have seen her. 'What about that soldier?'

'Which soldier?' Elizabeth asked sharply.

Laurence exclaimed in horror. 'The one she promised not to write to more than once a month? You mean to say that Phoebe is still communicating with him?'

'I don't know,' George faltered, feeling a complete Judas. 'But he's in France anyway.'

'Perhaps he's on leave?' Elizabeth suggested.

'Has Phoebe lied to me?' Laurence asked, his face dark with anger.

'I don't know,' George yelled, exasperated at his father's inability to grasp essentials. 'Anyway, it's not a lie.'

'What is it then?' Laurence demanded.

'Only a sort of not telling all the truth.' George grew scarlet.

'It seems to me I have failed in my duty,' Laurence said heavily, 'if my son cannot tell the difference between truth and falsehood.'

Arriving by carrier's horse wagon was not the way the Rector of Ashden would normally have chosen to arrive in Buxted village, but it was convenient and much quicker than the roundabout train route. Harold Mutter's horse was slow but reliable, and had his mind not been beset with worry about Phoebe, Laurence would have enjoyed the ride. Even in the dead month of November the forest was beautiful, with the morning chilly mists still lingering on the late gorse and birds calling in the rapidly baring tree branches.

It was a different forest in wartime to the one he had known when he first came to Ashdown. Now he could see army camps everywhere, and army vehicles clogged the roads. The animals had learnt to stay within its secret depths, and those that didn't often fell victim to a staff car's wheels. The army had promised the Board of Conservators that all damage to the land would be made good when they left at the end of the war. But would it happen that way?

Some of the wildlife would be gone for ever; refuse, human and inanimate, sullied the once clean waters, and barbed wire encampments now covered the place where kings had stood to watch the Royal Chase.

Harold waited in the station yard while Laurence spoke to one of the porters, who infuriated him by intimating that young, unaccompanied ladies were not as rare as once they had been with so many army camps around. Laurence retorted that Buxted was not a large station, and a rector's daughter of eighteen would bear little resemblance to ladies of the night.

Realising he was addressing a gentleman of the cloth, a fact hitherto hidden from him by Laurence's heavy muffler, the porter called to the ticketman who thought he might have seen her.

'I thought it queer; here she was coming to Buxted, then she said she'd changed her mind and wanted to go back right away. Feeling sick, she said. So I sold her a ticket and she caught the next train.'

'Where to?'

'That was the queer part. Her ticket was from Crowborough and she wanted to go on to Tonbridge. Or was it London?'

'London,' Laurence told Elizabeth three hours later. 'I'm sure that's where she's gone.'

The news depressed Elizabeth even more. 'Joe Ifield has called. Harry Darling is in France so far as the camp knows. His family lives in Stepney and Joe has their address. He's telephoned the Stepney police who visited them, but they've no knowledge of Phoebe.'

'Where else could she have gone in London? To Caroline?'

'I rang her on the chance she might have seen her. She hasn't. You don't think – oh Laurence, Phoebe couldn't have gone to *France*, could she?'

'If she had,' Laurence grappled with this nightmare, 'she won't get very far.'

'She is very resourceful. And determined. Suppose she's tried to become a nurse?'

Despite his anxiety, Laurence smiled. 'No one would take her.'

'Over here, perhaps, but don't you remember Felicia telling us that once you got to France they weren't too particular about qualifications if you were willing and there?'

'Felicia!' Laurence exclaimed. 'Perhaps Phoebe has tried to make her way to join her and Tilly.'

'But why should she?'

'To be near this soldier of hers?'

'Surely even Phoebe isn't muddleheaded or romantic enough to think that she'd be allowed anywhere near him even if she knew where his battalion was. I think your idea about her setting off to find Felicia is more likely, but how do we find Felicia?' Elizabeth looked at Laurence, and they answered together: 'Lord Banning.'

'Good morning, Rector.'

Laurence was surprised to see Beth Parry descending his staircase. 'I'm here to see Agnes Thorn's baby,' she explained, adding, 'I'm very sorry to hear you are so worried about your daughter. If I can help when she returns, I should be very glad to do so.'

He was grateful, so grateful for the 'when'. 'That is

good of you, Dr Parry. I hadn't heard about the baby, I'm afraid. Is she ill?'

'I'm afraid she has chickenpox.'

'I'm sorry. In so young a child that is no light thing.'

'You're right. The rash has just appeared. There are several children with it in the village and Agnes thinks she may have picked it up when she took her to visit her mother two weeks ago. I've given Agnes instructions for a dusting powder for the spots.'

'Thank you, Dr Parry.' He hesitated. 'Do you find your way easier in Ashden now?'

'Thanks to Len Thorn, yes. He's taken my place as the football between Mutters and Thorns.'

'In what way?'

'The remaining eligible Mutters have all signed the blue cards to attest their willingness to serve.'

'And Len Thorn has not?'

'He seems to have disappeared.'

'I thought the forge was taking a long time with my bicycle. Has he left the village? I must admit, it would be no bad thing.'

'I agree, Mr Lilley. I do hope you find your daughter quickly.' And Beth Parry went on her way.

Elizabeth was surprised to find Laurence in the drawing room before dinner, instead of in his study. 'Are you well?' she asked him.

'Just tired. Did you want me?'

'We must decide on the rooms for your mother, and get Percy to clear them. She arrives on the eighteenth, and that's just over a fortnight away.'

Laurence groaned. How could he cope with his mother when he did not know whether Phoebe were alive or dead? He should be out looking for her now, not slumped in here.

Isabel poked her head up from the sofa where she'd been hidden from their sight. 'Why don't you put her in the boudoir?'

'My boudoir?' Elizabeth was horrified.

Laurence considered it. 'You know, that isn't a bad idea. She'd be well away from us.'

'And from the bathroom,' his wife pointed out.

'Give her the two adjoining rooms and she can have the old hip bath up there.' Isabel was inspired.

'Myrtle won't like that.' Elizabeth was dubious. 'She's not been used to taking jugs of water up to fill the old bath.'

'It's better than our running into Grandmother with her moustache net on.'

Elizabeth and Isabel laughed, then seeing Father's face Isabel hurriedly suggested, 'Suppose we get Harold Mutter to put in a new water closet?'

'We can't afford it.' Trust Isabel to come up with the expensive solution.

'It may be we can't afford not to.' Laurence thought about this too. 'There's water that side of the building. I'll talk to Harold and see if he can do it quickly.'

'What about the Honourable Pecksniff?' Isabel asked. Caroline's nickname for Grandmother's butler had been adopted by them all. Indeed, his real name was quite forgotten now. 'And there's that awful maid.'

'How many is she bringing?' Elizabeth asked in growing dismay. 'The maid can go in Harriet's old room,' Laurence said quickly. 'We can't put Pecksniff up in the attics.'

'I'm not having that old Count Dracula near me,' declared Isabel.

'Suppose we clear out the lumber room,' Laurence suggested wearily. 'And put him the far side of the attic rooms. It means them all sharing a bathroom, but it can't be helped. There's the old earth closet outside, of course.'

Isabel giggled. 'Oh yes, Father. Tell Pecksniff he's got to use that. I'd love to see those shiny boots underneath the door.'

'Isabel, I realise you are a married lady, but sometimes you go too far.'

'Not where Pecksniff's concerned,' Isabel replied.

Caroline replaced the receiver. Over two weeks now and still no news of Phoebe; was that bad or good? If she had run into trouble, either here or in France, surely something would have been heard by now? She blamed herself for not taking more care of her sister. She of all people had known how wayward the girl was. She should have kept a closer eye on her, especially after she went to work at the army camp. Yet she had been so preoccupied with her own concerns that she had dismissed all other worries.

Caroline felt frustrated that there was nothing she could do. Or was there? Suppose she sat and thought it through from Phoebe's point of view.

Father had told her about the letters, and she remembered meeting Harry Darling briefly at the tennis party. It was all too probable Phoebe had defied Father and continued writing to Harry, and *not* merely as a friend. So where did that get her? Caroline paced round the room, then looked down on the small garden at the back of the Norland Square house, which was tended by the housekeeper and her husband. There were a couple of bee hives there. It was a pity you couldn't ask the bees the answer to your problems, instead of merely telling them all your troubles. Percy Dibble had been very zealous about his bees; they were on the march again, he had informed Father solemnly. In the 'old days' there was no sugar, only bees, honey and beeboles, and now people were resorting to them again with sugar the most hard-hit commodity. Even Mrs Dibble had grudgingly agreed to cook with honey if she could.

Well, if she couldn't ask the bees, she would ask God. She had been praying every night for news; perhaps He wanted her to do something herself. But what?

Suppose Harry had leave and he and Phoebe were together somewhere? That was the most likely explanation, in her view. Somehow she couldn't see Phoebe going to France. But where was she, if not in Stepney? Or suppose Harry were ill or wounded?

Caroline thought this over again: *if not in Stepney* ... The police had called there and had been told that she wasn't there. But if Phoebe was determined not to be found that's what they *would* be told. The police would not have searched the house, and in any case Phoebe might have been out.

Caroline was suddenly convinced – his family must know where Harry was, and where Harry was, it was probable Phoebe was too. It was Saturday, a half day, and she decided to postpone her visit to Ashden for a few hours and go to Stepney instead.

With its rows of small terraced houses, each with its neat white doorstep Stepney was a new land to her. But the clothes of the children playing hopscotch on the pathway would have revealed its poverty even had Caroline not known about it from Sylvia Pankhurst's work in the area.

Consulting once again the address which she had written down on a piece of paper, she found number twenty-two Dakin Street, and knocked tentatively on the front door. Inside she could hear a child crying and for a while nothing happened. Then the door was opened by a little girl who peered curiously round it.

'Is Mrs Darling in, please?'

Caroline realised that in her tailored suit and felt hat she must look like Authority. The door was slammed in her face though not apparently as a rebuff, since after a few moments a small bird-like woman opened it once more. She didn't open it wide, though, nor invite her in.

Caroline decided on shock tactics. 'I've called to ask how your son is, Mrs Darling.'

'Poorly.' The answer was sharp, suspicious.

'I'm Phoebe Lilley's sister.' At least she had been right about something being wrong with Harry.

'Who?'

'I think you know her, don't you, Mrs Darling? I don't want to interfere, I just want to know she's all right so that I can tell Father. He and Mother are very worried, and think she may have gone to France.'

'To France?' The woman was clearly taken aback. 'Why's that then?'

'To look for your son.'

''E's not in France. 'E's here. Shooter's 'ill.'

Why on earth hadn't they thought of that at the beginning? And Shooter's Hill military hospital – of course that's where he'd be. 'Is Phoebe staying nearby? I'll go there, if you give me the address. I only want to see her, not drag her away.'

'You'd better come in.' The woman led her into the downstairs living room, crowded with photographs, with a musty smell from the fire where a batch of kitchen rubbish had just been placed. The little girl was banished to the kitchen beyond, and the door firmly shut. ''Arry is bad,' she said flatly. 'It's that gas. Wicked it is. Phoebe and me, we take it in turns. She's living 'ere, not there.'

Where? Caroline wondered. In this tiny house?

'She sleeps down here on the sofa. She don't make a fuss, for all she's a lady. Real fond of 'Arry, she is.' Mrs Darling looked defiant.

Caroline looked at the photograph of Harry on the mantelpiece, sporting his newly acquired uniform. 'Is he your only son?' she asked gently.

'No, there's Tom. 'E's out there an' all. And there's young Danny. Can't wait to go 'isself, for all 'e's only twelve. Lucky 'is dad's forty-five, or 'e'd be off too. And what we'd do then, God only knows. You'd best wait, miss. Miss Phoebe'll be back soon.'

Caroline waited for two hours, knowing she was in the

way, but determined to stay until Phoebe returned. She was overcome with relief. Phoebe was safe.

At last there was a knock on the door.

'That's 'er,' Mrs Darling said, jumping up. 'That's 'er special knock.'

Seeing the fear leap into Mrs Darling's face, Caroline felt ashamed that her thoughts had been for Phoebe alone. This woman's son was lying in hospital, gravely ill, and Phoebe would be bringing news of him. At first Caroline hardly recognised her sister as Phoebe came in. She looked thinner, older, and the pink cheeks had paled into sallowness.

Caroline stood up to greet her sister, suppressing her emotions until she had gauged what was wrong with her. But Phoebe showed no surprise or pleasure at her presence, nor even registered that there was anything odd about seeing Caroline here.

'What's wrong, lovie?' Mrs Darling asked sharply.

Phoebe drew a deep trembling breath. 'He's dead, Mrs Darling. Oh, Caroline, he's dead.'

She burst into tears, and hurled herself into her sister's arms.

'Laurence, Phoebe's been found. She's safe.' The door of the study flew open and Elizabeth burst in, tears pouring down her face.

Laurence closed his eyes. 'Thank you, Lord. Thank you.'

'She was at Mrs Darling's all the time.'

He groaned in exasperation for not having thought of this himself.

'Caroline found her. That soldier friend of Phoebe's was in the Shooter's Hill military hospital and she's been staying with his parents.'

'When is Caroline bringing her home?'

'She says she's not.'

'Then I must.' He attempted to move, but his legs and arms seemed to be refusing to obey his instructions.

'Caroline begs you not to. That poor man has died, and Phoebe's very upset. She wants to stay until the funeral and then come home. And Caroline suggests that you might wish to take the funeral.'

The East End of London seemed an unimaginable distance away. The whole idea was impossible.

'It would mean a lot to Phoebe, Caroline says,' Elizabeth added, watching him.

'After what she has done to you, Elizabeth?'

'She is safe, Laurence. That's the main thing. If you took the funeral service, it might help us to understand her.'

Even the prospect of walking to the station seemed unthinkable – that hot, dusty unending road.

'Is anything wrong?' Elizabeth's voice seemed to come from a great distance.

'I'm not feeling very well,' he admitted. 'I don't seem able to move.'

'You've a chill. I'll ask Mrs Dibble for the *nux vomica*.'

'I'm hot, not cold.'

She came over to him, felt his forehead, and said in concern, 'You have a fever.'

He put up his hand to follow hers and she exclaimed again, 'Spots. You've a rash. And look at your neck.'

Laurence took off his jacket and waistcoat and undid his shirt. He could see it himself. An ugly red rash. Already he was beginning to itch.

'It's chicken pox!' Elizabeth cried in dismay. 'Oh, Laurence, you've got chicken pox. And your mother is arriving next Thursday.'

Chapter Fourteen

Mrs Dibble tried to burst into seasonal Advent song. 'Hills of the North, rejoice.' But her efforts soon petered out. Whatever the hills of the north might have to sing about, she, Margaret Dibble, had little to rejoice over.

'What's to become of us, Percy, I don't know.' She had to talk to someone, and speaking to Myrtle was beneath her. Agnes, who was nursing the Rector, was in semi-quarantine, although she paid fleeting visits to the kitchen now and again. She was a lucky one, she was, Mrs Dibble thought grimly. She didn't have to grapple with the recent comings and goings. 'A house divided against itself cannot stand.' She sighed. 'And the *Rectory*, of all places.'

'But it is still standing.' Percy was engrossed in his Saturday morning egg.

'Bricks and mortar, maybe,' his wife retorted darkly.

'The Rectory's built on rock.' Percy had a sudden flash of inspiration.

'Wealden clay.' It was Mrs Dibble's turn to be literal.

'And the rain descended, and the floods came, and the winds blew and beat upon that house; and it fell not: for it was founded upon a rock.'

'Mayhap you're right, Percy. Mayhap. Seems to me more like the rocks are melting one by one, like that bloke with the elephants.'

'Elephants?' Percy looked up, puzzled.

'Poured vinegar on them.'

'On the elephants?'

'The *rocks*, Percy.' Her exasperation returned. 'The Alps. And vinegar's what we've had all too much of here, ever since *she* came.'

In Mrs Dibble's view things were going from bad to worse. Miss Caroline, who was only here for the weekend, would be going back to London tomorrow evening and then there'd be just Mrs Lilley, George, and Her Ladyship again – the Rector being shut away in quarantine upstairs for a good while yet, so the doctor said. And there was a storm brewing between the Kitchen, as Mrs Dibble liked to term herself, and Her Ladyship. When Mrs Lilley had suggested to Her Ladyship she took her meals separately in case she caught chicken pox, the mistress hadn't thought about how it would affect the kitchen. Twice the amount of work, and her having to do the serving herself. She couldn't leave it to Myrtle – she'd have the gravy all over Her Ladyship in a trice, and then the balloon would go up.

And then there were Pecksniff and that Miss Lewis,

otherwise known to Master George as Count Dracula and Moaning Minnie. Mrs Dibble had chuckled to herself when she heard that. At mealtimes, Peck looked as though the food the good Lord and Mrs Dibble provided was not good enough for the likes of him, and Miss Lewis who, in her mistress's presence, was all yes your ladyship, and no your ladyship, was complaints and wails in the servants' hall. Not that the Rectory's old comfortable chairs and sofas constituted a servants' hall in their High and Mighties' opinion. After a few days she and Percy had taken to eating in the kitchen with Myrtle.

Mrs Dibble eyed the mixture in the bowl before her. Once there had been many hands to stir the Christmas pudding mix: Joe, Lizzie, Miss Caroline, Miss Phoebe – now there was only her.

At that moment the kitchen door opened and Caroline put her head in.

'I heard it was time for pudding stirring,' she announced. 'I can't let the Three Wise Men think they're not being honoured.'

'Never could resist a few currants, could you, Miss Caroline?'

Mrs Dibble tried not to show how pleased she was.

'Nor sultanas.' Caroline took up the wooden spoon with great ceremony, and poised it over one of the three basins.

'Three times round for the Wise Men,' Mrs Dibble instructed unnecessarily. 'Then shut your eyes and wish.'

Caroline shut her eyes obediently and forced the spoon round in the heavy mixture.

'I am sorry to see you taking up kitchen work, Caroline.'

Aghast, Mrs Dibble looked up to see the unthinkable: the Dowager Lady Buckford had entered her kitchen without so much as a by your leave. Even Mrs Lilley knocked in courtesy before she entered.

'I'm stirring the Christmas pudding,' Caroline replied brightly, seeing the ominous signs of war on Mrs Dibble's face. 'Would you like a stir?'

'I would not, Caroline. You may leave. I have come to speak to the cook.'

'About what, your ladyship?' Mrs Dibble donned her most wooden expression and Caroline, remained where she was.

'I have decided to prepare a broth for my son,' her grandmother stated. 'He is not receiving enough nourishment.'

Mrs Dibble bristled. 'He does not like broth, your ladyship. But if you insist, I will prepare one.'

'I shall prepare it myself.'

Mrs Dibble nerved herself for battle. 'Not in my kitchen, madam.' There it was, out. Said. Done. When old Boney comes straight at you, all you can do is prepare for Waterloo.

Grandmother paused. 'I understood you are a servant here.'

'Mrs Dibble is our valued cook and housekeeper, Grandmother, and fully capable of nursing Father,' Caroline intervened.

'You too are willing to jeopardise your father's recovery?'

'Father is recovering excellently.'

'I do not believe in discussion before servants. Your father shall hear of your behaviour, and this cook's.'

'If you wish, Grandmother. But it would be more suitable to complain to my mother. She runs this household.'

'I see few signs of it.'

It was Mrs Dibble's turn to intervene. 'Mrs Lilley's who I answer to, madam, and that's that. And now, if you'll both excuse me, the Rector's waiting for his *egg*.'

After her Pyhrric victory, Mrs Dibble made herself a cup of tea and sat down. Never in all her years at the Rectory had she made one mid-morning. Today she needed it. She had had a shock. Over the years the house had had plenty of cuckoos in its nest in the way of guests, yet somehow life had gone on as normal. Now, well, she shouldn't say it of the Rector's mother, but there were three black crows here, bent on taking over: Her Ladyship, Dracula, and Minnie the Moaner.

Mrs Dibble squared her shoulders. If the Germans hadn't succeeded in conquering her domain, no mere ladyship was going to.

He would go mad closeted in this room much longer, Laurence thought to himself, as he wondered what mischief his mother was wreaking on his family. He had few clues. Elizabeth was loving, but he sensed the strain. Nothing was said overtly but, on the other hand, no one spoke to him naturally any more. They all spoke soothingly as though to a petulant child.

To a limited extent, Agnes was his companion, but he couldn't ask her what was going on point-blank. When she brought his meals in, she sat with him while he ate, talking of this and that; sometimes she talked too while she cleaned his room. When he asked if family prayers were still being said, she guessed that what he really wanted to find out was whether his mother was attending them and worse, if she was insisting on reading them. The answer had been no on both counts: her ladyship held separate prayers for herself and her own servants. Did this relieve or perturb him? He did not know; he only wanted to be back in harness again and to take control of the Rectory's affairs.

'Is all well,' he had asked, 'in the servants' hall with the extra work?' Even he and Elizabeth had adopted Mrs Dibble's rather grandiose name for the comfortable, though far from elegant, room to which the servants repaired in their free time.

Agnes had been circumspect. 'There's a war on, sir.' And with that he had to be content.

Laurence's only other visitor was Dr Parry. To his surprise, he did not find it in the least disconcerting to be attended by a woman doctor. In fact, he looked forward to her bi-weekly visits, although he was somewhat concerned for her safety, despite the curious mask she wore yashmak-style across her face.

'Are you immune to catching this ridiculous disease?' he enquired, looking in distaste at the scabs which were now falling off rapidly.

'I'm immune to everything,' she answered lightly. 'Another three or four days and you may re-enter the world. I've brought some zinc lotion for your new tender skin.'

Why, of all the people in this house, Laurence fumed, had it to be him who caught chicken pox? A rector needed to be seen, to be available, not hiding in one room. It was ironic that he had so often longed for the opportunity to read through the recent revised edition of Whiston's translation of the complete works of Flavius Josephus, and now it had come, it was proving a dull companion.

Today was his *seventeenth* birthday! At least, George exulted, he had reached an age when he might begin to have some control over his life. Another two years before the Army would take him under the Derby Scheme, a year before the Royal Flying Corps. Officially, that is. Amongst his birthday post there had been an interesting-looking letter, and he couldn't wait to get breakfast over to see what it was. Father's eagle eye would have noticed it, but Mother was less observant. Nowadays anyway. Fortunately the Howitzer, as he called his grandmother, didn't have breakfast downstairs. Moaning Minnie took it up to her, now that Mrs Dibble had declared war. Not before time in George's opinion.

A lowering cloud now hovered over the house, partly because of Father being in quarantine, but mainly because of Grandmother. It wasn't even so much what she said and did, though that was bad enough, but it was the effect she had on everyone around her. Still, he brightened up, surely even Grandmother couldn't ruin his birthday luncheon.

He ripped open the envelope in the privacy of his room, and caught his breath as he saw the letter heading: *Punch*. He read on incredulously. They had been given his address by his printers, and had he any more cartoons like the postcard they had recently seen? *Punch* was actually asking him; he'd never dared approach them. 'They would be grateful if he could call at his convenience to discuss the matter.' Be grateful. He hugged the words to himself in excitement.

Birthday luncheon followed a ritual and, as usual, he had been allowed to choose the menu: rabbit pie and mash. Caroline had made a face, but he had insisted. It was his birthday, after all. He'd been hoping Eleanor would come, but she was 'on duty', she explained. He hardly ever saw her now; she always seemed to be on duty, and her visits to the Rectory, which had been as familiar to the Hunney children as Ashden Manor, were few and far between. Still, as a consolation prize he was taking her to a picture palace in Tunbridge Wells next week, to see not only a Charlie Chaplin film but Mary Pickford as well. Not that he thought much of Mary Pickford, all curls and round eyes. He liked girls like Eleanor, whom you could talk to almost as if she were a chap. It wasn't fair that she was a few years older than him. He had a suspicion she didn't see him as a man at all. Just wait till he was flying aeroplanes in the RFC or RNAS.

His mind was abruptly brought back to the luncheon table as he heard Grandmother breaking the silence that fell all too often nowadays with a forbidding 'Mrs Lilley—'

Caroline had positioned herself, Isabel and George to keep Grandmother and Mother as far apart as possible, but with so few of them this was difficult. Grandmother was looking more like a howitzer than ever, and had obviously now decided to fire. On his birthday too, George thought peevishly.

'Mrs Lilley, I fear you are not aware of what is happening in your kitchen. This pie appears to be composed of rabbit. Do we have the servants' meal in error?'

George said the first thing that came into his head. 'You must find it difficult living here, Grandmother.'

'Difficult?' The first shell shot out at him. 'In what way?'

'Well.' George thought quickly. 'After not seeing us for so long, here you are plunged in the middle of us, and at such a bad time. Phoebe not here, Caroline away a lot of the time, Father ill, and . . .' His voice trailed off.

There was a pause. 'There is something of your grandfather in you,' his grandmother commented.

George thought with horror of the dark oil painting that hung in state in Buckford House, depicting a gloomy-faced, balding and bearded gentleman of venerable years.

'He was a diplomat too,' the Howitzer continued. 'Mrs Lilley, I compliment you on your *son's* manners.'

George saw his mother opening her mouth to reply when they were interrupted by the sound of the front door opening. She stood up, but before she had a chance to reach the hall, the door opened and her youngest daughter entered hesitantly.

'Phoebe! Oh darling!' Elizabeth threw her arms around her.

'I can't help being late,' Phoebe said when she had disengaged herself. 'The train just stood and stood outside East Grinstead.'

'We're not cross, darling.' Elizabeth half laughed, half cried. Caroline and Isabel leapt up to kiss her too.

'Good to see you back, Phoebe.' George contented himself with a manly pat on the back, still keeping an eye on the stony face at the table. The Howitzer had obviously decided even rabbit pie was preferable to greeting her granddaughter.

Phoebe came forward, emboldened by her welcome. 'I'm pleased to see you, Grandmother.'

The Howitzer raised her head. 'You are not yet changed for luncheon.' Phoebe was still wearing her bright Petticoat Lane skirt with her old Rectory coat slung over it.

'Phoebe can be excused—' Elizabeth began, but Phoebe forestalled her.

'No, I'll go immediately.'

How strange, Caroline thought. The Phoebe she knew of old would have retaliated.

'Where's Father?' Phoebe asked anxiously as Caroline went with her to change.

'Still locked away in his prison. He thinks Mother's thrown away the key.'

'Nonsense.' They looked up to see Laurence coming down the stairs, clinging to the banister rail for support.

'Don't come too close!' Elizabeth cried warningly, hearing the voice and rushing to intervene. 'Dr Parry said Tuesday at the earliest.'

'Contagious or not, I heard my Phoebe's voice.' Laurence came down a little further.

'I'm so sorry.' Phoebe stood still, not convinced of her welcome.

'I am glad you have returned, Phoebe,' Laurence told her.

Her face lightened. 'I thought you'd still be upset.'

'Upset that it happened, but of course I'm relieved and happy to have you back. How could you doubt it, my love?'

Her lips quivered. 'I'm very glad to be home.' She began to cry.

'I say.' George came out to join them. 'The pie's getting cold and it's my birthday.'

'Quite right,' Laurence announced briskly. 'Phoebe, take that coat off and we'll go straight in and have luncheon together, a family luncheon. I shall remain at one end of the table in splendid isolation, while you cower together at the other end.' He paused. 'With your grandmother.'

At her mother's request, Caroline had agreed to return to the Rectory on the Thursday before Christmas in order to spend the whole of Friday, Christmas Eve, helping with the family preparations. Normally, she would have delighted in it, but this year she felt as though she were marching into battle. And there were battles enough at work. The government had discovered the location of the WSPU's secret printing press in a Kensington garage, and had seized it and the magazine last Saturday. The press had erroneously reported it as a raid on Lincoln's Inn House, and the consequent outcry from branches all over the country had kept her so busy all week that she feared she would be unable to get away.

The familiar walk down Station Road soon cheered her up, however. At least Father was out and about again and almost his usual self. But when she arrived home, there was no sign of her mother.

'She's at the school house, Miss Caroline,' Mrs Dibble informed her.

Caroline's heart sank. Grandmother would be sitting in the drawing room like a bird of prey waiting for a victim. Well, it wasn't going to be her. She decided to call on Isabel who was hiding at Hop House to keep out of Grandmother's way, according to Mother. She would go by the Mill Lane route, longer and muddier though it was, in order to avoid Reggie. She had heard nothing from him; and assumed he must be nearly better since he was to return to France in the New Year. No, she would not think of Reggie, she told herself sternly.

She arrived at the back entrance of Hop House, and hurried up the path amid the tangle of weeds and undergrowth that had once been its garden. Reaching the tradesmen's door, she was puzzled to find it ajar. She knocked, and when no one answered took off her muddy boots and went in just as she usually did.

'Isabel,' she called softly. There was no reply. Don't say she's out too, Caroline thought crossly. Where could she be? The Towers? She looked into the drawing room – empty. Then she heard a noise upstairs. Thinking that Isabel must be packing to come to the Rectory for Christmas and could not hear her, she ran up the stairs in her stockinged feet and along to Isabel's slightly open bedroom door. Simultaneously rapping and calling 'Isabel!' she pushed the door wide open and entered.

And then she saw. Isabel was lying on the bed in her underwear, and a man was lying on top of her, his back to Caroline. It was Robert, home on leave, and she had burst in on them. In her horror at her tactlessness, some kind of noise must have come from her throat, for Isabel looked towards her and the man rolled over.

Was she going to be sick? Somehow Caroline managed to leave the room, and slam the door behind her. She had to get out of the house. She found herself in the garden, struggling to cram on her boots, hopping on one foot, then the other. She ran along the path and soon she was swallowed up in the anonymity of the hopfields. She drew a gasping breath. She was all right, she told herself, she was completely calm, if a little wobbly. She just needed . . . needed time.

The man on the bed had not been Robert at all. It was Reggie.

She struggled on through the hopfields, half walking, half running, while the horror overwhelmed her. She clung to a hop pole marking the ends of a row of bines, as if it were a life support. Then physical reaction caught up with her in deep choking retches that tore at her chest and her stomach.

'Caroline – Miss Lilley, are you ill?'

What on earth was Beth Parry doing in the middle of the hopgarden? With a supreme effort Caroline let go of the pole. 'Go away,' was all she could manage to say.

'Go away!' she shouted again, when Beth did not move. 'I don't want help, especially from you!'

Why had she said that? She didn't know and she didn't care. In any case, Beth ignored her. A firm arm was placed around her waist, and something was thrust under her nose.

Caroline gave a shudder, then pushed it away. 'What's that? Smelling salts?'

'No. It's an oil – an old herbal remedy of my grandmother's. It has vervain in it, a touch of rue and a couple of other wild flower essences. With so many people in mourning, I find it useful. Just sniff.'

'Please go away.' Caroline made a last attempt, but Beth would not be shaken off.

Unable to move, Caroline sniffed, then sniffed again. There was nothing else to do. As she felt her physical pain subside, misery took its place. She tried to pull herself together.

'Thank you. I'm sorry I shouted at you.'

'It's natural after shock.'

'How do you know I've had a shock?' Caroline felt anger rising again.

'I've seen a lot of it. Look, I don't know what's happened, but you're distressed and, being a doctor, I should help.' She still showed no signs of moving.

'Why are you always so bally competent?'

'I've had to be. I'll stay until you feel better and then you can hit a few more hop poles.'

Illogically, Caroline felt irritated at this offer. 'No. I'll go now,' she replied. 'Then you won't feel any obligation to stay at all.'

'Why don't we both go?' Beth suggested. 'You can come to my cottage if you want somewhere to be alone. I don't imagine you want to go to the Rectory for a while. If we go the back way to Tillow House, we won't meet anyone.'

Caroline clutched at this offer of escape. 'It's good of you. But I can't talk about it,' she added fiercely.

They set off in silence. When they reached her cottage

in the grounds of Tillow House, Beth made some tea while Caroline hovered uneasily in these new impersonal surroundings. A *competent* cottage, she thought crossly, and she'd been stupid to come here.

'It's Mr Hunney, isn't it, and your sister?' Beth poured tea as though she were asking about the new captain of the stoolball team.

'How do you know?'

'It was a guess. I've visited Hop House in the last week or two, and on two occasions I saw your sister out with someone in uniform who'd been wounded. It wasn't too difficult to guess who it was.'

'They were . . .' If she could frame the words, she might make the nightmare go away '. . . on her bed.' Caroline remembered belatedly that her sister was a married woman. 'I shouldn't have told you that,' she added wearily. 'You won't say anything to anyone, will you?'

'I'm very good at not telling anyone anything. Doesn't your sister love her husband?'

'I don't know. I don't even know my sister any more.'

'Loneliness can make people do strange things.'

'But I'm lonely too!' Caroline cried, in sudden self-pity. 'Reggie can't love me, and can never have done so. How could he do it? How could *she* do it?' She took a steadying sip of tea.

'Being on a bed with her doesn't mean Reggie loves her, Caroline.'

'Then it's even more terrible.' When Beth said nothing, she added, 'Do you think I'm making a fuss about nothing?'

'No. In your place I felt the same.'

'You?'

'Why else do you think I'm here in a small village and not in France or in a hospital somewhere?'

'I did think it strange,' Caroline admitted.

'I was married. I was the luckiest woman on earth, or so I thought. Then my husband volunteered; he was in the Royal Medical Corps, and was killed by a shell at Ypres three months later. I received his effects home even before the telegram arrived – they were not so well organised in those days. Amongst them was a packet of letters from another woman, and an unposted one by him to her. She, too, was the luckiest woman on earth, she claimed. I even forced myself to go to see her. She'd seen his name in the Roll of Honour lists. She was rather nice.' She paused. 'We'll say no more of this, Caroline. You have to steady yourself for Christmas?'

Caroline shuddered. 'Don't. How can I endure seeing her? How do *you* manage?'

'By pretending I'm someone else.'

'Perhaps I'll pretend I'm Grandmother Buckford.' Caroline laughed shakily.

'You could try,' Beth replied. 'But I doubt if your father could take two of you in the same house.' She was silent for a moment and then said, 'Don't run away too far if you can help it. He needs you there, and he is a very fine man.'

A little calmer, Caroline walked back to the Rectory. She hoped to reach the refuge of her room unseen, but there was little chance of that. As soon as she entered the house, Mrs Dibble came rushing up to her from the kitchen. 'Oh, Miss Caroline, such a to-do.'

Why did she worry, she thought bitterly. No one had time to notice her concerns.

'Just look who's come,' Mrs Dibble continued.

Isabel? Her heart jumped in fear.

Then Caroline heard familiar, well-loved voices. She rushed into the drawing room and with sudden, unexpected pleasure saw them both, talking to her father. Felicia and Aunt Tilly were home for Christmas.

Chapter Fifteen

For the next hour, Caroline tried to forget about her own concerns, as she exchanged news with Tilly and Felicia. Not that they talked very much about their work; they merely told her they were back in the front in Belgium, and that trench life was relatively quiet – which meant, Caroline knew, only the usual amount of shelling and sniper fire. London's Victoria Station had been packed with Tommies coming home on Christmas leave, Felicia said, and her father had told them that several Ashden families had been lucky, though not poor Agnes nor even Joe Dibble. Both looked tired and thinner, their faces showing a wiry strength and vitality that had not been there before, and their serviceable clothes were hard-worn. After a while Felicia excused herself to go to her room. Caroline had decided to leave too when Tilly stopped her.

'Did your mother tell you there's another guest for Christmas at the Rectory?'

'No. I haven't seen her yet. Who?'

'Simon.'

'Does that mean what everyone will think it will mean?' Caroline asked lightly.

'It means a man who would otherwise be on his own can now share Christmas with friends,' Tilly replied calmly.

Caroline hadn't seen Simon for about two weeks as he had been overseas and then at his house in Tunbridge Wells. She knew he was very concerned about Penelope. German troops had just taken over Skopje and, according to his sources, their occupation was brutal and complete. He had been even more worried to hear a rumour that his daughter was no longer with Lady Paget's hospital unit but had accompanied some of the wounded Serbian soldiers crossing the mountains in the hope of reaching the safety of Albania.

'And now,' Tilly asked, 'tell me about your work. How is the WSPU faring?'

'You must have heard.' Caroline was grateful for her interest. 'There's a tremendous row going on between the Pankhursts and the rest of the leadership.'

'There usually is.'

'Quite a lot of people resent the way they behave like queen bees.'

'They *are* queen bees, of course.'

'But the funds are for the WSPU, and Mrs Pankhurst and Christabel seem to think they have sole control of them.'

'And whose side are you on?'

Caroline tried hard to answer her. In truth she was so tired she did not much care. Now, dulled by shock, she found she could say not a word.

Tilly laid a hand on her arm, concerned. 'I'm not going to ask you what's wrong, Caroline. I can see you're still grieving for Reggie.'

She made an effort. 'If I felt I was still working for women's war effort, the office fighting wouldn't matter. But I don't any longer. I feel I'm working for the Pankhursts, and admirable though they are in some ways, that's not the same thing.'

'You need a fresh vision.'

Caroline hesitated. 'I've been thinking about going overseas, to help with the driving and organisation of Lena Ashwell's concert parties, perhaps.'

Tilly was silent for a moment. 'Going overseas means you must have your prime commitment to what you are doing there, not use it as an escape from what you can't have here. You must heal yourself first, or you won't be able to heal others.' There was compassion in her voice.

Caroline wanted to shout at her, to tell her she was wrong. Instead, she found she was close to tears.

'Now the government is seeing sense about women working there will be plenty for you to do here. This war has no end in sight, and the organisation of man and woman power at the front is becoming more formal. Today Felicia and I could not have established ourselves so easily as we did a year ago. And when general male conscription comes in, as it surely must,' Tilly continued, 'the door will open even further for women to take up work.'

313

'We'll be conscripted too?'

'Some kind of Derby Scheme for women perhaps.'

'We signed the National Register in August and last March, but the government took little notice.'

'I don't think we will have to wait much longer. I could see even in our short journey home that it was beginning. We had a female bus conductress!'

Caroline rose to dress for dinner. She gave her aunt a quick kiss of welcome before she left. 'I'm so glad you're here.'

'I doubt if The Towers will rejoice so enthusiastically,' Tilly said cheerfully, coming to open the door for her.

Laughing, Caroline turned her head to see Grandmother Buckford, in full evening dress, about to enter the drawing room. The Howitzer looked at Caroline, then her gaze settled on her errant daughter. 'Matilda!'

A terrible thought occurred to Caroline: surely Tilly had known Grandmother was staying here? Caroline herself had avoided the subject in her own letters, realising how complete the breach still was between the two, but Mother or Father must have mentioned it.

Tilly was white-faced. She tried to speak, but could not.

'No one informed me that you would be here, Matilda,' Lady Buckford said 'Naturally I would have arranged to stay with Charles, had I known.'

'No one told me either,' Tilly replied. Then, to Caroline's admiration, she added, 'However, the Rectory is large enough for both of us.'

'It appears that Buckford House was insufficiently large for you, Matilda, so why should the Rectory prove otherwise?' Lady Buckford regarded her daughter's clothes with a disdainful eye. 'I hear you are a nurse.'

'No. I drive motor cars and carry luggage,' came the swift reply. Nurses could be considered socially acceptable; transporting mutilated men from the mud of Flanders would not.

Grandmother did not comment, and Caroline and Tilly escaped to their room upstairs.

'She's like something out of the Great Exhibition of '51,' Caroline exploded. 'A monstrous invention of the Victorian age. The household's been upside down for weeks. I'm so sorry. You will stay, though?'

Tilly laughed. 'Since Simon is galloping down here like St George, I can hardly leave him to be devoured by the dragon alone.'

'Good. It will be like Christmas after all with you and Felicia here.'

'Do you think Felicia has changed?'

'She appears stronger somehow – and thinner, of course. I'm beginning to think Edith Cavell must have been very like her. Did you know her?' Caroline asked, momentarily deflected from Felicia.

Although Edith Cavell's execution in October had attracted only a brief mention in the newspapers, public outrage had gradually grown, and her last words to the British chaplain were quoted everywhere: 'Patriotism is not enough.'

'Her training school for nurses was in occupied Brussels, and so I never met her. But I do know she played a central role in the organisation which helped hundreds of British soldiers stranded or wounded behind the lines after Mons to reach the Dutch border, where they could return home. It wasn't just Edith Cavell who was arrested, you know. The whole organisation was betrayed, and thirty-five stood trial. I think nine were acquitted but five received the death sentence. Edith Cavell and Philippe Baucq were shot immediately but, because of the outcry, the Kaiser, so it's said, ordered that no more women should be executed. There are still clandestine groups operating in Brussels, I hear. Anyway,' Tilly added, 'you are right, Caroline. Felicia has Edith Cavell's steel.'

'And you too.'

'No, I could turn my hand to anything, munitions, woodchopping or embroidery if it were for the war effort. Felicia is different. She has the steadfastness of a nun.'

Caroline was horrified at the comparison. Beautiful Felicia, with all the love she had to bestow, locked away in a convent? Surely God must have some other purpose for her.

'I can't understand it. Isabel has telephoned to say she's decided to stay at Hop House.' Elizabeth was greatly upset. 'And that she'll merely come here for Christmas Day. Naturally I told her not to be so foolish.'

'When is she coming, then?' Caroline hid her trembling fingers in the folds of her skirt.

'I persuaded her to come late tomorrow evening. For the midnight service.'

So that was when she would have to face her. What would she say? It did not help that Isabel was obviously feeling as bothered as she was about their meeting. Caroline had decided that the only way of surviving Christmas was to attempt to push the sordid, ugly image of Isabel with Reggie into the back of her mind. She must tell herself that Beth Parry had been right and that was not love she had witnessed.

On Christmas Eve, Tilly and Felicia elected to go Christmas shopping in Tunbridge Wells in Tilly's old Austin, which had made a proud reappearance from the stables where it had been housed in her absence. Caroline did not go with them. Perhaps in the kitchen, helping Mrs Dibble with mince pies and stuffings, some semblance of the joy of Christmas might come to her. In the entrance hall the Christmas tree, parcels already heaped beneath it, seemed to mock her. Last night she and Felicia had decorated it with baubles and garlands they had made themselves and cherished over the years. Two lantern-shaped decorations had even been created out of an old Bradshaw railway timetable, its pink printed pages giving a decorative touch. Yet somehow even the shiny gold and silver stars could not succeed in making the tree look other than forlorn and tawdry.

As soon as Caroline entered the kitchen, she could see something was wrong.

'My mince pies,' declared Mrs Dibble without preamble, 'are real mince pies.'

'Of course,' Caroline soothed.

'They don't need brandy in them.'

'Of course not.'

'My recipe's been good enough for the Rectory for over twenty years.'

317

'I love your mince pies.'

'That Peck was sent to tell me to put brandy in the mincemeat.' Caroline's heart sank. Not another battle in the Campaign for the Kitchen.

'She'd sent him out to buy a whole bottle of that Napoleon brandy. The devil's drink. I won't put up with it and that's that.'

'Quite right, Mrs Dibble. I'll have a word with Mother.'

Mince pies were a serious matter. If Mrs Dibble refused to make them, they could not eat their ritual mince pie a day during the Twelve Days of Christmas, and that meant ill-luck for the year. Caroline found her mother, who was sitting in her outside 'boudoir' despite the poor heating, and told her what was happening.

Elizabeth was perturbed. The smooth organisation of the Rectory was being threatened at one of the most important times of the year. She took a deep breath.

'She's in the morning room, Caroline. Let's go together, but leave me to do the talking.'

Grandmother was sitting at the desk writing letters. She looked up when Elizabeth and Caroline came in.

'It is good of you to buy the brandy, Lady Buckford,' Elizabeth began, 'but we can't ask Mrs Dibble to go against her principles.'

'She is a servant, Mrs Lilley,' was Grandmother's reply. 'These mince pies are for the family. Do you expect me to make them myself?'

'No, but Miss Lewis is welcome to make a special batch of pies for you, provided Mrs Dibble agrees to the use of her kitchen.'

'Louise is a lady's maid. Not a cook.'

Elizabeth could not resist it. 'She is a servant, Lady Buckford.'

Caroline held her breath. 'My son shall hear of this,' was her grandmother's only reply.

'No doubt. This is my concern, however, and I make it a policy not to disturb him at his work.'

'So it would seem from the way this house is run.'

Elizabeth gasped in disbelief at this attack. 'I would remind you you are a guest under our roof.'

'One with eyes, Mrs Lilley.'

'No,' Elizabeth retorted quietly. 'There you are mistaken. You have no eyes to see, only to perpetuate your own bigotry.'

By ten o'clock on Christmas Eve there was still no sign of Isabel. Once everyone knew Grandmother was keeping to her rooms, dinner had been enjoyable. Phoebe and George were in ebullient form, Felicia was glowing with happiness and Tilly had driven up to meet Simon at the railway station. The only fly in the ointment of peace was Father, who looked rather puzzled to see his mother missing and announced his intention of visiting her after supper.

If only Isabel were not coming at all, Caroline felt she could enjoy Christmas.

She dressed with care for the coming carol service, in a new dark blue velveteen gown with a full skirt, and a warm wrap over it. After all, the Eucharist proclaimed the beginning of Christmas, and a large part of the village would be packed into St Nicholas. Reggie would be there.

With this unwelcome thought in her mind, she descended the staircase – and there was Isabel. She had been expecting it, of course, but shock still ran through her.

'Hello, Isabel.' Strange how normal her voice sounded.

Isabel gave a theatrical start. 'Goodness, how you startled me. Oh, Caroline, you do look nice.'

The worst was over.

When the Rectory party arrived at the church, the choir was already singing. Caroline walked straight up the aisle with the rest of her family, avoiding even a glance at the Hunney pew. The Norville pew would be unoccupied of course – or so she thought, until she realised Grandmother was no longer with them.

Looking around, Caroline saw Lady Buckford, Peck and Miss Lewis sitting in state in the Norville pew. Then she understood. Lady Hunney would be sitting in the Hunney pew with Sir John. By taking over the rival pew, Grandmother was making a bid for power.

Try as she might, Caroline could not resist turning to look at the Hunneys' seats. Lady Hunney and Sir John were there of course; so were Daniel and Eleanor. But Reggie was not.

I must have no bitterness, Caroline reproved herself. Not tonight. But, as she sat between Mother and Phoebe, every inch of her was aware of Isabel just a few feet away and, as her father began the Communion: 'Because thou did give Jesus Christ, thine only son, to be borne this day for us . . .' she found herself unable to forgive her sister.

On the way home she walked ahead, but Isabel soon caught up with her. Surely, Caroline thought in agony, she wouldn't talk about it? On the contrary, Isabel seemed determined to do just that.

'I'm sorry you came in that moment,' she said.

Caroline cringed at the memory. 'The door was open.'

'It was stupid of us. You see, Caroline,' the large blue eyes fixed on her earnestly, 'Robert is so far away. I haven't seen him since July, and goodness knows when I will again.'

Caroline stared at her. 'What difference does that make?'

'Every difference.' Isabel managed to sound indignant. 'You don't understand. You're not married. There are needs.'

What about my needs, Caroline thought. 'And Reggie?' She could hardly get his name out.

'He too,' Isabel answered in a low voice. 'The trenches, you see.'

'But he loves me, Isabel. I know he does, despite what happened between us. Did that not affect your "needs"?'

'He's been so lonely since you broke it off—'

'Me?'

'Refusing to do the one single thing he asked—'

'Stop it, Isabel!' Caroline's voice was so sharp that Isabel obeyed instantly. How could you live all your life with someone and not know them, she wondered. She and her sisters and brother had been brought up with the same set of beliefs and values. She had tried to hold on to them, and had assumed Isabel did the same. How very foolish of her.

Mrs Dibble put her feet up on Christmas afternoon with some satisfaction. All in all, it hadn't been too bad. And her *real* mince pies had gone down a treat! It was nice to have Muriel and Lizzie here, and the children. Agnes had gone home to her parents, but Peck and Miss Lewis had stayed on with them.

To her amazement, Peck was playing with the children, Fred had joined in, and Miss Lewis had shown an unexpected flair for banging out music hall songs on the old piano, in which they all joined. Irreverent, even vulgar perhaps, on a holy day, but they sang a carol or two as well to make up for it.

Muriel was looking happier too. She heard from Joe regularly – so regularly, in fact, that she reckoned he was not in the fighting line. 'He says he might even get leave soon.' Leave. That would be good. They were always hearing about it but it never seemed to happen.

Only one thing bothered Mrs Dibble. Lizzie was oddly quiet. Perhaps she's regretting moving in with that Mr Eliot, she thought smugly, and missing Rudolf. One letter in over a year she'd had; it had been smuggled out by a friend sent to Switzerland on duty, and dropped in at the British Embassy. Nothing since last November. 'He'll be back, you mark my words,' her mother said severely to her over the washing up, 'and then what will you do? When folks tell him? And they will, believe me.'

Lizzie did not reply, and Mrs Dibble looked at her sharply. 'What's wrong, my girl? That hop man working you too hard?'

'No, Ma.' Lizzie's voice trembled. 'You'll have to know sooner or later, I suppose. I'm expecting.'

'You're what?' Mrs Dibble sat down heavily on a chair, the dish mop still in her hand.

'Don't look like that,' Lizzie pleaded. 'I'm pleased, really I am.'

'Pleased?' her mother cried. 'To be having a bastard?'

'Don't say that.'

'Did he force you? I told Percy that's what he'd do.'

'No, Ma, he didn't. It's not his fault I'm expecting.'

'That it should come to this,' Mrs Dibble moaned, rocking to and fro.

Lizzie was quiet. She couldn't believe it when Dr Parry told her what was wrong with her. After so long with Rudolf, she didn't think she could start a baby at all, let alone so easily.

'Don't look so gloomy, Ma. It's Christmas.'

'If it weren't, my lass, I'd turn you out here and now. Bringing disgrace on me and the Rectory. Lizzie Dibble, how could you?'

'Stein, Ma. My name's Stein.'

'*You* forgot that, my girl. Not me.'

Laurence changed into his cap and bells costume, the traditional one he always wore for the ritual game of 'Family Coach' on Christmas afternoon, though this was far from a normal Christmas. It was true that all his family was gathered together, but the atmosphere was strained. They had invited the Hunneys to join them for Christmas afternoon as a formality, hardly expecting them to come. Instead, to poor Caroline's obvious horror, shortly after luncheon, not only Sir John but Lady Hunney, Daniel,

Eleanor and Reggie had arrived. What could he do? He could hardly turn them away.

Now it was time for the 'Family Coach.' Lady Hunney had never joined in the game, and he could not envisage his mother doing so. The tradition had been inherited from Elizabeth's family, not his. However, he decided, now that it had become a Rectory tradition, it should be played by all, no matter who was here. Luncheon had passed off reasonably amicably, thanks, he acknowledged, to Phoebe.

When the Christmas pudding had been borne into the darkened room with due ceremony, flaming its blue alcoholic flames, his mother had commented, 'I see your cook has liberally sacrificed her scruples so far as this pudding is concerned; it is a pity that mince pies are not accorded the same status.'

'Oh, but Grandmother,' Phoebe had broken in immediately, wide-eyed with apparent shock. 'On a Christmas pudding the alcohol has *religious* significance. Didn't you know that?'

Laurence jangled his bells in private satisfaction as, attired to begin the game, he made his entrance into the drawing room to cheers from his family and even louder ones from Daniel and Reggie. Especially Reggie. Probably he felt awkward being here, in view of his treatment of Caroline in August, though that didn't quite explain the odd signals Laurence's intuition was receiving. He noticed that his mother, who had chosen the most uncomfortable chair in the room, took no part in the cheering.

'Today, our subject is—' he paused, as his audience

waited expectantly. 'The Mistletoe Bough.' Cheers and claps.

Phoebe ran to the piano and began to bang out the old Victorian song.

'This afternoon our text is drawn,' Laurence continued in his most pompous voice, 'from Mr Thomas Haynes Bayly's scholarly study of the mediaeval verbal treatise on the lamentations of young Lord Lovel upon the disappearance of his beauteous bride in a game of hide and seek during the celebrations following their nuptials; and, after many years wandering the world, of his discovery of her skeleton in an old chest.'

'The mistletoe hung in the castle hall . . .' bawled Phoebe at the piano.

'Later,' Laurence pontificated, 'when the house is dark and quiet and full of secrets, we shall examine the mysterious disappearance of the fair bride and the dramatic search that then took place.' ('Oh!' groaned his audience.) 'Meanwhile, we shall consider the journey of the happy bridal party to the castle, unaware of the ghastly tragedy that will ensue.' (Indrawn hiss of excitement from his flock.) 'Had there been mishaps along the way that they should have noted as omens of disaster to come?' ('There had,' Caroline shouted.) 'Let the journey begin!' Laurence cried. 'Mother, you play the coachman. You and Lady Hunney and Daniel are excused from jumping up. Just wave your hands in the air.'

He held his breath, half expecting his mother to walk out of the room, but his gamble paid off. She hesitated, then barked out: 'Kindly inform me what this entails.'

He had reasoned to himself that his mother could not refuse to lie for she had no means of knowing what Lady Hunney would do. If Lady Hunney agreed, Lady Buckford would look churlish, and Lady Hunney could now not refuse for the same reason.

Much relieved; he gave everyone else a part. ('Bags I the wheels,' George shouted). Once the bride, her father, her mother, the little bridesmaid; the footman; the horses; the doors and the baggage had all been distributed; and he had explained to Lady Buckford that on any mention of the word 'coachman' she must wave her hands in the air (in lieu of leaping up and turning round) the game started.

By the time the family coach had run through an hour of vicissitudes and finally rattled triumphantly over the drawbridge into Lord Lovel's castle, the entire company was exhausted, and a harmonious atmosphere reigned. It even wafted around Lady Buckford – partly because Laurence had cheated and allowed her to stay in the game long after her slow reactions should have knocked her out.

'Though we cannot know what lies before us. Lord, as our coach rattles into the future,' Laurence concluded with his usual brief prayer, 'grant that Thy grace which is with us now may strengthen us in the darkness outside and be a lantern to guide us to Thy ever-lasting light.'

Felicia drew the role of bride for the hide and seek that followed the game from the screws of paper in her father's panama. She went to change into an old cream wedding dress from the dressing-up trunk and then disappeared to look for a place to hide. A few rooms had been declared out of bounds: Grandmother's was one, Mrs Dibble's stillroom another, and the servant's hall and bedrooms were all inviolate. That still left a large part of the Rectory, not to mention the outbuildings.

At last they were ready, assembled with candles and torches in the drawing room, the only room now with lights. To Caroline's surprise, her grandmother still remained in the drawing room to watch the proceedings.

'Alas, alack,' called Laurence, 'during our festivities his lordship's bride has disappeared. Let us seek for her!' And the stampede began.

Caroline decided to keep as far from Reggie as possible; bumping into him by mistake would be terrible. She thought she saw him going upstairs in the dark, so started her own search in the stables outside. Her nerves were on edge, however, and when she bumped into someone, she screamed. Luckily it was only Eleanor, and her pounding heart subsided.

'You've been quiet today.' Caroline said to her when she caught her breath. 'Is anything wrong?'

'Martin's been called up. He attested, you know, and though there's no general call-up yet under the scheme, there's a need for vets in the Army Veterinary Corps. He goes off on Monday week.'

'Oh, Eleanor, I'm so sorry.'

'So am I. We carved his initials on the tree last night.'

'And what about you?'

'You mean us?' Eleanor made a face. 'We wanted to get married before he left.'

327

'You're not going to let your mother stop you?' Caroline asked in alarm.

'She asked Father to talk to Martin and he managed to convince him it wasn't honourable to marry me before going to war.'

'He didn't convince you, I take it.'

'Of course not. I know very well it's nothing to do with honour; Mother doesn't want me to marry a vet. The Prince of Wales might do at a pinch.'

'Can't you talk to Martin about it?'

'I've tried. But now he's got this idea about bally honour stuck in his mind. Look at Reggie, he says. He went off to war without – oh, Caroline, I'm sorry. I shouldn't have mentioned that. Does it still hurt very much?'

Look at Reggie, indeed, Caroline thought bitterly. What a splendid example of honour!

'Would it be crass of me to kiss you under the mistletoe, Tilly?' Simon crept up behind her while she was searching the wardrobe in Caroline's bedroom.

Tilly shut the wardrobe door, very conscious of how near Simon was in the dark. She looked at his face, flickering in the glow of the candle. 'There is none in this room,' she pointed out.

He kissed her lightly, then harder, finding her lips more welcoming and eager than he had expected. 'It's not easy sleeping in this house,' he said as he released her. 'I want to be in your bedroom, not mine.'

'Then let's swap rooms.'

'Don't laugh at me, Tilly.'

'I apologise,' she said contritely. 'That was crass of me.'

'Is it a defensive weapon?'

'No. Or, if it is, I'm not sure whether it's permanent.'

'Because of your war work?'

'Yes, but also because of me.'

'Has anyone made love to you before?' he asked gently.

'I'm fifty-one.'

'That's not an answer.'

Tilly sighed. 'Someday, I promise you, I will tell you the story of my life. But not today, and not here.'

'Very well.' He took her hand and kissed it. 'I'll hold you to that promise. Be sure of that.'

'Come down, Felicia,' Daniel hissed up the narrow winding staircase behind a well-camouflaged door that led to the secret room they had all used as children for meetings. 'I know you're there, and I can't bally well get up. Is that why you chose it?' There was silence.

'If I get my peg leg in the New Year,' he continued, 'I'll come over and climb the Eiffel Tower for you, but for now you'll have to indulge my infirmities.'

Still silence.

'Damn you,' he shouted. Angrily, he hunched his tall body over the crutches, but there wasn't room to manoeuvre himself up the narrow staircase on them.

'Blast you to blazes, Felicia.' Tears of anger combined with self-pity came to his eyes as he hurled one of the crutches away. The anger won. He collapsed on to one of the steps, threw the other crutch away too, and sitting on the step heaved his weight by his arms, up and back to the next step. And the next, and the next. It took him ten minutes before he reached out and found no step behind him, only a woman's foot and a long silk dress.

Felicia swung the lantern she had been given in honour of her starring role, and he saw her long dark hair framing the pale face. 'I suppose this was an obvious place. I hoped it was so obvious no one would bother to look,' she said.

'What the hell do you think you're playing at? I thought the Lady of the Lamp was supposed to show some kind of womanly gentleness towards injured soldiers, not put them through torture.'

'You're here,' Felicia pointed out, sitting down beside him.

'No thanks to you.'

'Why come then?' Her voice was gentle.

He was aware of every inch of her, breathing quietly beside him. Desire was in the mind, the eyes and the heart, not just in the body. How easy to say, 'I wanted to reach you.' But he wouldn't do it for there could be no future for them. 'I wanted to win the game,' he said instead.

She sighed. 'You have, Daniel.'

He had to touch her, so he kissed her cheek. 'When I get my artificial leg and the war's over, I shall travel, just like I wanted to. And I shall owe it to you.'

She did not comment. 'Do you want to go down to claim the prize for finding me?'

'Not yet. Tell me about your work, Felicia.'

'I can't.'

'Why not?'

She tried to answer his question. 'To do so would

make it seem unreal. This is one world, that is another. They co-exist, and one is as real as the other.'

'I've seen a battlefield, Felicia, and I can guess something of what it's like out there. Perhaps you need to talk to someone.'

'I have Tilly.'

'Are you shutting me out?'

'You have done that to me.' There was no bitterness in her tone.

'I had to.'

'But you made your decision without understanding anything of me.'

'Then tell me about what you're doing,' Daniel pleaded. 'About the men you look after, about the life, anything. I may not deserve it, but I want to hear about it and, in return, I'll bore you with tales of ancient Greece.'

In the dark of the room, with only the lantern lighting them, how could she resist him? She felt his lips on her cheek, his hand lying over hers. Perhaps any bridge was better than none? Felicia took a deep breath and began to talk.

'Simon—'

The name died on Caroline's lips as she peered into a chest in the glory-hole and a man's hand was laid on her arm. The chest top banged as she jumped in horror. It wasn't Simon. It was Reggie.

'Caroline, don't go.'

She struggled to release herself from his grasp.

'You've no idea – what it's been like,' he continued jerkily.

'There's no one left, you see. My battalion lost nearly all its officers at Loos. The gas – we couldn't see – those awful flannel masks. I looked round and there were only three or four men behind me. We saw the rest after they yelled at us to get back. They were all lying there. Dead. All we had to do was reach a road, then the Hohenzollern Redoubt and a small village; we didn't reach any of them. I'm a full lieutenant now. Do you know why? Because there's no one else. That's why I can't—'

'No, Reggie.' She tried to say it as gently as she could. Only a month or two ago, it had been her making the same plea, a plea which he had humiliatingly ignored. He had rejected her three times. It was not his fault, she laid no blame; but she knew now that the gate to the apple orchard of that last glorious summer was closed forever.

Chapter Sixteen

Caroline read the second paragraph in the letter from her mother with incredulity; in fact she read it three times to ensure she was not mistaken. It was All Fools' Day, but surely her mother would not joke about such a serious matter? It was a miracle the letter had reached her at all with the enormous disruption caused by Monday night's freak gales and heavy snowstorms. Railway lines had been out of service all over the country and many still were, telegraph and telephone communications were cut, houses had been damaged, thousands of trees uprooted, and bridges washed away. Even today, five days later, the newspapers were full of the storm damage. Caroline turned back to the storm in her letter: Mrs Dibble, it appeared, had announced her intention to leave the Rectory.

'Things haven't been right since your grandmother came, Mrs Dibble maintains, and she's decided that enough is enough, and she, Percy and Fred are going to live in Hartfield.'

Thoroughly alarmed, Caroline read on, imagining her mother at the battered writing desk carefully penning the words, resting her left elbow on the desk and clutching her hair at the temple, as she so often did when under strain.

'Now I am writing to you, dearest, so that you may consider this very carefully, rather than making the instant decision I know you would, were I able to telephone you.' The Rectory telephone was out of service due to the storm.

'I have talked to your father,' her mother continued, 'but he sees no way of dislodging your grandmother for the moment, especially now the Zeppelins have started their antics once again.' Antics was an understatement. Only last night there had been a heavy raid on London and East Anglia with many people killed and injured. Caroline had been at Drury Lane, enthralled by the magnificent new American film *Birth of a Nation*, and hearing about the raid on her return home had been a grim reminder of last October's horror. The film had been about the American Civil War, and had made her wonder if America would be joining the Allies in their fight against Germany.

'There is some relief, however. Your grandmother has begun to appear regularly at church, which pleases your father, though I doubt if it is for the reason he imagines.' Caroline remembered the rivalry between the Ladies Buckford and Hunney on Christmas Eve. 'She presides also over a tea for wounded officers in the Rectory drawing room. This has proved an unexpected success since Miss Lewis has an astounding aptitude for thumping out cheap music on the piano, which (unaccountably!) has proved more popular with the soldiers than teas at the Dower House. It has become a regular arrangement, and develops into quite a rowdy sing-song. It deflects your grandmother's attention from Phoebe, George and myself, and I encourage it. Your father is less enthusiastic, however, as on more than one occasion I have been forced to remind the soldiers that they are in a Rectory!'

'Come on, Mother.' Caroline was growing impatient at this rambling.

'After great persuasion, I have managed to persuade Mrs Dibble to remain.' Thank goodness! Caroline relaxed – but only for a moment. 'There is, unfortunately, a condition. Mrs Dibble insists that I resume my role as mistress of the Rectory. I have therefore decided to give up my place on the local Women's Agricultural Committee.

'Caroline, my darling, could you bear to return and take my position on the WAC? Phoebe, I am sure, will continue to assist us on the Ashden rotas, so that you may still have the time to help the cause of women's work locally, if not in London.'

Go back to Ashden? Rather to her surprise, Caroline found she was weighing the matter up objectively. Outside in the London streets the flowering almond trees were in full bloom, the hooping season had begun in the parks, and the people she passed in the streets looked more cheerful. Nevertheless, she was finding her work for the WSPU increasingly frustrating. It certainly hadn't been dull – in February, Scotland Yard's Special Branch had again seized copies of *Britannia*, this time raiding WSPU premises in Mecklenburg Square. Why, she asked herself despairingly, when the Pankhursts seemed proud of having aroused so much attention, did they waste time fighting the government?

In February too, the new Women's National Land Service Corps had been formed. An offshoot of the Garden and Farm Union, it had full Board of Agriculture support. And Lord Selborne had announced a scheme for village registers of women ready to undertake farm work. Letters to the newspapers also reflected a need for more help from women on the land. Now, with her mother's letter before her, Caroline knew her choice was clear. In Ashden, she thought with excitement, she could join the local WAC and help with organising similar rotas in other parishes.

Then she remembered Reggie.

For a moment she had almost forgotten her most pressing problem. It was true that Reggie would not be there all the time, but Isabel would. Caroline looked at her mother's letter with its oh-so-innocent request, then into the bleakness of her own heart. Somehow or other she had to face it. If she let Reggie and the Hunneys continue to stand between her and what she wanted to do, the pain would never go away. She would go!

She ran to the telephone in Simon's entrance hall, remembering belatedly it was out of action because of the storm. She decided to try anyway. To her delight, the operator was able to put her through to the Rectory and, less than a week later, she was back in Ashden in time for Friday luncheon.

* * *

To Caroline's surprise, the first person to greet her, as she opened the front door, was Eleanor Hunney.

'Martin and I are to marry.' Eleanor's face was pink with excitement. 'Martin's talking to your father now. The service is to be held *tomorrow*, Caroline.'

'I've been away too long,' Caroline laughed. 'I thought Martin had left for the Army already.'

'So he had. He's a week's leave and a special licence, and then he's going overseas.' Eleanor pulled a face. 'Still, as a vet he won't be in the front trenches, will he?'

'Has your mother relented?'

'I'm afraid not. She has refused even to attend the wedding, though Father says he'll try to come down. Daniel will be there, of course, prancing around on his new leg. And your mother is holding the wedding breakfast. She's –' Eleanor choked slightly – 'she's always been as much of a mother to me as my own; more in many ways. You'll find her in emergency conference with Mrs Dibble in the dining room.'

'And the wedding's tomorrow? Oh, Eleanor, I'm so happy for you. But what will you wear?'

'I haven't even begun to think,' Eleanor said cheerfully. 'I suppose you wouldn't come over and give me some advice? The Dower House is like an ice house at the moment; I could do with some friendly warmth.'

Caroline tried to sound enthusiastic. 'Of course I'll come – if your mother will let me past the door.'

In the event, Caroline found that going to the Dower House no longer caused her any concern. Lady Hunney had done her worst, and there was nothing more to fear. Nor were there happy memories of former times with Reggie to distract her. Once in Eleanor's bedroom, however, Caroline looked through her friend's wardrobe with increasing concern. Nothing was suitable; everything bore the hand of Lady Hunney and not a skirt was off the ground.

'I could get married in my trousers,' Eleanor suggested hopefully.

'Let's go into Tunbridge Wells. Now,' Caroline said.

'*Ready-made*? My dear, the skies will tumble. All right, but I'm not, *not*, having a long white dress with bones and lace. Martin wouldn't recognise me.'

They compromised. Eleanor bought a cream turban hat with a veil, and a fashionably short cream silk and wool afternoon frock with a full skirt.

'Legs,' said Eleanor, peering down at her ankles. 'They'll be surprised to feel the air.'

'We haven't finished yet,' Caroline declared. 'We need stockings, shoes, and gloves, not to mention a trousseau.'

Her friend groaned.

True to her word, Lady Hunney did not make an appearance at Eleanor's wedding, and caught by an emergency on the Verdun front in France, Sir John had to send his apologies too. It was left to Daniel, now walking merely with the aid of one stick on his new wood and metal leg, to give the bride away. Grandmother Buckford, Caroline noted, from her proud position as bridesmaid (in the fashionably smart blue jumper dress Eleanor had insisted on buying her) took the opportunity the Good Lord had sent and sat in the front pew on the bride's side, taking precedence even over Mother. For once Caroline applauded and when, back at the Rectory, a photograph was taken of the group, she encouraged her grandmother to take a central position. Eleanor winked at her, fully aware of what she was doing.

A wedding was always nice. Mrs Dibble contemplated the plates of sandwiches with satisfaction, remembering the last wedding here twenty months ago. Miss Isabel's, and what a day that had been. Still, everything had all gone off well today, even if Miss Eleanor was marrying beneath her. Miss Caroline didn't seem to mind a bit that her friend was wed before her. Poor Miss Caroline. Still missing Mr Reggie, she could tell that.

With some surprise, she remembered that only a week or two ago she'd been set on leaving the Rectory. My word, she was glad she hadn't. It would have been dull in Hartfield, just keeping Muriel company while Joe was away. She brightened at the thought of Joe. He'd come home on a week's leave in March, and what a grand time that had been.

'Mrs Dibble!'

Agnes rushed in, looking agitated. What was it now, Mrs Dibble wondered. Had they run out of tea in there, or was it Fred and the baby again? Fred had taken a fancy to Elizabeth Agnes and, despite Agnes's initial concern, he had been allowed to look after her now she was beginning to walk; he took the same care with her as he devoted to his wounded animals and birds.

'Jamie's coming home!' Agnes cried, waving a telegram. 'I thought it was to tell me he was dead, but instead he's on his way. He's got leave. He'll be here tomorrow for a whole four days.'

'Here?' Mrs Dibble repeated.

Agnes's eyes filled with tears. She and Jamie had no home, she remembered. 'I'll ask Mrs Lilley if he can stay here.'

Mrs Dibble pursed her lips. 'You ask her, of course, but tell her if she says no, she'll have me to deal with!'

Their eyes met, and Agnes laughed in relief.

'That's it, my girl. A bit of laughter never did the blackleading any harm. Nor the sponge cake neither. Mop your eyes and remember you're in your black.'

'I'm enjoying it. It's nice, a wedding.' Agnes thought a little wistfully of her own hurried affair last Christmas.

'The Rectory needs more of them. There's more funerals at St Nicholas than marriages, it seems to me, and baptisms are down.'

'They'll be up next winter, what with compulsory military service coming in.'

'Then the weddings had best be up to the same number,' Mrs Dibble retorted. 'Those that can.' She thought of her Lizzie and the terrible shame of it. 'Now Agnes,' she finished briskly. 'It's time to stop talking, and get back to work.'

Chapter Seventeen

Robert flicked idly through the *Illustrated London News*. Home from Gallipoli, he was convalescing after a nasty bout of dysentery. He still hadn't told Isabel of his decision, and this weighed on his mind. He would do so this very evening, he vowed. She was being so solicitous and he didn't want to mar this new happy atmosphere. She was even making an effort in the house, partly he suspected because she didn't want him to move to The Towers. With Isabel cheerful and busy, home was beginning to feel like a home. Which made what he was about to tell her all the more difficult.

'Isabel,' he said, as she brought in the tea. 'I have something to say to you.'

'You're not going back? You've resigned?' she cried hopefully.

He smiled. 'You don't resign after you've taken the

King's shilling. You're in until the end of hostilities.'

'I suppose the battalion is going somewhere even more dangerous.'

'No,' Robert replied quietly. 'The Royal Flying Corps in Ismailia is asking for volunteers. I've put my name down.'

'The RFC. Oh, Robert!' Isabel saw him winging his way through the heavens, dipping his wings in salute, battling it out with enemy aircraft over the Western Front. 'That's wonderful.'

'You're pleased?' He was surprised. 'It might mean officer training, after all, as otherwise you can't be a pilot.'

'But that's even more splendid.'

Did Isabel know that the life expectancy of a pilot in the RFC was measured in weeks? Probably not, and he wasn't going to tell her.

'At least I'll be around a little longer. It takes some time to train.'

'Never mind. The war is not over yet,' she replied.

'You're right.' On and on and on, battling against an enemy, getting nowhere; Turks or Germans, it was all the same. Eight feet lost in France, eight feet gained in Gallipoli. A battle lost in Gallipoli, another won in France. Robert burst into bitter song. 'See saw, Margery Daw/Johnny shall have a new master.' Johnny would have a new master indeed, the air. He began to laugh.

Isabel looked at him in consternation. 'Robert darling, you're still not well. It's that horrid germ you caught.' She paused. 'Let's go to bed early, shall we?'

* * *

342

'Caroline!' For a moment Caroline thought the voice at the other end of the telephone was – no, of course it couldn't be. 'It's me, you chump. Penelope.'

It was her! 'Are you ringing from Serbia?' she asked in disbelief.

'No! From Tunbridge Wells. It's cheaper.'

'Are you all right? Oh, Penelope, we've been so worried about you.'

'I'm fine. I survived the trek over the mountains to Albania – just. The whole thing was appalling, what with disease, the cold, and the ambushes by Albanians who didn't agree with their country's decision to help the Serbs. And we were all starving – you know how I like my food. Still, I'm here now to fatten up again.'

Caroline shivered. 'You're not going back to Serbia again, are you?'

'No. I thought I'd go somewhere really dangerous!'

'You'll have to choose, Phoebe.' Caroline chose her moment carefully, while they were walking to Seb Grendel's Farm. 'Choose what?' Phoebe looked mutinous.

'You'll be eighteen soon. Are you going to work for Mrs Manning in the recreation hut? Or are you going to throw in your lot with me?'

For the last few months, Phoebe had been officially 'helping' Caroline with her duties in organising village rotas, but the 'help' had been somewhat less than eager. It had seemed to Caroline that Phoebe was avoiding a return to the camp at Crowborough Warren rather than embracing a cause in which she wholeheartedly believed.

343

She was as uncommunicative now as she had been as a sixteen-year-old and that, as Caroline knew, might be storing up trouble. Phoebe had a great deal of vital energy, but there seemed to be nothing in Ashden that inspired her to use it.

Almost as if reading her thoughts, Phoebe burst out, 'I know it's valuable work you're doing here, Caroline, but you don't know how much I long to get away – anywhere – like Felicia, or like you when you went to Dover. Then I'd be able to think about something other than Harry.'

'It doesn't always work that way,' Caroline replied gently, 'Sometimes it's better if you confront the pain. As I'm trying to do each day.'

Phoebe looked puzzled. 'But at least Reggie's alive; there's still hope for you both.'

'No.' Caroline cut across her gently. 'There's no hope. We weren't meant for each other after all.'

'I thought you were.'

'We wanted different things, Phoebe, as I think you and Harry might have done after a while. At first I thought it was Lady Hunney's fault for turning Reggie against me, and that he had allowed himself to be talked into it. Now I see that to some extent at least, he agreed with her, and that our relationship would never have been happy in the long term.'

'But what will you do?' Phoebe looked genuinely concerned.

Caroline smiled at her younger sister. 'Don't look so stricken. The world is a large place, and the future even larger. It's you I'm worried about.'

344

'You really think I should go back to Crowborough if they'll have me?'

'Yes, though I don't want to lose you from my team.'

'Janie Marden will take my place.' Phoebe began to brighten up.

'So you'll go?'

'Yes.' For the first time in months, Phoebe sounded enthusiastic. 'After all I don't have to stay for ever, do I?'

Caroline was pleased to see Daniel at the Rectory. He looked well, his new leg was working properly and he continued to use just the one stick for walking.

'Dearest Daniel,' she placed her hand on her heart, 'you have but to ask and I am yours to command.'

He grinned. 'Good. I need someone to drive me to Ashdown Park in the Lanchester. I can't quite manage it yet, and I refuse to order the carriage. Or the dog cart.'

'Can the Lanchester risk its reputation being seen with me?' Caroline asked.

'It's not that far.'

She aimed a mock blow at him, and he laughed. She had learnt to drive as a VAD, and now drove regularly. She enjoyed the feeling of independence it gave her. The Lanchester was as daunting as Lady Hunney herself, however.

'How about tomorrow?' Daniel suggested.

Formerly the home of a captain in the Army, Ashdown Park had been converted into a hospital and convalescent home for Belgian army officers by Lady Brassey who lived nearby. Caroline had visited the estate as a child, and was curious to see it again.

'I met Henri Willaerts at Dover House in the Roehampton hospital, while I was having the leg fitted,' Daniel explained of the friend he was going to see. 'Henri was a lieutenant – a grenadier regiment – and was even more unlucky than me. He was in for two, but one stump became infected so he can't wear the second leg. He's been packed off here for a few weeks to recuperate before having another go. Then he's going to be sent to the re-education institute at Port-Villez in France. It only opened last August, and does marvellous work with weights and straps and the right exercises. The patients even play sports. I'd thought of going there too, but my progress has been good enough not to need it. Besides, I've got a rather pretty massage nurse here. We have enormous fun in the douche.' He broke off. 'I'm sorry, I shouldn't have said that.'

'I'm wearing a mental peaked cap today.' His words, however, had instantly recalled what Isabel had said about Reggie and another nurse. But the memory no longer hurt. Oh glory be, it no longer hurt.

As they turned into the road – if it could be dignified by such a name – to Wych Cross, the forest still showed signs of the terrible March storm more than four weeks earlier. Branches torn off in the gales lay starkly over the new spring growth on the ground, and the earth was still muddy from the snow and subsequent heavy rain and sleet. Caroline turned into the driveway up to the house with some relief. It was only five or six miles from Ashden to

Ashdown Park, but Lady Lanchester seemed to resent her driving every one of them.

The nurse on duty at Ashdown Park directed them through what must have been the morning room to a rear door into the garden where they could find Henri. What curious inscriptions were carved into the panelling, Caroline noticed. One above the morning room door showed a porcupine and underneath it: 'Those who are uncomfortable had better go out'. She could hear the sounds of voices from the communal room beyond: French, English and a more guttural sound she took to be Flemish and, with the porcupine in mind, she thought perhaps she should wait here until Daniel returned.

'Shall I come?' she asked Daniel uncertainly.

'Of course. Henri likes ladies. You can leave us alone after a while to enjoy soldier-talk.'

The rear gardens were even more magnificent than those in front of the house, with superb wooded areas and lawns, and flower gardens which would look splendid when the roses came out. It was obvious, however, that the storm had taken its toll. Trees could be seen lying uprooted by the lake, mighty monsters of oak and elm caught by the gales.

'There he is – in that invalid chair. Henri!' Daniel waved his stick, and set off towards his friend so fast that he was almost dragging Caroline along. Henri was being wheeled across the grass on the far side of the flower garden by a tall man in what Caroline recognised as Belgian army uniform: dark blue tunic with red piping over blue-grey trousers, and a shako on his head. Presumably he too was visiting Henri, since he showed no signs of injury other than a slight limp.

'Henri, my dear fellow!' Daniel pumped his hand up and down.

'*Content de te voir, Daniel.*' Henri twinkled at Caroline. '*Et Mademoiselle? Ta femme?*'

'*Pas sa femme. Je suis une amie,*' Caroline informed him, conscious that her accent was not all that could be desired. She liked the look of Henri, a plump man, already balding and with expressive dark eyes. Daniel began to introduce Henri to her formally, but suddenly his voice seemed to come from far away. She was seeing everything – the trees, the chair, the house, the people – through the wrong end of a telescope. Even the bird song seemed muted. For a moment all that remained in focus was the pair of hands gripping the invalid chair. Surely, surely, she recognised those hands?

'*Mademoiselle Lilley, je vous presente mon ami le Capitaine Yves Rosier,*' she heard Henri saying.

The captain bowed. He was in his thirties, and his face bore a scar and the set and bitter look of those turned out of their homeland. She had seen it so many times on the faces of Belgian refugees.

Henri waved a lordly hand towards his friend. 'Yves knew Miss Edith Cavell.'

The captain frowned, and Caroline could see that he was displeased at Henri's happy-go-lucky comment.

'She was a very brave woman,' Caroline said, and quickly changed the subject. 'I'm sorry to hear about the problems with your leg, Lieutenant Willaerts.'

Henri was deflected into a breezy account of the sports

he would be playing once he was running around like Daniel, only, so far as Caroline gathered from his broken English, he would be better than Daniel as he would have two wooden legs, not one.

Daniel turned to Captain Rosier again. 'And what do you do in England?' he asked. 'Are you convalescing here?'

Caroline sensed a tiny pause before he replied, also in English, which he spoke better than Henri, 'I am a refugee, like many of my compatriots.' His voice was deep and heavily accented.

Caroline longed to ask why he wore a uniform, but it was none of her business. Anyway, she must have been mistaken about the hands. They looked quite ordinary now only one was lightly resting on the chair and the other was at his side. For a brief moment, she had fancied them to be those of the man who had assisted her on the night of the Zeppelin bomb.

'I'll leave you gentlemen to talk.' Caroline remembered Daniel's suggestion. 'I'm so glad to have met you, Lieutenant Willaerts, and you, Capitaine Rosier.'

The captain gave a little bow. 'I hope we shall meet again, Miss Lilley.'

Caroline strolled towards the trees under which the last of the daffodils were trumpeting the way to summer in a yellow splash of bloom. Despite the war, despite the Easter uprising in Dublin, despite the Zeppelin raids, despite all the awfulness that man could do, here in the wood the ferns were unfurling as they had done for thousands of years. Branches were starting to show their greenery, and a few lilies of the valley announced the imminent arrival of May.

For no reason at all, Caroline gave a little skip and twirled herself by one arm round the trunk of a silver birch.

There would be storms to damage and destroy, but spring would always follow. Days of clear blue skies, new growth to cover dead bracken. At last the sun was beginning to shine, and might, if it tried hard enough, even spot Caroline Lilley far below it in Ashdown Park. Beneath her feet, all around her, and now within her heart, there was life. There was hope.

Acknowledgements

An author has two best friends, her editor and her agent, and I have been exceptionally fortunate in both: to Jane Wood and Dorothy Lumley, my grateful thanks for their support and expertise. I also owe much to Selina Walker for her perceptive comments and guidance.

I am also grateful to Norman Franks, Martin Kender, Mary Lewis, Jean Robinson and Carol Tyler for their help and interest, and to Jan Boxshall for her painstaking and constructive copy-editing.

With thanks, also, to all at Allison & Busby for bringing the Seasons of War quartet to a new generation of readers.